TWILIGHT of KERBEROS

SHADOWMAGE

Startled now, and worried by what might have stirred the thieves into breaking their silence, Lucius started to run to the main deck, but was halted by the sound of movement from the stairs leading to the lower deck. The crew of the ship would have been awoken by the thieves on board, and Lucius crouched, sword drawn, ready to skewer whoever came up the stairs first.

Seeing a shadow move, the stench he had smelled before suddenly strengthened and he realised someone was approaching. He felt the comfort of the threads of magic spin in his mind's eye, ready to be unleashed if his sword alone proved insufficient. Stepping forward, blade ready, Lucius prepared to thrust his weapon into the chest of whoever emerged and then sprint out to see what danger the rest of his team faced.

A loud cry of fear and alarm rang out, resounding in the confined space. Dimly, Lucius realised it was he that had screamed. The figure before him climbed up the stairs inexorably, but he was rooted to the spot, unable to move as he watched the horror approach.

An Abaddon Books™ Publication
www.abaddonbooks.com
abaddon@rebellion.co.uk

First published in 2008 by Abaddon Books™, Rebellion
Intellectual Property Limited, The Studio, Brewer Street,
Oxford, OX1 1QN, UK.

10 9 8 7 6 5 4 3 2 1

Editor: Jonathan Oliver
Cover: Mark Harrison
Design: Simon Parr & Luke Preece
Marketing and PR: Keith Richardson
Creative Director and CEO: Jason Kingsley
Chief Technical Officer: Chris Kingsley
Twilight of Kerberos™created by Mathew Sprange and
Jonathan Oliver

ISBN 13: 978-1-905437-54-2

TWILIGHT of KERBEROS

SHADOW MAGE

Matthew Sprange

WWW.ABADDONBOOKS.COM

PROLOGUE

Shouts for his blood echoed off the walls of the narrow alley, the worn buildings bouncing the sound so it seemed as though he were surrounded. Casting an anxious glance over his shoulder, he saw nothing through the shadowy gloom and guessed they were still on the street behind.

Not wanting to push his luck, he ran faster, legs straining under the effort and ankles aching from the unfamiliar exertion. A shape shuffled from the darkness of a doorway to his left. He nearly screamed in panic, thinking the murderers behind had caught up with him. The grey-haired beggar gave him a curious look, perhaps wondering why a wild-eyed man was in this region of the city at so late an hour, then shuffled back into his temporary home.

The alley jinked crookedly and, rounding the last corner, he saw the expanse of Meridian Street opening up before him. He slowed down, trying to control his breathing and appear normal, lest he draw attention from revellers or some of the less desirable types he knew frequented the thoroughfare. Drawing his hood up, he wrapped his cloak about him and continued north at a measured pace. The shouts were gradually receding and he began to give a silent prayer of relief. While the events of the evening had been painful, there was still a chance that something could be salvaged from the disaster.

Meridian Street was lit only by the torches and lanterns of the taverns, clubs and brothels that choked its wide midway stretch as it reached, arrow straight, to Turnitia's northern gate. Even those lights were slowly being doused as all but the most stubborn establishments, or those most patronised, depending on how you looked at it, began to call an end to the evening's trade. Only the pale blue giant overhead continued to provide an eerie grey illumination, its cloud strewn surface leering down on the city as the sphere dominated three quarters of the night sky.

He hoped his ancestors, soaring high in the clouds of Kerberos above, were watching over him now, providing whatever aid and protection the true God permitted. Discretely, he made the sign of the Brotherhood under his cloak, and then hurried north. Hoping to appear like a young party-goer finding his way home, but fearing he appeared more like an old man on the run.

Few others were on the street, and even fewer paid him more than a scant glance, having the delights of heavy drink and loose women on their minds. For this, at least, he was grateful, for he could not afford any sort of confrontation, not tonight. The Faith had eyes everywhere, it seemed, and it might not take them long to arrive here if some sort of altercation broke out.

Crossing the cobbled road to avoid two young men obviously, and loudly, looking for a tavern that was still serving new arrivals, he strode purposefully onwards, eventually reaching the point where Meridian Street narrowed. A few closed shop fronts marked the undeclared barrier between entertainment and residential district, and he stopped for a few seconds, watching the road behind to see if any furtive shapes broke from the shadows to continue pursuit. Seeing nothing, he released the breath he had unconsciously been holding, though he knew he would not feel completely safe until he reached home. Perhaps not even then – that, however, was something to deal with in the morning. If he could just survive this night...

He continued his frightened trek and, a few hundred yards further along the road, he turned into a side street he had come to know well. Another turn and he was in the alleys that ran behind the row of close knit dwellings, the simple two storey town houses of a type that sheltered the majority of the inhabitants of the city. Such humble accommodations were perhaps surprising for the man he was to call on, but he had learned they were entirely fitting for the Preacher's outlook on life. In Pontaine, the man would have been revered as a bishop, at the very least, but here, in subjugated Turnitia, the Faith and its lackeys in the Empire of Vos had ensured even this great man remain hidden.

Pausing once again to make sure he was not being followed, ears straining to hear soft footfalls in the twilight, he quietly entered the shadows cast by the house, and tapped on its back door, flecks of paint breaking loose from its ragged surface. Three taps followed by a pause, then two more.

A middle-aged woman opened the door, peering anxiously past him into the alley before focussing on his face. He could sense the fear emanating from her as she hustled him in quickly but that did little to stifle his own relief at, finally, reaching safe territory.

Inside, the kitchen was small and the same as in every other house in the street. A small cast-iron stove sitting under the chimney flooded the room with warmth, the fires behind its latticed grate combining with the lantern on the central dark wood table to provide a homely atmosphere, something he was glad of. The man seated at the table grabbed a bottle and poured a generous amount of wine into a clay cup.

"Tabius," the man nodded in welcome. "You look as if you could use this."

"Preacher," Tabius acknowledged. "We should get you to safety. The Faith could have discovered your location by now. They have taken enough of us tonight."

The Preacher waved his concern aside. "I did not run when the Empire descended on our city, even though we all knew they would bring the Final Faith with them. I am not going to start now. Have a drink man, steady your nerves. We don't believe it breaks the divine connection between man and God."

"I heard the Anointed Lord had passed that law," Tabius said, finally accepting the cup and relishing the first sip as it warmed his throat and stomach. "Think her followers will accept it?"

"They had better, if they know what is good for them," the Preacher said then, with a wry smile added, "Whether the Anointed Lord and her closest cronies follow it too, ah, that would be the question. Still, what can you expect when women are allowed into religion? Now, sit, and tell me how we fare this evening."

Tabius sat across from the Preacher and smiled in thanks as his wife laid out a plate of bread and ham, though he did not touch the supper, instead cradling the cup of wine in his hands to warm it.

"They knew where we were and what we were doing," he began, wincing slightly as the screams of dying friends echoed in his ears once again. "Someone gave us up. Tanner, maybe. He was a little too ready to offer us his cellar, knowing the risks it carried."

The Preacher shook his head. "I find that difficult to believe. I have known Tanner a long time, and would declare him righteous. He accepted the risks because he knew they were necessary. However, we have taken in new believers recently, and who knows whether they are all truly genuine? Even with recommendations, it is within some men to only deceive."

"Truly. The Rites of Protection and Good Health had barely finished when the Faith arrived. They were among us before we knew it, striking with swords at anyone within reach. Not just the men – they were after everyone."

He stopped to take another sip of wine, hoping the motion would conceal the shaking he felt enter his hands. The compassion in the Preacher's eyes told him he had failed, and he took a deep breath before continuing.

"It was complete chaos. People were running in all directions, trying to get out. And the screaming. It filled the cellar. We were slipping on the blood running across the floor, men were struck down as they tried to help their wounded sons. Gregor rallied first and began to fight back – I remember a hammer in his hand. We followed him as he headed for the stairs. I saw him cut down, but some of us, I don't know, maybe a dozen, managed to get out. Once we were on the street, we just ran."

"And you were chased?"

"Yes. We split up. I don't know if the others escaped. I was hoping I would find some of them here, as I went all the way round the Five Markets before coming back towards Meridian Street. I know Sanser, Mikels and Dornire got out with me, and I think I saw Kurn as well."

"Did the guard not come?"

"I saw a couple but..." Tabius paused. "The thing is I could have sworn they were in on it. Or, at least, some of them were. Since the city fell, the guard step in if you so much as knock a barrel over in the market. They must have seen what was happening, they just had to – but I did not see any of them act."

The Preacher nodded. "We have no friends in the Empire of Vos, and the Faith is fast taking root in the highest levels of their leadership. This Katherine may be a woman but as Anointed Lord, she has garnered a great deal of support among the Lord Dukes. I shudder to think what favours she has granted them, but her power is undeniable. Even here, in Turnitia, we feel the weight of her growing authority. We will find no justice from the city guard."

He reached across the table to top up Tabius' cup, though it had barely been touched. Tabius took this as a sign to drink, and he dutifully raised the cup to his lips.

"Gregor gone, you say? He will be missed in this hour of need." The Preacher sighed as he watched his wife fussing over the stove. "Aldene wants us to pack up and head for Pontaine. Perhaps even Allantia, she says. The Brotherhood is welcome there, she believes, or is at least not persecuted."

This caused his wife to glance over her shoulder with a reproachful look at her husband, and he smiled fondly back at her. Tabius shifted uneasily as he witnessed the love between them speak silent volumes.

"Perhaps that would be for the best," he ventured.

The Preacher hooted at that. "Would you?" he asked. "Really? Leave behind everything you have built up here for a new life? The grass is always greener, as they say but, in truth, you have sweated and worked too hard to leave behind your little empire here. I have worked just as hard, my boy. While you have amassed a small fortune in gold with your warehouses, I have become just as rich in spirit, bringing new blood into the Brotherhood and guiding those who believe to the best of my ability."

He fell silent for a moment, and Tabius stared into his cup. "No," the Preacher finally said. "I will stay and do what must be done. Our people will be scared after tonight, and will need reminding that the trials God puts before us are necessary for the salvation of all of us. Yes, even those poor misguided fools of the Faith. They have their part to play in his grand design too."

"So, what do we do now?" Tabius asked. Though he knew, come morning, a thousand problems would be waiting for him in his growing business. The Preacher had a knack of inspiring him to always work that little bit harder for the Brotherhood. His money and connections among the merchants of Turnitia had already benefited their congregation. All the Preacher had to do was ask, and he would serve as best he could.

"We start again," the Preacher said confidently. "Our beliefs are strong enough to survive the cruelty of the Final Faith. No matter how many of us they threaten, bully or kill, you cannot stamp out the truth my boy. And truth is on our side. They have twisted the word of God beyond all recognition, turning it into a dream of conquest. But that is all it can be – a dream. We carry the burden of God's will Tabius, and so we cannot fail. Whatever the tests put before us, we are God's chosen. Take comfort in that."

"As you say, Preacher."

"Now, come morning we will have a clearer idea of what our losses are. We will need a new meeting place – you can help with that, I trust?"

Tabius thought hard. Though one of his many warehouses by the docks would be a perfect venue for their gatherings, they had avoided it up to now, as it had seemed too dangerous with agents of the Final Faith constantly looking for signs of the Brotherhood growing in the city. Still, he had several that were away from the main trading areas, and his own name was nowhere near their legal documents of possession.

"It may be possible, yes," he said slowly, still thinking. "I'll start making arrangements tomorrow. I might be able to have something ready by evening."

"Please make sure you do. I must address our people by then at the latest. They will be terrified and in need of guidance. Perhaps just in need of assurance that everything will turn out the way it should." He smiled. "One thing is for sure, though. If we can –"

A loud crash of splintering wood resounded in the tiny kitchen. Tabius jerked in shock, looking past the Preacher to where the sound had come from.

"They're here!" cried the Preacher's wife, and she raced across to her husband to put a hand on his shoulder.

The Preacher looked at Tabius. "Go," he said simply.

Tabius stood immediately, as much out of habit of doing whatever the Preacher told him to do. Only then did he hesitate, looking into the man's eyes. He opened his mouth to speak, but the Preacher cut him off.

"Go! Quickly, while you still have time!"

Another crash, this time followed by a triumphant cry, and there were heavy footsteps in the hall outside the kitchen. Panic took over, and Tabius bolted through the back door, leaving the warm kitchen, the Preacher, and his wife behind. He heard shouts and a scream cut short.

Outside, a cry went up from a shadow in the alley to his right, and he dashed blindly left. Stumbling past houses on either side, he heard heavy footsteps with the chink of mail following, and fear gave him extra speed.

Behind, someone called out. "By the law of Vos – halt!"

That only served to drive Tabius on. A gap between houses to his left beckoned, and he dove into the darkness, crashing into a barrow that had been left casually propped up against one of the walls. The noise of man and barrow clattering onto the cobbles seemed deafening to him, and he scrabbled to his feet, ignoring the sting of grazed palms and shins as he burst out into another small street. Looking to each side, he ploughed forward into another alley that ran behind the next row of houses, changing direction to head back to Meridian Street.

Breathless after several minutes of fear-filled flight, he stopped, leaning against an abandoned cart outside a provisions store. His pursuers had been outpaced for now, no doubt weighed down by their armour and weaponry. Behind, he saw an orange glow silhouetting the city's skyline, and he strained his ears to hear massed cries in the distance. Smoke rose in columns from fires near the centre of Turnitia to lazily float in a growing cloud across the face of Kerberos, the massive sphere uncaring and unchanging in the face of human misery, even on this scale. The city, he saw, was descending into riotous chaos, and fellow members of the Brotherhood, people he knew, were the target of the mob, whipped into a frenzy by the Faith.

Slowly, his mind tried to come to terms with what was happening, but the implications of the city guard openly helping the Faith to track down their rivals – or dangerous heretics, as the Brotherhood was no doubt being described – filled him with a sick, creeping dread.

Had he been recognised at the Preacher's house? Tabius thought not, his escape had been too quick, and there had been no time to see his face clearly. Then he thought of the Preacher, and what he might be forced to tell his captors. If, indeed, the man was still alive.

Though weary, he pulled himself up straight and, doing his best to ignore the riots claiming the roads, markets and homes of the city, he carried on up Meridian Street until the north gate came into view. Taking the road that ran behind the city's fortified ramparts, he turned east until the tightly packed houses gave way to much larger dwellings, with their own gardens and protective walls hiding their grounds. This district was known intimately to Tabius. It was home.

Even through his fear, despair and fatigue, he possessed enough awareness to circle his own property twice, staring into the shadows for any sign of movement or presence of the guard. There was nothing, and he guessed the guard would not permit the riots to extend to this part of Turnitia, as there were too many men of power and money living here. Such men rarely entangled themselves in religious conflicts and, living here high on the hill on which Turnitia's foundations were built, they demanded nothing less than a total separation from the common rabble.

Gingerly opening a small wooden gate in the side wall of his home's compound, he silently slipped in and, closing it behind him, he breathed a heartfelt sigh of release. For the first time that night, he was truly safe. He opened his eyes and looked at his home, a large and finely built town house that took enough space to accommodate perhaps six or seven dwellings of the type the Preacher lived in. Light radiated from several of the downstairs rooms, and Tabius suddenly yearned to see his family, to make sure they were still safe, even though he knew no harm would reach them here.

His wife whirled round as he entered. Standing in front of the roaring fireplace in the drawing room, he guessed she had been pacing fretfully until he returned. With a cry of relief, she ran into his arms and, for a moment, they just held one another.

"Arthur came by earlier," she said once tears had been choked back. "He said the whole city has turned against you."

Tabius hushed her. "We will be safe. The mob won't climb the hill. There are too many interests to protect here. For once Vos might actually help us, however unintentionally."

"I hope you are right. Arthur said –"

Tabius held his wife at arms length and smiled reassuringly. "While I appreciate Arthur looking after my family while I am away, he is an old man, and I really must have a word to him about scaring you unnecessarily."

"He said people were being killed in the streets. And the fires, I saw them from the landing. Half the city is aflame..."

"It is not as bad as all that. Where are the children?"

"Maggy is asleep. Lucius is pretending to be. He wanted to go down into the city to find his father."

Tabius grinned at that. "Thank God you convinced him otherwise. Now, I have a great deal of work tomorrow. Let's have supper and get some rest. Everything will seem better in the morning, I promise."

She wiped away a tear and nodded. "I'll rouse the kitchen."

Leaving Tabius' side, she walked proudly away, causing him to admire her fortitude, not for the first time. She paused at the door, then turned round. "Tabius... do you hear that?"

Straining his ears, he listened hard, not sure what his wife was getting at. Then it suddenly hit him – the mob was ascending the hill. He could hear their cries, muffled and distant now but slowly growing stronger.

"Impossible," he muttered. "The guard would not dare let them loose. Not up here."

His wife rested against the door for support. "Tabius," she said, worry and strain evident in her voice. "Are you sure about that? Really sure?"

One glance at his wife, standing by the door, strong in her faith but unsure of what to do, convinced him.

"Get the children. Do it now!"

As his wife fled upstairs, Tabius crossed the hall to his study, striding to the unlit fireplace to unbuckle the sword that hung there. Though it had belonged to his father and the blade had not been drawn in anger in decades, the lessons hammered into him during adolescence began to flood back as he grasped the hilt and drew the weapon. He fervently hoped he would not have to use it, especially in front of his children, but he would not permit anyone to hurt his family.

Striding back into the hall, he saw his wife leading little Magallia down the stairs, still in her night clothes and rubbing sleep from her eyes. Behind them was Lucius, his pride, about to enter adulthood and take on the responsibilities of the family business. Spying the sword, Lucius had just one question.

"Are we fighting them, Father?"

"I sincerely hope not," Tabius said, though he could not fully suppress a smile at his son's spirit.

A rap at the main door of the house caused them to freeze before it was followed by several more. Three raps, then a pause, followed by two more.

Tabius looked at his wife as he went for the door. "Arthur."

Unbolting the door, he opened it a crack at first, then threw it open when his suspicion was confirmed. Arthur, a stooped man in his seventies but with all the energy of someone far younger, shuffled in.

"You are preparing to leave?" he asked.

"Right now," Tabius said. "I'm not taking any chances. Have you seen anything?"

Turning to gather his family, Tabius stopped when he realised Arthur had not answered. He looked at the old man, and saw tears in the familiar face.

"The guard are already outside," Arthur said. "They are funnelling the mob straight here, avoiding everyone else. When they let me through their line, they said they were happy to let me burn with the rest of you."

Tabius sagged against the door, furiously trying to think what to do. His first thought was for the children. He walked slowly to his wife and took her hand.

"Get the children into the cellar. They will be after the three of us, not the children. They may be... missed in the confusion."

She put a hand to his cheek, and his heart broke at the look of anguish on her face.

"Tabius..." she said, searching for the words. He had nothing of comfort to tell her.

"It is too late."

CHAPTER 1

Once again, he found himself waiting for his opponent's decision. Leaning back on two legs of his chair, Lucius propped his feet up on the table and closed his eyes, knowing this could take a while. He held three cards to his chest, feeling the hard, rounded edges of mail beneath the hardened leather of his tunic. Two long, thin daggers were concealed in his boots and any member of the city guard shaking him down might quickly find the short sword strapped to his back, beneath his grey woollen cloak. The taverns on the Street of Dogs had not been noted as rough places when he was last in Turnitia, but too many changes had happened in the city during his long absence to take any chances.

The tavern was heaving and, judging by the other establishments he had visited earlier in the evening, business was good in the Street of Dogs. Whether it was the boost in the city's economy by the occupying power or the result of a subjugated populace seeking to forget the realities of the day, he had yet to tell. Certainly some had profited from the occupation, but as he knew too well, others always had to suffer for it. Here, at least, there seemed little evidence of the long war, as the soft tones of flute and harp from somewhere near the back of the common room floated over the raucous cries, laughter and shouts of the patrons.

His eyes snapped open as his opponent, a luckless man in rough clothing and sporting a thick dark beard, grabbed the dice and took a breath. Lucius had taken him for one of the labourers that toiled in the city's warehouse district, perhaps hoping to turn a week's wages into a year's salary in just one fortuitous night. This was not to be his night, Lucius knew, as he focussed his attention on the dice in the man's hand.

"I'll stay," the man said confidently, ignoring Lucius' provocative raised eyebrow. With another glance at his hand, the man shook the dice, blew on them, and then scattered them on the table.

Lucius narrowed his whole world to the tumbling dice and, under the table, the fingers of his free hand twitched as he sought the invisible threads that had become so familiar to him, and he felt the other-worldly power flow under his control. Tiny wisps of air streaked across the table to envelope the tumbling dice. As the dice bounced, Lucius lifted each one by the smallest fraction, buoying them up on a current, while spinning each slightly. When they landed and came to a rest, both cubes of carved bone presented the number four on their top face.

"At last!" the man cried, and his relief was palpable. Lucius had already seen that his belt pouch was getting light, but he had no desire to prolong his opponent's pain. The man took a card from his hand and proudly laid it on the table.

"Eight Princes!" he declared. "Your luck has turned, my friend!"

"Alas, I think not," said Lucius as he produced one of his own cards, also showing the number eight but with a smiling nubile woman seated on a golden throne. "The Queen trumps all but the Fool. I win again."

So saying, Lucius swept the coins lying on the table into his own pouch before snatching another card from the face down deck between them. "Another round? I believe I'm getting the feel for this."

The man, however, was not swayed by Lucius' demeanour. "The ills of Kerberos be on you, no one is that lucky," he spat. "How many times is that now? Eleven, twelve hands in a row? You've played me."

Seeing the man begin to rise from his seat, Lucius swept his legs off the table and stood, reaching into one of his boots for a blade. It was done in one well-practised, fluid motion that caught the man completely off-guard. He had no idea of the danger until Lucius was leaning over him, the dagger planted firmly in the wood of the table with a dull thud.

"I'm sorry, *friend*," said Lucius. "But I have the idea that you were about to call me a cheat."

Looking into the man's eyes, Lucius could see what he was thinking. The man was no coward, and he likely had friends here that, in the very least, he would not want to see him backing down. On the other hand, Lucius' weather-beaten face, out-of-town air, and readiness to display a weapon marked him as someone not to casually entangle with. An ear-beating from the wife for losing a week's earnings was infinitely preferable to a knife in the belly.

The man spat again. "Your kind never last long around here, you know that? The guard will have you. Sooner or later, you'll push your luck too hard, and then the guard will have you."

Standing up to face Lucius briefly, the man then turned to grab the long coat thrown across the back of his chair before storming through the crowd of revellers to the door. Lucius glanced around to see if anyone had taken an undue interest in his naked blade – the man had not been wrong about the guard, after all – before sliding it back into his boot and gesturing a maid for an ale.

He slipped the maid a silver tenth with a wink when she returned, then settled down to sip his drink, searching for another mark. He caught men's eyes several times with a pointed look at the dice and cards, but no one was biting. Either they had seen the outburst just now, or their female companions were of greater interest than a game of chance. Cursing his previous opponent for forcing him to draw a weapon, he quickly decided to move on. Downing the last remains of the ale, a Vosbrew he had little love for anyway, he surreptitiously checked his weapons and belt pouch and, finding them to be present and in order, slipped through the throng towards the door.

Outside the tavern, he took a deep breath, glad to have air somewhat cleaner than that inside. Looking up, he saw the huge blue-grey globe of Kerberos hanging above, dominating the sky as it cast its dull twilight glow upon the city while bands of white gossamer clouds played slowly across its surface. The eternal sphere had meant much to his father, his faith rooted in the belief of salvation among those clouds, but Lucius had come to know better.

Glancing to the east, he saw the Street of Dogs sweep downwards towards the cliffs, perhaps a couple of miles away, where they formed a natural defence against the ocean. The waters constantly raged against the land either side of the city, gouging chunks from it every year, and Lucius wondered at the sanity of the original settlers in building a port here. Only maybe one day in ten could a ship brave the barriers shielding the port from the churning waters to dock at the massive stone harbour built at the bottom of those cliffs, and then only with great risk – and that was assuming the harbour could accept another vessel, as one section or another was always under repair. Once a great marvel of engineering, the harbour had fallen into various states of disrepair over the years as the change in the city's leadership began to favour other priorities. It was certainly no coincidence that many of the Vos nobles now running Turnitia had their own existing interests in the mercantile activities of companies that relied on horse and wagon to transport goods, rather than the dangerous and intemperate sea.

Even from the centre of Turnitia, he could hear the roiling surf blasting itself against the barriers, conjuring a constant dim roar that the citizens of the city soon learned to tune out. For someone who had been away for so long, however, it was a reminder of just how precarious the city's position was. One day, the land must succumb to the angry waters and collapse into the sea, taking Turnitia with it. Perhaps that would not be so bad a thing, he thought. It would save many people a great deal of trouble.

"That's the whore's son." The voice brought Lucius back to the present and he turned around to see if it was indeed him being spoken of. It was. The beaten card player had evidently found some friends in a nearby tavern and had either been convinced to take his money back, or was somewhat braver than Lucius had thought.

There were seven of them, though only two had the presence of mind to bring weapons. One brandished a knife, while the other wielded a crude cudgel. They had come from the high end of the Street of Dogs and were fanning out in a loose semicircle to trap him against the row of buildings behind.

"I really don't need this," Lucius remarked, as much to himself as to the men. His original opponent appeared to take the comment personally.

"Well, I don't need to be cheated out of me money by a charlatan like you. Breezing into the city, hitting up a few of the locals, and then breezing out again with your pouch clinking with our coin. Is that it?"

"Friend, I beat you fair and square, no cheating," said Lucius, raising a hand in an attempt to forestall any violence. It was not true of course, but there was not much else he could say.

"Hey, no need for us to start trouble," the man said with a crooked smile. "Just hand me the money back – and your other coins, which you no doubt gained from your games – and we'll call it quits."

Lucius sighed, wondering how far he had fallen to have his own marks trying to rob him. He was not worried about his own immediate safety. A half dozen or so labourers, a little worse for drink no doubt, were of small concern. The city guard, however, were another matter and while he spied no patrols nearby, open violence on the street would bring them running in no time. *That* was something worth avoiding.

"I'm sorry, I can't do that," he said, knowing exactly

how this was going to turn out. "I warn you now, walk away. Just walk away. There is nothing you can do that will end this well."

"Cocky, 'ain't he?" said one of the man's companions.

"He'll be less cocksure with this wrapped round his head," the thug with the cudgel growled. He took a step forward and drew the weapon back as if he were aiming to knock Lucius' head clean off his shoulders and send it sailing down the street.

Lucius ran. Behind him, the men whooped and hollered, their blood rising at the sight of prey fleeing. Hearing their footsteps just a few yards behind, Lucius was faintly surprised they had reacted so quickly, as he had bolted without hesitation when it became clear a confrontation was inevitable.

Keen to get away from the main street where any number of well-meaning citizens might raise a call for the guard, he had already spotted a side alley between the tavern and a hardware stall, one of thousands linking the main thoroughfares of the city. He darted for the narrow entrance, feet skipping over the dull cobbles.

Once veiled by the shadows of the tall buildings either side, Lucius smiled. With darkness as his ally and no witnesses, the odds now swung massively in his favour. Skidding to a halt with his back to a greying stone wall, he momentarily closed his eyes and concentrated, feeling the shadows rise up to cloak his body.

The men rushed around the corner, the one in the lead suddenly stopping. Those behind cursed as they ran into one another before the first raised his hand.

"Well... where on Kerberos did he go?" he said.

They all peered into the alley, squinting to penetrate the gloom. Running straight as an arrow, they could clearly see the length of the alley, just as they could clearly see there was no rogue silhouetted against the lights of the establishments in the next street.

"Maybe he climbed to the roof," said one, eyeing up the side of the buildings.

"Idiot," retorted another.

"There's people that can do it!"

"Not in just a few seconds."

"A master criminal, are you?"

"Idiot."

Lucius watched the men, reaching behind his back to clasp the hilt of his short sword. The closest stood no more than two feet away, but they were oblivious to his presence. Wreathed in arcane darkness, Lucius had effectively become invisible. The other things that might give him away, an involuntary movement, a slight sound, those he could suppress from years of practice. It was a fearsome combination and one that was more than a match for an irritated gambler and his friends.

As the squabble spread to the other men, all with theories on what to do next, Lucius moved. Whipping his sword clear of its inverted scabbard in near silence, he reversed the weapon and brought the steel pommel down on the neck of the nearest man. The target sank without a sound, and Lucius was among the rest of them before they realised one of their number had hit the ground.

A foot sank into the stomach of another, while the sword descended once more − pommel first − into the face of a third. The man's shriek bubbled as blood welled up from his shattered nose, but it was enough to alert the remaining thugs.

The mark acted before thinking, and reached for Lucius' throat with both hands. Lucius took a step back and felt threads of energies rush through him as he sought to harness their power. Selecting a strand, he focussed on its structure and form, consciously moulding it into something he could use. He felt its strength swelling inside his body as it always did in battle, somewhere near his heart, and he extended an open palm to the charging man. A crack resounded down the alley, like a miniature bolt of lightning, and a faint, crimson wave of force sprang from his palm, catching the man full in the chest. With no chance of avoiding the blast, the man was picked up off his feet and hurled against the unyielding building opposite. He collapsed to the floor, winded.

"It's a damned wizard!" one of his friends cried out, now panicking.

"Could be the Lord of the Three Towers himself, he still won't bespell us without a head." This came from cudgel-man, and Lucius turned to see him winding up for another swing. The blow, when it came, seemed painfully slow and obvious to Lucius, who raised his sword to block the attack. The sharpened blade dug deep into the club, trapping it briefly.

Two others, seeing an advantage, both rushed Lucius from behind. He felt a hand grab his shoulder and instantly buckled his knees, rolling forward and dragging his weapon free at the same time. Tumbling away, he came up in a crouch, ready for their next move.

While cudgel-man was wondering where his enemy had gone, the other two were not so slow. Both yelled in triumph as they saw what they thought was a beaten man on the ground. As they ran to start raining kicks and blows down upon him, Lucius took another breath, narrowed his eyes in concentration, and then slapped his free hand on the cobbles. A wave of energy spread out before him, pushing up stones as it shifted the ground. All the men still in the fight were thrown off their feet by the pulse, fear registering in their eyes.

Three turned and fled without another word, though a curse from cudgel-man followed them. Another, the first to fall, lay motionless on the ground, though Lucius knew he would wake up in an hour or so with the world's worst hangover.

Cudgel-man faced him once again, seething with anger but unsure of what to do without anyone backing him up. Knife-man helped the mark to his feet, before turning to face Lucius, blade held at arm's length.

"We can still take him," said cudgel-man, sounding as if he needed the encouragement himself.

"I advise you not to try," said Lucius, raising a hand in an attempt to start a parley. "A beating in an alley is a hazard of the city. But if either of you try to use those weapons, I'll start getting serious."

The gambler was suddenly less than sure of himself and started to mumble something, but Lucius caught the flash of the knife's movement from his friend.

"Fool!" Lucius hissed as the knife span through the air. The man's aim was true, but Lucius gritted his teeth as he released the same energy he had used on the dice earlier. This time there was no effort at finesse or style, as he desperately sought to slow and steady the blade. A blast of wind gusted in a narrow line, striking the knife with a low whistle. The weapon stopped suddenly in mid-air, hung motionless for a brief second, then fell to the stones with a clatter.

Knowing a distraction when he saw one, cudgel-man judged the moment right to finally unleash his skull-splitting swing. It was a poor decision.

Ducking under the wild blow, Lucius sprang forward,

lunging with his short sword. The blade buried itself in cudgel-man's stomach, and the man gave a curious mewing sound as his brain began to register that the wound was mortal. Knife-man started to back away, but Lucius reached forward with his outstretched hand and grasped him by the throat.

The rage of battle now well and truly upon him, Lucius dug within himself to find the darkest, most vile, and terrible of threads. He felt a chill sweep through his body as he channelled the force from his heart, down his arm, through his hand and into the man. The power mustered was the antithesis of life and it reacted with the living flesh it raced into. The man gasped as he futilely grabbed at the hand holding him, but his strength was already waning. Lucius stared into his eyes, watching them grow dim in seconds. The man's skin greyed and withered, while his cheeks sank into his face and muscles shrivelled, hair falling out in clumps. When Lucius released his grip the corpse looked as if it had been dead for months.

Angry at the men for attacking him, and for forcing him to use such power, Lucius ripped his sword clear of cudgel-man then rounded on the gambler. With blade held menacingly, he turned his free hand palm upwards and conjured wisps of fiery energy, his hand now wreathed in flames of lavender and turquoise.

"You've lost two friends tonight because of your folly," Lucius told the man. "Believe me when I say you got off lightly. Now go!"

Lucius jerked his head to reinforce his command, but it was wholly unnecessary. As far as the man was concerned, death itself stalked that alley, and he wanted no part of it. Spinning on his heel, the man scrabbled for the bright lights of the Street of Dogs, and a life that held no terror.

Briefly regarding the men lying on the ground, Lucius exhaled as the tension left him. Wiping his blade on the tunic of cudgel-man, he sheathed it then cursed. He had not intended to give knife-man so gruesome a death, no matter how much it might have been deserved or forewarned. Lucius knew many different ways to kill a man but, in the heat of battle, there was rarely time to plan and consider. He had reached for the most devastating attack needed at the time, and taken the first that came to his command. That it was the most loathsome of the energies he was able to use and control was almost pure chance, as he had reached blindly, by instinct. The coldness of its touch still caressed him, and he could feel the dark evil lurking just beneath the surface. He would be paying for its help with a couple of sleepless nights at least, as the old dreams flooded back.

Trying to stem images of past haunted nights, he gathered his wits and resolved to put as much distance between himself and the bodies as possible. Heading away from the Street of Dogs, he briefly considered trying to find another tavern friendly to gamblers, but he quickly dismissed the idea. The earnings tonight would keep him for a day or two at worst, and he was in no shape to beguile anyone after the fight. All they would see would be a rogue, a desperado. Or murderer, maybe.

He decided to head away from the lights and aim for the merchant quarter. The inns there were usually sombre affairs, dedicated to traders and other businessmen visiting Turnitia. They catered for higher classes who demanded peace, security and thrills less blatant than those on offer in the Street of Dogs. The peace and security at least were things Lucius could appreciate at this moment.

Stepping cautiously out the other end of the alley, Lucius scanned the wide road it spilled onto. From old memories, he believed this to be Lantern Street, which ran down the hill parallel to the Street of Dogs before jinking north toward the merchant quarter. Houses lined both sides of the street, punctuated with the occasional bookseller, jewellers, or other trader dealing in luxuries. This area marked the boundary between the masses living alongside the cliff-side warehouses and those in the considerably wealthier area higher up the hill. Drawing his cloak about him, he set off with a safe room, warm bath and comfy sheets in mind.

"A display some would find impressive."

The casual remark caused him to whirl round, his hand instinctively reaching up behind his cloak to grasp his sword once more. A woman stepped from the alley he had just left, slipping easily from the darkness as if she had been there all along. Lucius was not so certain that was not the case.

"Who are you?" he said warily, expecting any kind of trouble after events this evening.

"Do you not recognise me?"

Lucius stared at the woman for a moment, racking his mind. Her dark hair was tied up high on her head, in the style common to women used to fighting, and both her poise and manner indicated she was well accomplished in battle. In age, she was beginning to reach her middle years, but he thought she was no less attractive for that, for the leather tunic studded with small metal discs could not conceal the fact her body was extremely well-toned. Lucius had met such women before and he knew they could drive a blade through a man's body as easily as he could. A tell-tale and familiar bulge in one of her boots told him she was armed with at least one blade and he began to wonder what other weapons may be concealed.

Her eyes were the most striking feature though, dark pits that seemed impenetrable and yet likely missed nothing. They assessed him and the potential danger he posed, even as he weighed her in return. Upon seeing that gaze cast upon him once more, he knew exactly who he was talking to.

"Aidy," he said finally. "I hadn't counted on you still being here."

CHAPTER 2

Eyeing Aidy warily from across the table as she sipped her wine, Lucius was a little unnerved to realise she was returning his own suspicious stare. It had been eight years since he had last seen her but under the lanterns of the inn, the years had seemed only to brush against her. Those dark brown, almost black, eyes watched him with the same disapproval he began to remember all too well. They were bordered by a few lines he thought had not been there before, but the biggest change was in her demeanour. She seemed... harder. Colder. Half a decade older than he, Adrianna Torres was obviously just as dangerous as she was in the past.

"Damned chance us running into each other," he said, beginning to feel uncomfortable at the easy way in which she carried the silence.

"Fool," she said dismissively. "Have you forgotten

already the lessons of Master Roe? There is very little in this world that happens by coincidence."

"Then how... ?"

"Your arrival here was like a beacon. I would be surprised if every Shadowmage remaining in the city did not feel it."

Lucius was perplexed at that but did not feel like pushing the point and risking a lecture. Adrianna had been more advanced in the craft than he had ever been, and she was certainly more committed. He had always seen his control of the magical threads that made up the Shadowmage's art as a tool, a means to an end. For Aidy, it had been something more akin to a religion, with their shared Master the high priest. Still, at least there was some common ground there.

"So, still learning under Master Roe?"

Her eyes suddenly narrowed, and he mentally kicked himself. He should have guessed things had taken a turn for the worse after he had left Turnitia.

"No, I am not."

It was a leading statement, but Lucius found himself hesitating over the obvious question. Not for the first time, he felt as if he were being led by Aidy in the direction she wanted.

"What happened?"

"What do you think happened? The Empire of Vos increased its grip on the city after their occupation, and the Shadowmages were at the top of their list. Some fled." At this she looked pointedly at him. "The rest of us tried to fight. Without support, we were crushed. Master Roe, as one of the most visible among us, was captured by the Vos guard and taken to the Citadel."

"They killed him?"

"Well, they don't pamper you with whores and wine in the Citadel," she said, caustically.

"I'm sorry," he said. She let it pass but continued to stare at him witheringly over the rim of her glass. Her self-righteousness was beginning to grate on him.

"You do remember I had some problems of my own back then?" he said, trying not to sound defensive. "The war affected everyone in this city, not just the Shadowmages. The Final Faith was their vanguard, and they made damned sure the Brotherhood was in no position to raise objections. I lost my whole family, Aidy, and I would have been next. They knew who I was. I had no choice but to leave."

"You always had a choice."

"What, stand and fight?" he asked incredulously.

She leaned across the table, setting down her glass. "Yes," she said fiercely. "We needed every friend we had. Instead, you chose to run. And for what? What are you now? A vagabond, thief for hire, mercenary?"

"What possible difference could I have made? If you were not powerful enough to stop them taking the Master, what could I have done?"

Adrianna did not answer straight away. Finally leaning back in her chair, she broke eye contact with him for the first time since they had sat down. "It might have made all the difference in the world. You have no idea what you..."

She paused and seemed unwilling to continue.

"What?" he prompted, but she did not answer. As the silence between them grew, Lucius began to feel uncomfortable again. He cleared his throat.

"So, what are the Shadowmages doing now?" he asked.

"We are a pale... shadow of our former selves. Hunted by Vos, whose nobles are convinced we are unstoppable assassins, and used by Pontaine nobles who think much the same thing. The guild is directionless with so many members dead and no one training young blood."

Lucius frowned. "Aidy, it was never much of a guild..." he started.

"It was more a guild than many others in this city. We pledged to never attack one another, to re-assign ourselves when contracts clashed, and to take any and all action when one of us was in danger. Some of us still adhere to the old ways." She gave a short, bitter laugh. "Old ways! It has only been eight years, and yet it seems like ancient history."

Draining her glass, she seemed in no hurry to order another, and Lucius presumed their meeting was drawing to a close.

"So, Lucius, just why have you returned? Come to claim your inheritance? Cause more trouble for your former allies? Why have you come back to Turnitia?"

Lucius shrugged. "I've spent the past eight years wandering the Anclas Territories and Pontaine. I wanted to see home again. I've kept out of the strife between the Empire and Pontaine, but I thought there might be someone here who could use my talents."

"Ha!" Adrianna cried, drawing the attention of the few remaining merchants and traders scattered on the tables around them. "I was right – playing the mercenary."

"I have a right to make a living," said Lucius, giving her an injured look. "The guild could help me with that. Just a few jobs, and then I'll be out of here."

"The guild no longer exists, Lucius," Adrianna said firmly. "Not for you. Not for those who ran."

She stood abruptly and threw a few coins on the table to pay for their wine. "You are not welcome in Turnitia, Lucius Kane. Leave. Now. You are not wanted."

Left staring at her back as she departed, Lucius nursed

what remaned of his wine, wondering just how he would continue working in the city if Adrianna decided to make life difficult for him.

The sun was peering past Kerberos as Lucius paced Ring Street, its full daylight strength beginning to warm Turnitia as the citizenry stirred. As the fiery ball moved inexorably clear of Kerberos' shadow, its rays warped and shimmered through the clouds of its giant companion until it coalesced into a solid sphere.

Ring Street was the thoroughfare that bound the Five Markets together, and it was heaving with traffic. Lying east of the merchant quarter and the docks, the Five Markets were the centre of commerce in Turnitia and on any given day they would be thronged with traders and peddlers, all calling and shrieking for custom, be it from the city's own population or foreign merchants looking to secure new goods for their own home markets.

At the centre of the Five Markets lay the Citadel, a giant fortress that leered over the city and its people. As he looked up warily at its ramparts and the guards that lined them, Lucius recalled that it had been merely a single tower used by the watch when he was last in Turnitia. When Vos had fought with Pontaine, the city had been quickly conquered and the Empire, keen not to lose any territory of value, had dedicated its energies to rebuilding the tower, turning it into an unassailable fortress. A double line of high walls had been thrown up around the tower, causing many to speak of terrible crimes being committed within the hidden interior. The tower itself was expanded into an entire keep within just three years, and a law was passed that no other structures in Turnitia were permitted to be built taller than the

Citadel. The message was clear; nothing was above the Empire of Vos.

The original tower still stood, but it had been reinforced and built, to match its four companions, each of which loomed over one of the Five Markets. At the pinnacle of each tower, a flagpole rose bearing the fluttering standard of Vos, a black eagle on a red field.

Lucius felt the presence of Vos in the streets too as he wandered this part of the city. Patrols of the guard, now cloaked in the livery of the Empire, were frequent and terribly efficient. Wherever he found himself on Ring Street or within one of the Five Markets, a patrol of five or six red-tabarded guards were always in sight. What he found curious was that the people of Turnitia seemed to readily accept the presence of the guard, even act friendly towards them. Some chatted amiably with one patrol, while others stood dutifully to one side as another hurried past on some errand.

It seemed as if he were the only one to remember the dreadful days after the army of Vos had routed Turnitia's pitifully small guard and entered the city. The persecutions, the dismantling of the existing law and order, and the carefree violence; women violated in the streets and in their homes, men killed casually while trying to defend them, shops looted then burned. The religion of the Brotherhood wiped out and the Shadowmages decimated.

Looking around as he passed through the Five Markets, Lucius began to understand why the people of his city had been so quick to forget those times. Despite the many guards patrolling the streets, despite the constant, foreboding presence of the Citadel in the heart of Turnitia, business was clearly going well.

The Five Markets were packed with crowds, and there were not enough stalls for all the traders, many being forced to set up shop in alleyways and on street corners. Fine Pontaine wines brought in from the captured Anclas Territories were sold alongside clothes of the highest fashion worn in the Vos cities of Malmkrug, Scholten and Vosburg. The people of the city moved easily, dressed in clothing finer than he remembered them wearing eight years before, and the traders themselves seemed to be doing a great deal of business.

He had to admit, it was not the city he had grown up in. The population had forgiven Vos for its crimes in return for an economy that had flourished, the city's coffers swelled by the presence of the invaders. So what if a little freedom had been curtailed and new taxes imposed? Everyone was better off.

Except himself, Lucius thought. Perhaps the old saying was true, and you really could never go back home. Turnitia was no longer the place he had thought it was, and it was unlikely to welcome one of his sort. Adrianna had been right in one thing; he had grown into an adventurer and mercenary.

He was not entirely sure when it had happened, but he thought of his time in Pontaine and the Anclas territories, working as a sword for hire, trading his skills for gold and silver as the opportunity struck. It had not been a bad life, he decided, and he certainly appreciated the freedom he had experienced more than the people of Turnitia mourned its loss.

As he wandered through a crowd gathering around a stall whose rotund trader cajoled them into buying trinkets all the way from Allantia, or so he claimed, Lucius made the decision to make what money he could in the city, then leave. He needed gold for a horse and supplies. Then he could perhaps lose himself in the Anclas Territories once more, or perhaps journey deep into Pontaine to discover what lay within the Sardenne. Maybe head north to Allantia, he thought as he eyed the trader. Why not? He was free to do as he wished. Money permitting.

Lucius flicked his eyes to each side as he paced the Five Markets, looking for an opportunity, some sign of the old city he would find familiar and could turn to his advantage. An old acquaintance, perhaps, who could push work his way. A rich trader in need of a capable guard. A ship's captain recruiting marines to work the dangerous trade routes. Anything that provided quick and ready gold.

Much of his morning was spent in this way, but Lucius found little that presented itself. He feared he might be reduced to gambling as a means to an end, but even his special skills might not guarantee win after win. There was a reason they called it gambling, of course, and there was always the risk he might meet someone whose luck or skill at cheating might exceed his own abilities; and then he would be back to square one.

Trying to think a little more laterally, he began to eye up the various stores he passed, and his gaze fixed upon a trader whose accent gave him away as Vos born and bred. His stall was bedecked with chains of gold and silver, bracelets and brooches sparkling in the strengthening sunlight as their gems glinted with every colour Lucius could imagine. He stopped in the street and stared, thinking fast. A quick distraction would be easy enough to create, and a faster hand could sweep a cluster of jewels under his cloak before the trader's attention was brought back to his wares. Glancing about, he looked for the telltale red of guard patrols and, sure enough, he saw two at opposite ends of this market. However, they were both at least a hundred paces away, and would have to fight their way through the crowd.

The trader was engaged in an animated discussion over a thin gold chain with a young lady wreathed in silks. He was anxiously assuring her that the chain would bring focus to her neck which, he declared, could not remain unadorned another minute. Lucius cast a look at the two patrols, and then began to search for escape routes. He knew he would have to move fast once the goods were in his possession. The alleyways in the area were too crowded for his comfort, with peddlers and customers spilling over the boundaries of the markets. He knew he could make a crowd work for him, but it would be better overall if no cry of alarm went up until he was well on his way. He took a step forward, preparing to draw upon otherworldly energies to create the distraction he would need.

"I wouldn't if I was you," a gravely voice behind him said.

Lucius turned then looked downwards to find the source of the comment. He saw a filthy man sitting on the cobbles, leaning against a rusting horse trough. The man's clothes were a patchwork of cast-offs, each thread entangled with dirt, crusted food and other, less describable stains. A terrible stench of sweat and foulness reached Lucius' nostrils, and he gagged as he tried to form a retort.

"You'd never make it out of the market in time," the man continued as he quite openly scratched at his nether regions. "See, people here don't like thieves too much. Don't like beggars either, as it happens, but we just get moved on from time to time. You'd go straight to the Citadel, make no mistake. And then you really would be in trouble."

Lucius stared at the man for the moment, peering through the dirt and wild greying hair to detect any deceit. He had the feeling he was being played, but could not quite put his finger on how.

"What business is it of yours?" he asked, quickly glancing about to see if the beggar had any accomplices that were about to assault or rob him.

The man shrugged. "Call it some advice from someone who knows. That much I'll give you for free. If you want more, it'll cost." With this, the man produced a tin cup from the folds of his rags and proffered it upwards to Lucius. "Spare a coin for the sick?" he said with a grin that revealed ruined and blackened teeth.

Trying hard not to wrinkle his face in disgust, Lucius shook his head. "You've caught me at a bad time, my friend. I am as desperate for coin as you."

"Oh, I'm not so sure about that," the man said, winking at Lucius. "A man like you is never far from gold."

That checked Lucius and he gave the man a hard look. "And just what do you mean by that?"

The man shook his head noncommittally. "I've seen you about."

"I haven't been in the city long."

"Last evening, for example. Six men was it? Or seven?"

Lucius narrowed his eyes. "How do you know this? I saw no one else."

The ruined teeth grinned at him again. "That's the point. No one sees us beggars. Just part of the scenery. There I was, just minding me own business, trying to get some kip in the door of the local book-seller. But I have a clear view down a certain alley, and what I saw there was... intriguing."

Lucius glanced about nervously, seeing if anyone else was taking an interest in the conversation, but the crowd seemed to be far more intent on securing deals on food, clothing, or luxuries.

"And what, exactly, would a beggar find intriguing about it?" Lucius said dangerously, though he was a little unsure of what he could do to this man while so many people were close by.

"Just going to dismiss me because I am a beggar, is it? Of no use to anyone, a stain on the backside of Turnitia? Well, I'll tell you, my foolish friend. We beggars are the eyes and ears of the city. What we don't see 'ain't worth knowing. The wise man knows this, and rewards a beggar for the information he has." Again, the tin cup was shaken in front of Lucius.

Pursing his lips, Lucius considered the man and his words. Opportunity had so far eluded him this morning, and the beggar clearly understood the city and its workings. If the man's intention was to call the guard and get a reward for finding a Shadowmage, if indeed he truly understood what had taken place in the alley the evening before, then surely he would already have done so. The greatest danger was, surely, that the beggar was simply fleecing him for a coin. Despite Lucius' own financial circumstances, the beggar certainly looked as if he needed the money more than him. His face full of distrust, he reached into his pouch and flipped a coin into the cup.

The beggar grinned openly as he scooped the coin out. "Ah, blessings of the Faith be on you."

Lucius watched as the coin disappeared in the folds of the man's rags. He coughed to bring attention back to himself. "And you have information for me?"

"Well, it seems to me you're looking for good money."

"How perceptive."

"There's a peddler across the way, near the fountain

in the centre of this market. You'll recognise him, has a green awning above his stall. Sells pans and ornaments, foreign junk."

"And?"

"Ask for Ambrose. You'll be thanking me later."

The beggar shifted his position, then stood, brushing himself down as if removing the dirt of the street would have any effect on his hygiene.

"That's it?" Lucius asked, frowning.

"That's it. Can't do everything for you. My thanks for the coin," the beggar said as he waddled away. Then, he stopped and turned back to Lucius. "Oh, and a word of advice while you are in the city. Always pay a beggar. You never know how fortune may smile upon you."

Lucius was left standing as the man disappeared into the crowd. He shook his head in disbelief, for if this had been a scam, it was a lengthy process simply to gain a single coin. Quickly, he reached down for his pouch to make sure that it was still there and was reassured by its bulk, filled with the proceeds of the previous evening's gambling. Giving one more glance at the jewellery on the stall in front of him, he walked past it, heading towards the centre of the market.

Finding a single stall with a green awning was not a simple task, he soon discovered. The market was a riot of colours, with many traders shadowing their goods and potential customers from the sun with gaudy parasols, awnings and wind-breakers. These clashed with the silks, wools and furs, which in turn competed with brightly coloured signs proclaiming that only they had the best deals in the city.

The fountain was likely a new construction, for Lucius remembered no such decoration in this market years before. As he neared its carved grey stone, his thoughts were confirmed as he saw the tall and familiar figure of the Anointed Lord Katherine Makennon. Her statue stood as depicted in the many paintings that were spreading throughout the Empire as signs of piety and faith; plate-armoured, sword held high in readiness to strike down unbelievers and infidels. Long hair flew from beneath an elegant helm, its front plates open to reveal a stern faced woman. One hand was held low, as if offered for a kiss of fealty, and from this water flowed into a marble basin. People sat around the rim, but all were at an awkward angle, for one did not turn their back on God's own true representative. A squad of guardsmen were never far away to ensure this observance was followed in public.

After circling the fountain, Lucius finally found the stall he was looking for. The awning was indeed green but, unlike many others nearby, it looked as if it had seen better days. A quick inspection of the goods on display revealed that they were indeed best described as foreign junk. A few largely disinterested passers-by were collared by the animated man behind the stall, perhaps looking for a rare, yet cheap, relic or artefact among the detritus spread across the cloth-covered surface of the stall. Another man sat to one side, whittling away at a wood carved feline creature, either having fashioned it from scratch, or more likely, repairing some sign of damage.

Lucius sidled up to the stall, suddenly unsure of himself. He picked up a model of a ship, one of its masts twisting under the movement to hang by a thin strip of wood across the deck. The trader immediately turned his attention to the newcomer and started a practised spiel that described the model as a rare work of art from Allantia, honed by a fine craftsman whose name would soon spread throughout the peninsula, raising the value of investment in any of his works purchased now.

Lucius quickly looked at the other patrons of the stall then, seeing them take not the slightest notice of him, said quietly, "I am looking for Ambrose."

The trader immediately lost interest in him, quickly jerking his head toward the man whittling wood before turning back to more likely prospects. Lucius took the sign and placed the ship back on the stall.

"You Ambrose?" he asked, standing over the man as he worked. The man did not bother to look up from the carving he drew a knife over, and Lucius saw it was actually some fantastic creature that stood on two legs, with fierce gouging fangs. The man himself was middle-aged, thin, and dressed in a cheap black tunic.

"Depends," the man answered lazily. "You after a commission? Come back next week, I've got enough for now."

"I'm after work."

"Any good with wood?"

Lucius frowned, not certain he had approached this conversation properly. "I don't think that is the kind of work intended."

The man looked up at him curiously. "Who sent you?"

"Some beggar," Lucius said lamely with a shrug.

"You pay him for my name?"

"I did."

"Good. You looking to work inside the law?" Ambrose asked.

Lucius smiled at that. "I have a feeling that if that was what I was after, I wouldn't be talking to you. No, I have no great desire to work purely within the law of Vos."

"Willing to take risks?"

"Of course. So long as the reward matches them."

Ambrose put his wood carving on the ground and stood, looking Lucius up and down as if weighing his worth.

"You look fit. Can you run?"

"Faster than you would think."

"And fight?"

"If I have to. Haven't been beaten yet."

Ambrose shook his head. "Everyone gets a beating once in a while. The sooner you learn that, the better." He paused for a moment, then seemed to make up his mind. "You'll start at the bottom – means you'll be working with the kids, but do well and we'll see what else you are capable of."

"What's the work? And where?"

"Right here," Ambrose said, sweeping a hand across the market. "I'll put you on a team, you'll work the crowd. Earnings get pooled and split, with the guild taking its forty per cent. Listen to the kids in your team, they know more than you do. And stay away from the stalls, we don't rob them – we have too many friends among the traders, and we don't want you pissing them off."

Lucius frowned. "You want me to work as... a pickpocket. That it?"

Ambrose cocked an eyebrow. "Too good for that line of work, are you? Let me tell you, I – and every thief I know, for that matter – started off on one of these teams. And I never regretted a minute of it. Learn the trade, and then we'll see what else you are capable of. If you are as good as you seem to think you are we'll find the right place for you."

"I was hoping for some real money," Lucius said, a little disenchanted as he saw his future boiling away to nothing more than petty crime and humiliating spells in the stocks. If, indeed, the Vos guard bothered with anything as trivial as stocks for captured thieves. He was surprised to see Ambrose smiling at him.

"I tell you what," said Ambrose. "You give me a week on a team. If you don't like it, if you decide it is not for you, if it is not bringing in the sort of money you are after, then we'll call it quits. You can just walk away, no harm done."

Ambrose sat back down and picked up his carving again. "But I have a feeling that once you see what a noble and skilled profession you have joined, you'll be less than ready to give it up."

CHAPTER 3

The Five Markets had changed, at least for Lucius. No longer were they thronged with crowds wandering aimlessly between traders while trying to save a few coins on their latest purchase, nor was a chance opportunity floating elusively away from him. Instead, this place of commerce had become his hunting ground.

Ambrose had assigned him to a pickpocket team that same afternoon, and his new comrades were Markel and Treal, twin brother and sister no more than twelve or thirteen years old. The previous member of their team, a lad named Harker, Lucius learned, had been promoted to work within the guildhouse of the Night Hands, the title given to this band of thieves. Lucius was taking his place, but neither Markel nor Treal made any comment about his advanced years, even though pick-pocketing was a child's game.

Their acceptance of an adult as an equal, if anything, made Lucius even more self-conscious of what he was doing, and more than once he wondered how much further he could possibly fall. Still, Ambrose had promised that he would not regret the money that would soon be flowing through his hands.

The veteran thief kept a close eye on Lucius' team, and several others, directing them to different areas within the Five Markets, rotating each so suspicious guards would inevitably lose track of the children they had started to watch. The proceeds of their work were transferred to Ambrose regularly, and he quickly sorted the guild's percentage and scribbled down what was owed to each team in his own code, to be returned to each member by the end of the day. It was a well-practised system, with more valuable goods, such as jewels and cut stones, quickly fenced through the Night Hands' own network of dealers and traders, to be returned as hard currency at the day's final accounting.

Lucius' first day was humiliating for him, taking instructions from two children barely old enough to piss in a pot, while his own efforts at grabbing purses and pouches without notice were more often than not dismal failures, forcing him to beat a hasty retreat before his mark realised just what he had intended. By the end of the second day, Lucius was about ready to walk away from the deal and take his chances running cards in taverns. What stopped him was partially the realisation that he was getting better in his role, but mostly because Ambrose made good on his promise of real money. Lucius had not been bothering to keep track of the pockets he, Markel and Treal had picked during the day as he descended ever further into depression, and he actually took a step back in surprise when Ambrose read them their total day's

takings as the sun fell beneath the rooftops of the city
and the Five Markets began to clear of custom.

His share amounted to twelve full silvers, plus a little
change, which he gratefully took from Ambrose and
swept into his own pouch.

"You see, lad?" Ambrose had said. "I told you there was
good money in this."

Treal had told him that skilled teams that had worked
together for many months could easily triple or quadruple
this on a good day, and he slowly came to believe this
was more than just an idle boast. While it was true that he
could earn more than this in a single evening's gambling,
particularly when he brought his magic to bear, this work
carried far less risk of discovery. It was easy, and despite
their tender young years, Markel and Treal were solid
partners with honed tactics that had been passed down to
them from thieves with years of experience.

A pick pocketing team always consisted of three.
During his work in the Five Markets, Treal pointed out
the 'independents,' as she called them, desperate men
who worked alone. Watching them ply the crowd, Lucius
saw the flaws in their plan. With no backup or support,
they risked their lives and liberty with every mark they
robbed. One bad move, one moment of inattention
inevitably led to a cry of "thief" being raised, and then
it was only a matter of time. The guard would be on
the scene in seconds, and there were many in the crowd
willing to play hero and delay the thief's escape long
enough for him to be collared by a mailed hand. True,
the independents shared their ill-gotten gains with no
one else, but they would always, *always*, be caught in
the end.

In a Night Hands team, every member had their own
specific role to play, though they would often switch

throughout the day in order to spread experience and practice, as well as throw off any suspicions a mark, or the guard might have,

Once a mark had been picked out of the crowd, the first member of the team created a distraction. This could be as straightforward as actually approaching the mark and asking for, say, directions to a nearby tavern (something which, being an adult, Lucius found easy, as marks were more likely to pay him attention). The second team member then moved in to grab the belt pouch, purse, sack of valuables, or whatever had been deemed worth the effort. Small and high value items were the most desirable, and pouches were at the top of the list. It was the role of the third member of the team that impressed Lucius the most. Once the snatch had been made, the second member would disappear into the crowd, where the third would be waiting for them. The goods would then be passed between them and the third would leave the market for a pre-arranged rendezvous. This was done so that if they were made by the mark – that is, the second team member was caught in the act – no incriminating stolen goods would be found upon him when searched. The Vos guard would find it difficult to arrest someone if an accusation appeared blatantly false.

Distract, grab, switch. The secret to making a small fortune from picking pockets.

Of course, even the dullest guard would soon become suspicious if the same group of children were being collared every hour, and this was where Ambrose came in. He monitored the activities of all the pick-pocketing teams working the Five Markets, and he would regularly rotate their patches so the same team would not be stealing from under the noses of the same guardsmen all the time. The guard rotated their patrols as well, but

Ambrose kept a close eye on their activities, all noted down in his own code, and was good at keeping his kids one step ahead.

It worked. It worked very well. By the end of the first week, Lucius had earned more than a hundred full silver, less the Night Hands forty percent, of course.

He had grown to like Markel and Treal too, though for all the world he could not see why, as he had little in common with them. They had made no judgements as to why an adult had been placed on their team, and they soon spotted that Lucius was a quick learner. By the end of the third day, they had begun to defer to him when selecting marks, and he was able to execute distractions, both subtle and calamitous, with far greater ease.

They had only one brush with the guard during the week and, for that, Lucius was grateful. As had become the norm, he had picked the mark, a lady of good money if not good breeding, escorting her young daughter through the dressmakers of the Five Markets. The girl was perhaps in her late teens, perhaps looking for something suitable to wear in a coming society function in which she hoped to impress. Lucius, however, had first noted her mother's bulging purse, looped around a belt behind her back.

After pointing her out to Markel and Treal, then agreeing a plan, Lucius approached them while they turned from one stall to search for another carrying the fabrics they sought.

"Ladies, I am so sorry to trouble you," Lucius began as he stepped in front of them. He wore a now well-practised smile, feigning a little embarrassment, keyed to set a mark at ease. "I arrived in Turnitia yesterday, and am hopelessly lost."

As Lucius started to ask for directions to the Street of Dogs, where he ostensibly hoped to find an old friend, he kept his attention on his peripheral vision. Markel had sidled up to the woman and, with a short blade, cut the strings of the purse, allowing it to easily drop into his hand. Making no eye contact with Lucius, he turned and walked quickly away.

"Mother! That boy!" The girl's voice was high and shrill, and it caused her mother to immediately reach behind her back to find the purse gone. She looked back at Lucius accusingly, and he felt a rise of panic.

"You've been robbed!" he cried with as much conviction as he could muster. "There, that boy, there! Thief!"

Knowing that the daughter had already made Markel, he could only pray the boy would slip the purse to his sister with all speed. The cry of "Thief!" was picked up quickly by the crowd, who themselves were split between wanting any criminal brought to justice and seeing an exciting pursuit through the market.

Lucius saw some of them make a grab for Markel and he winced as he thought of what Ambrose might say about him giving up one of his own team. His heart fell further when he heard the next cry.

"Make way! Guard! Make way!" Six red-clad and very well armoured men were making their way through the crowd, which readily parted before them.

"I have him!" another voice cried, and a struggling Markel was held aloft as the guard closed in. "Here's the thief!"

"I am no thief!" Markel shouted and Lucius thought he saw tears in the boy's eyes, though whether they were genuine or part of his act, he could not say.

The lady, trailed by her daughter, forgot all about Lucius as she stalked imperiously toward the guard, who had formed a circle around Markel. Her demands for her purse were met by flat denials from Markel, and two guardsmen soon had him hoisted into the air by his arms as another searched his tunic thoroughly. Lucius began to think that they might actually turn him upside down and shake him, but no purse was found.

With no apologies, Markel was released, and he disappeared. Lucius looked about, thinking he might see Treal poking her head from amongst the crowd, a sly wink on her face letting him know the switch had been made and that she now had the purse. She was nowhere to be seen and Lucius reminded himself that, despite her age, she was utterly professional when it came to work. The thought gave him some chagrin, as he was still standing there on the scene when he should have disappeared himself when the daughter had first cried.

With no more excitement seeming to be had, the crowd soon went back to its business and Lucius joined them in filtering away. He took a circuitous route around the market, as much out of habit now as wanting to throw off anyone who might have grown overly suspicious at his presence near the theft, and then headed back to his team's rendezvous. They had picked a sub-alley, which was probably an overly grand term. It was a dark and filthy place, full of discarded food, rags and, Lucius suspected, vermin. The key, however, was that it was quiet with no peddlers spilling over from the main trading areas, and no pedestrians taking a short cut from one market to another. Lucius' only worry was that they themselves might get robbed here by some desperate footpad, though he trusted in his own abilities to protect the kids.

Markel was already waiting for him when he arrived, perched on top of a stack of wooden boxes. He smiled as Lucius approached.

"Seen Treal yet?" Lucius asked.

"Nah. She'll be here soon. Good mark that one, I'll bet," Markel said by way of compliment.

Lucius shrugged. "Didn't go so well. Sorry about fingering you like that – I thought the woman had made me, couldn't think what else to do."

The fact he was making a heartfelt apology to a twelve year old boy did not strike Lucius as being odd in the least. After having worked alongside the two kids for the past few days, he had begun to treat them as equally as they had treated him from the start.

Markel shrugged the apology away. "Not the first time I've been collared – hazard of the job. Anyway, you did the right thing, throwing suspicion away from yourself. You have to trust in the other guy getting away – that's *his* job."

"And you made the switch?"

"Easy. Treal snuck in and took it just before they grabbed me."

Lucius looked at the boy, with a quizzical expression, prompting Markel to ask him what he was thinking.

"I've been wondering," Lucius said. "You earn good money doing this, and have been doing it for a while. What do you spend it on?"

"Oh, you think that kids can't spend money wisely," Markel said, mocking him. "Most of it goes to our parents right now. Doing this beats working at some butchers or tanners, and they don't complain when they see how much we bring in. The rest we mostly give to Caradoc for keeping."

"Caradoc?" Lucius asked.

"He's the lieutenant of the Night Hands. You'll meet him soon, I guess. He takes a special interest in kids who join the Hands, says they are the future. It was him who got Ambrose to start watching the teams in the markets."

"So what does he do with your money?"

"Holds it for us. Says we would just spend it on beer, and he's probably right. When we leave the teams and become proper thieves, we get the money. Spend it on the gear we'll need – lockpicks, a decent blade, silk rope. That stuff's expensive."

"When do you think you'll get accepted?"

Markel pursed his lips in thought. "A year maybe. If we carry on doing well. I'll probably see you in the guildhouse then."

"You think?"

"You won't be with us long. You're too good. They're just testing you, seeing how you work, and whether you can be trusted."

Lucius sighed. "Tell you the truth, wasn't planning to stay around long. Just wanted to earn some money, then leave."

"You mean leave the city?"

Lucius nodded.

"Nah, you'll stay."

"Oh, yes?"

"The money's too good. If you can avoid getting caught, that is, and I don't think you are planning on that any time soon."

Leaning back against the wall, Markel closed his eyes and dozed while he waited, leaving Lucius to his thoughts. Lucius marvelled in the kid's ability to switch off so quickly. He was hard to restrain at times but whenever there was nothing to do, he could fall into a light sleep almost on command.

Stifling a yawn himself, Lucius was surprised to find how weary he could become after a few marks had been worked. He started to chuckle as he considered the idea that thieving for a living could actually be hard work, but was distracted by a flash of movement within the alley beyond. Treal came tearing round the corner, skidding to a halt in front of them.

"Took your time," Markel said without opening an eye.

"Just met up with Ambrose," Treal said breathlessly, and she put a hand on Lucius' shoulder to steady herself as she panted. With her hair cut short and clothes carelessly chosen, she looked much like her brother, though Lucius thought she might become quite attractive in a few years.

"And?" he prompted.

"Just a few silver coins," Treal said, pausing as she savoured the disappointment in Lucius' eyes, before adding, "and a handful of emeralds and sapphires!"

Lucius smiled. Any cut stone that was green or blue was an emerald or sapphire to Treal, for she had yet to develop a thief's keen eye for detail. However, it would be a good haul nonetheless, and he looked forward to their meeting later with Ambrose when they would learn how much the stones had been fenced for.

"We're to move to the northern markets," Treal continued. "Ambrose saw what happened with Markel, and says there is no reason to push our luck. Vern's guys will take over this patch."

"We'd better get going then."

"Yeah – wake my brother up."

They switched roles in the afternoon, and it was Lucius' turn to be handed stolen goods, this time by Treal who would make the grab while her brother distracted the mark. The twins looked to Lucius to pick almost all their marks now, buoyed by their success earlier. They all smelled a good day's takings, and were eager to capitalise on their previous trade.

As the day wore on, the crowds thronging the Five Markets peaked, and then started to recede. There was still enough cover for the team to operate, with the ability to lose oneself among people paramount, and Lucius casually leaned against a plinth missing a statue, the original having been torn down during the city's fall. Treal was close by, while Markel sat by the market's edge a little further off, watching for the signal to move in on a mark.

Treal had been outlying a not entirely serious plan on how they could gain fame by being the first team to treat a guard patrol as a mark, perhaps lifting the sergeant's sword, when Lucius hushed for her attention. Nodding into the crowd, he indicated the unmistakable signs, to the trained eye at least, of a team closing in on a mark. They watched as a young lad purposefully tripped in front of an elderly man. Pretending to be in some distress, the boy persuaded the man to bend down to help him back up, even as one of the boy's friends quickly stepped up behind to lift the man's money.

"I thought Vern and his team were moved to our patch," he said.

"They were," said Treal. "That's not Vern. Damn them!"

Her exclamation caught Lucius by surprise, and he was mystified as Treal caught her brother's attention and directed it to the other pickpockets. Markel frowned angrily when he saw what was going on, and he nodded back to his sister.

"Go and get Ambrose," Treal said to Lucius. "We'll keep watch here and make sure they don't get far. Tell him that the Guild has moved into the markets."

Lucius was thoroughly confused. "Guild? I thought we were the guild?"

"Not this one, we're not. Quickly, get Ambrose," she said, shooing him away.

No wiser, Lucius did as instructed, pushing his way through the crowds to Ring Street, which was the quickest route to the knick-knack stall by the fountain. He began to hurry, not knowing what was going on, but driven by Treal's sense of urgency.

It was with some relief that Lucius saw Ambrose in his usual spot, talking to a young boy who he presumed was another pickpocket from a different team. Lucius paused, unsure of whether he should interrupt another team's business, but his seniority in years got the better of him and he marched up to Ambrose.

The veteran thief looked up in surprise, a querying look on his face.

"A message from Treal," Lucius said. "The Guild is in the markets."

"Damn it!" Ambrose cursed, with a virulence that made Lucius wonder just how bad the situation was. Ambrose turned his attention briefly to the boy standing with them. "Move to the east, like I told you. And not a word of the Guild to anyone, understand? If I hear any rumours floating about, I'll know where they came from."

The boy gave a hurried nod, then fled into the market. Ambrose stood and gestured for Lucius to lead the way.

Their pace was quick, with Ambrose driving Lucius on until his legs began to ache. "I am not entirely sure what is going on," Lucius said as they half walked, half trotted.

"The Guild is moving in on our territory. No damn respect, that's their problem. Today it's just pick-pocketing, but they'll be watching how we react. Any weakness here and they'll be all over our territory."

"I thought we were the only thieves guild in Turnitia," Lucius said, beginning to become a little breathless.

"Would that were so," said Ambrose with a grim tone. "Used to be just one, before Vos descended upon us all. They smashed the old Guild, broke it up. Didn't want any rivals in the city, you see. Took a few years for the thieves to get back together again and when they did, they could not agree on who should lead."

"So two guilds arose?"

"That's right. The Night Hands, under our Magnus, while Loredo started his Guild of Coin and Enterprise. Pompous man, pompous title."

"And they've been fighting ever since?"

"No one's died yet, been nothing more than a few brawls. The city got carved up into territories managed by them or us, but no one was completely happy with what they got. When we get to this Guild team, just follow my lead. Remember, they are just kids, whatever the provocation. I am not going to start a war because of pickpockets!"

They reached the northern market quickly and Markel's nod caught Lucius' attention from the people still milling around the stalls. They were quickly joined by Treal, who related what she had seen to Ambrose.

"Just three of them, seen no other teams. Don't recognise them. Could be they've been brought up from the docks. They're good – well practised. Definitely Guild, they've done this before."

"They still working?"

"Moved to the north edge, following the crowd and keeping away from the Citadel. I'll show you."

They followed the twins, threading through the waning crowd. Treal and Markel then stopped and, with a nod of the latter's head, they looked on to see the three young thieves. Lucius saw they were probably younger than his charges, lounging casually around the front of an open forge. To the casual eye they were just a group of kids lazing between chores, but Lucius saw the flickering glances, quiet muttering and sly movements that told him they were carefully combing passers-by, searching for another easy and rich mark.

Without breaking a step, Ambrose took the lead and marched straight up to them, Lucius in his wake and the twins trailing. At sight of the approaching man, the boys looked as if they were about to run but seeing nowhere to flee, one obviously decided to brazen it out, and his friends took his lead.

"Bugger off, the lot of you!" Ambrose's first words were not subtle in the least.

"Says who, old man?" said one of the boys, taking a step forward to meet the challenge. "We got as much right to be here as you."

"You know damn well this 'ain't your place. Now, clear off, or you'll be in for a beating."

One of the other boys threw a purse at Ambrose. It was empty, having been looted by them earlier, but the sign of defiance made Markel start, and he stepped past Lucius, fists raised. Lucius laid a hand on the back of Markel's neck, and then held it firm when he tried to struggle free.

"Not here," Lucius whispered. "Ambrose's orders."

That was sufficient to restrain Markel, but Lucius could feel his anger.

The lead boy took another step up to Ambrose and, completely unafraid, spat at his feet. "Your time's over, old man. The markets belong to us now."

"Oh, is that so?" said Ambrose and, like a snake, his arm shot forward to grab the boy. The boy struggled until

Ambrose cuffed him round the back of the head, and he was not gentle about it. The blow stunned the boy briefly, and he fell to the ground on his backside. When he heard Treal giggling at his misfortune, his eyes blazed with a fury that Lucius had thought only possible in frenzied warriors.

"You'll regret that, old man," he said, as he picked himself up. Despite his conviction, he started to back away, his friends following him. "Loredo will hear of this."

"I'm sure," Ambrose said. "He must take a personal interest in all the kids working for him. Well, you just tell him that the markets are our ground, and we won't stand for any pushing from him. Won't stand for it, you hear?"

The boys left, the last throwing an obscene gesture at the four of them before turning to follow his friends. Markel was still angry, while Treal jabbed Lucius in the ribs, laughing at the memory of the boy being knocked to the floor.

Sighing, Ambrose turned to Lucius.

"There'll be trouble there, mark my words. The Guild has been getting more aggressive over the past few months. Looks like we'll have plenty of work for you yet, and it won't be picking pockets."

Lucius stared past him, watching the boys disappear into a side street leading away from the market, wondering why every time he found an easy living, something always contrived to take it away from him.

CHAPTER 4

Markel had been right as it turned out, Lucius had not been kept on the team for long. A week later, Ambrose announced he was to be taken to the guildhouse of the Night Hands. Thus would start his true induction into the organisation.

He had not been sure quite what to expect of a thieves' headquarters. Something in the sewers, perhaps, accessible only by secret passageways and coded knocks, backed up by the password of the day. Maybe a rundown and dilapidated structure in the poorest quarter of the city, dismissed by passing guard patrols, and yet readily turned into a defensible fort when assaulted, with assassins and marksmen sniping from windows. Or it could be palatial, hiding behind the guise of some noble's holdings and filled with the proceeds of years of thieving, decked in gold and silver, with rare objects d'art scattered in every room in the most vulgar fashion.

It was none of those things. From the outside, the town house looked like every other in the aptly named Rogue's Way. The street had earned its title decades ago from a scandalous merchant who managed to rob several nobles blind before he was discovered and deported back to Pontaine. The house itself was a three storey structure with large bay windows protected from prying eyes by thick curtains and thicker shutters.

The front door appeared solid enough, but it was not until Lucius was permitted entry that he realised its heavy oak exterior was supported inside by metal bands and finely-crafted locks, and he guessed it would take at least a squad of guardsmen armed with a battering ram to break it down.

A short hallway led into a common room, which looked for all the world like that of a tavern. A bar was situated on the far side of the room, while tables were scattered about randomly, their occupants engaged in games of dice and cards, drinking or huddled together while whispering in conspiratorial tones. The furniture had certainly seen better days than that usually found in taverns, as it seemed thieves had better respect for their surroundings, but it was not of unusually high quality. No rare paintings adorned the wall, no golden sculptures graced the bar.

The rest of the ground floor was taken up by the kitchens, a couple of small store rooms (which held essential supplies, and were never used for hiding stolen goods), and several sleeping areas which were shared by guild members. Ambrose informed him that he was free to make use of them, and Lucius accepted, glad to be free of the financial burden his continued stay at an inn in the merchant quarter had imposed. Not that he could not afford it now, but why waste good coin when a perfectly good bed was available here? Rooms were not granted to individuals but instead shared by whoever was in the guildhouse at the time. There was little fear of having one's personal items go missing here, Ambrose informed him, as thieving from another member of the guild was grounds for immediate expulsion. As Lucius would find out, once granted membership, very few chose to voluntarily leave, as the perks were just too good. Access to the guildhouse, which was regarded as a safe bolt-hole for those running from the guard or an angry merchant, was really the least of these. Now he had been granted full membership, Lucius was considered to be on the payroll.

Money was still earned on a commission basis, based upon the success of individual operations, but there was plenty of work to be had in a city the size of Turnitia. Over the course of the next few days, Ambrose introduced Lucius to several thieves, most of whom agreed to take him on their next few missions.

The work was varied and Lucius was surprised to learn that the Night Hands were frighteningly well organised, operating with a professionalism he would not have believed possible among thieves. Though many of the more successful thieves planned their own operations, staking out likely targets, then gathering fellow members to make a hit on a warehouse or rich noble's townhouse, there was also a great deal of regular day-to-day work the guild needed completed in order to run efficiently. The pickpocket teams in the Five Markets were just the tip of this. There were confidence scams down on the docks, protection rackets run on shop owners and innkeepers, a growing prostitution ring that was quickly adapting to serve all tastes while keeping the women (and a not a few men) safe from both their clients and the occasional invasion by the Guild of Coin and Enterprise.

Ambrose arranged for Lucius to attend one of the weekly collections along the Street of Dogs, which was regarded by the thieves he spoke to as a lucrative business. Once you had the muscle, he discovered, protection rackets were among the simplest and yet most profitable ventures the guild invested its time in. It really just boiled down to standing behind the man collecting the money, looking menacing. None of the traders in the Street of Dogs put up any resistance, while some seemed almost grateful. After all, the racket worked both ways; if they experienced any trouble that could not be resolved with the intervention of the guard, they always had the Night Hands to call upon. This could range from tracking down vandals hired by a rival, to 'persuading' a money lender that his rates were too high.

However, Lucius earned less from his time on protection than he did from pick-pocketing and when he raised this with Ambrose, he was told the work was simply a way of him gaining experience in what the guild did each day, and his place had been obtained as a personal favour to Ambrose himself. Such operations, he learned, were treated as a franchise. One thief, a few years ago, had gathered a group of friends together and started the racket. The Night Hands took its usual percentage, and the rest was split between the thieves doing the work. When the first thief died or otherwise left the guild, control of the racket was passed on to one of his colleagues, who then would decide whether to bring more thieves into the enterprise and expand, or simply keep the current profits rolling in. It was very clear that such operations were run only by the most senior thieves, as they were also the most lucrative; the hard work in setting up the operation had already been done and, bar the occasional upset and non-paying shop owner, the money rolled in continually, week after week. Positions in such rackets were therefore highly prized, and to gain entry you either had to buy your way in, or be extremely good friends with a current franchise holder.

This system ran throughout the Night Hands, and Lucius began to realise that Ambrose was one such senior thief, with his franchise being the teams working the Five Markets. He could not help but smile to himself when he realised that despite all the money he had earned during his time there, he had likely been earning Ambrose a good deal more.

Lucius still felt he was being watched and weighed, with the other thieves gauging whether he could truly be trusted, but he was fine with that. Any business that brought in as much money as he suspected the Night Hands had access to was aided by continual suspicion, not hindered by it. So, he spent his time in the guildhouse common room making easy conversation with visiting thieves, taking up any offer of work, and slowly making his presence felt. The work at his low level was fairly easy, the earnings fair, and expenses non-existent. Even food and wine was free here, so long as no thief over-indulged. A quick mission to break into the apartment of a visiting merchant here, a scam to grab a precious cargo as it was unloaded from a wagon train there. And all the time, the money kept flowing in, at a steadily greater rate of coin.

Fundamentally, the Night Hands were no different to any other sort of business. It was just the nature of the work it specialised in that set the guild apart and on the wrong side of the law.

A fortnight passed, and Lucius began to consider setting up his own operation. He had little experience, but Ambrose promised support and, indeed, seemed pleased that his protégé was beginning to bear fruit. After a day spent aiding another thief – an Allantian born man of slight build – in timing guard patrols round a warehouse that was rumoured to hold spices from the Sarcre Islands, Lucius returned to the guildhouse. The common room was almost empty, and the few remaining thieves present informed him that the guildmaster, Magnus, had cajoled many of them to take part in an operation outside the city, though none offered any further details. The atmosphere was easy, and Lucius joined a group throwing dice, though they seemed more intent on discussing women they had recently bedded than the game itself.

A loud crash as the front door of the guildhouse was slammed shut froze their conversation, and angry voices from the hall had them all looking up in curiosity.

"Bastard!"

The man, swearing, blazed into the common room like a comet. He was tall and lithe, cloaked in black, with dark hair and a well-trimmed beard. A leather hauberk clad his chest, but Lucius was drawn to his eyes, which were fired with anger.

Two other men followed him, looking a little uncomfortable with their proximity to such fury. Lucius recognised them as thieves who had been keeping to themselves in the common room over the past few days.

"What's up, Caradoc?" asked one of Lucius' companions, and for the first time he realised that this was Caradoc Grey, the lieutenant of the Night Hands and second in power only to Guildmaster Magnus.

"That bastard Brink, he's only gone and declared for the Guild," Caradoc fumed.

"Eh?"

"Told these two, bold as brass," he said, indicating the men behind him with a sweeping arm. "Said he didn't need our protection when those Coin and Enterprise bastards were gaining so much power in the city. And he's hired mercenaries to back him up."

"What are you going to do?" asked another one of the thieves at Lucius' table.

"Teach him a valuable lesson in manners, that's what. And we're going to do it this evening. Now. You lot, come with us." So saying, Caradoc swept back out the door, leaving the common room stunned until one thief sighed and stood, giving the rest the cue to follow suit.

Lucius saw the others reach for knives and blades, and he put a hand to the small of his back to make sure his own sword was present. As they filed out, he touched another man on the arm who was winding a length of rope around his body.

"Who is this Brink?" he asked.

The man, who Lucius knew only as Hawk, gave him a grim look. "Hieronymus Brink, a money lender on the Street of Dogs. If the Guild is moving in on our territory there, they are stronger than we thought. This is a direct challenge, and they are forcing Caradoc to take action or watch his income drain away into nothing. Today it is just the money lender – if we do nothing, the merchants and shopkeepers will start to go over as well."

As they walked up the hill to the northern edge of Turnitia, Caradoc whispered sharp instructions to his men. In all, they numbered eight, which the lieutenant clearly felt enough to threaten the money lender. He told them that the goal was to scare the living daylights out of the man, to make sure he did not even think of switching allegiance. By striking at him in his own home, they were sending a message that the Night Hands could reach anyone anywhere, that there was no safety within the city's bounds. They were to employ all stealth to gain access to his house, track him down – his family too if he had any – and then leave them to Caradoc.

"And at all costs," Caradoc continued without missing a step, "avoid his mercenaries. They will be well armed and will know how to use a sword. You don't want to get into a running battle with the likes of them, so quiet is the key. With any luck they will be unprepared or even asleep at their posts. They won't be expecting us to do this, so the advantage is ours."

Lucius was less sure of this pronouncement, and he did not relish the thought of locking blades with trained killers.

The northern part of the city was quiet as they marched determinedly to the money lender's home, though the continual bass rumble of the sea breaking against the cliffs mixed with the raucous sounds of revellers in the taverns and inns further down the hill. One thief ranged ahead of them, diverting the group down side streets and alleys whenever he saw a guard patrol, for Caradoc did not want to be distracted by a confrontation with the law, particularly when his men were armed.

As they continued east, the houses grew steadily larger, more opulent, and further apart. The area reminded Lucius much of his old home, and it crossed his mind that he had not visited its grounds since he had come back to Turnitia. He knew the mob had burned the place after killing his father, but he had tried hard to forget the details of that night. He remembered being almost petrified with fear as he heard his parent's cries from his hiding place in the cellar, how his sister had clung to him painfully. The sounds of strangers rampaging through his home, the smell of burning, a hazy memory of bolting through the garden and streets, driven on by nothing but terror. The utter sense of loss when he returned the next morning to find little more than smoking ruins.

The money lender's house was similar to how Lucius remembered his own home, though it seemed smaller. The tall walls adorned with iron spikes looked more formidable though, and Caradoc drew back his men when they saw two mercenaries standing guard outside the main gate.

"We go in pairs," Caradoc whispered as he crouched down with his men around him. "Pick your own partner – Hawk, you take the new guy," he said, indicating Lucius.

"Sure," said Hawk. "What's the plan?"

"Avoid the rear gate, they'll have a guard there too. Probably just inside so as to draw a foolish thief in. We'll take the walls. Surround the place and pick your entry point. Cross the grounds and get into the house by any means you can. Remember, do this *quietly*. Brink is rich enough to have more mercenaries in the gardens, as well as in the house."

"Once inside?"

"If you see a mercenary with his back to you, consider him fair game. But I don't want any family hurt at all. Find Brink and restrain him. Do the same with the wife and any kids he may have. They will be the real problem, as their first reaction will be to scream. If that happens, we'll be drowning in mercenaries. So *don't let it happen*."

"You'll deliver the message?"

"Aye. Leave the speaking to me. Now, go. Begin your entry on the count of eighty."

They fanned out, each pair of thieves taking one wall surrounding the square grounds of the house. The walls were around ten feet high and built of tightly packed brick. The iron spikes atop looked wickedly sharp, but

Lucius saw they were spaced nearly a foot apart, enough to allow a careful thief safe passage. Hawk nudged him in the ribs and pointed up at a cherry tree whose branches stretched over the wall.

"That's our way in and out," he whispered. "Remember where it is once we get inside, case you and I are split up."

Lucius had absolutely no intention of letting Hawk out of his sight but dutifully nodded. Hawk unwound the rope he was carrying and threw it expertly upwards, curling it around a thick branch. He took the other end as it snaked back down to them, and made a loop knot before pulling hard. The knot shot upwards to hold firm against the branch and Hawk tugged to make sure it was secure. He held a hand up and waited. Lucius heard him muttering under his breath.

"Seventy-seven, seventy-eight, seventy-nine... up you go lad."

A little clumsily, Lucius reached hand over hand as he ascended the rope, trying not to gasp out loud with the effort. He ignored the ignominy of Hawk's hand on his rump as the thief tried to speed his partner up, and was soon straining a leg forward to stand on the wall. Letting go of the rope, he crouched, leaning against the cherry tree's branches for support and cover as Hawk followed him. Looking back, he saw Hawk swarm up the rope with practised ease before peering into the grounds of the townhouse.

Lucius could see that the garden was exceptionally well tended, with a paved path running alongside the wall, separating it from a flat lawn that ran to his right, round to the front of the house. A small apple orchard grew to his left, and he imagined the thieves that had gained entry around the back of the grounds were rejoicing in their good fortune, for they would be able to get within spitting distance of the house without any danger of being seen.

The house itself was perhaps a century old, though it had clearly been as well looked after as the gardens. A glasshouse had been built against the side facing him, close to a tall chimney that he guessed served the kitchen. Thick ivy clawed its way up the stonework, and he saw there were no windows on this side of the building.

Lucius took a branch in hand as he prepared to clamber down to ground level, but a quiet hiss from Hawk made him freeze. Movement to his left caught his eye and he watched as a man, thick chainmail glinting dully in the muted light of Kerberos, stepped out of the shadows at the rear of the house, and followed a meandering path that led to the orchard. Peering into the gloom, Lucius noted that the man had a large sword at his belt.

They watched as the man disappeared under the boughs of the trees, and Lucius thought of the thieves taking cover in the orchard, wishing he could warn them. He then considered that they were far more practised at this than he, and that they had no doubt seen the mercenary before he had. Perhaps they had stealthily crept behind the man as he entered the tree line, and even now he was face down in the dirt, a dagger protruding from his back. Another nudge from Hawk interrupted his thoughts, and he reached forward to grab a lower branch of the cherry tree, swinging down to dangle his feet in the air, before letting go and landing on a flower bed in a crouch.

"There's a door to the kitchens just round the side there," Hawk said, indicating where the guard had appeared. "Probably got a friend or two in there, so we'll avoid that. Head to the glasshouse, then go round the front. Stay out of sight. I'll watch your back, then get us in through one of the windows. Go!"

Taking a last glance round the garden to see if any more guards were close by, Lucius drew a deep breath then ran. Keeping low, he brought his cloak around his body, hoping to appear as no more than a shadow. The finely-cut grass of the open lawn provided no hiding places but allowed him to move quickly without a sound. He gingerly stepped over the gravel trail leading to the door of the glasshouse, then flattened himself against the thick ivy at the base of the wide chimney. Creeping round to the front of the house, he quickly spied another mercenary, this one slouching by the front door. A wide path led thirty or forty yards to the wrought iron gates in the front wall, and he saw two more armed men standing there. It was not long before he was aware of Hawk's presence behind him, and he jabbed a finger at the guards.

Hawk nodded to indicate that he saw the danger, then flashed a smile. Lucius looked on in surprise as Hawk crept past him, keeping flat against the front wall of the house, seeming to dare the guard at the front door to look to his right and catch the thief. He was not the only one taking risks, for Lucius looked up and saw another pair of thieves shinning up the ivy on the side of the house.

Having passed the first window at the front of the house, Hawk had positioned himself beneath a second, and gave a gesture for Lucius to follow him. Padding quietly forward, keeping Hawk's body between himself and the guard, he watched the other thief reach into his tunic to produce a curious device. Shaped like a small conical cup with a handle at the narrower end, Hawk placed it against the window. Slowly, he began to turn the handle, and it emitted a low whistling sound as he did so. In the still evening air, it seemed impossibly loud to Lucius, and he cast anxious looks at the nearest guard, thinking he must have detected them, but he made no movement at all.

After a few minutes, Hawk carefully cradled the cup in both hands and steadily moved it away from the window. Lucius saw that where the cup had been placed now lay a perfectly round hole in the window, the blades inside Hawk's tool having neatly cut a section out of the glass. With a last look around, Hawk reached inside the hole and unlatched the window, before pulling it open. Lucius could not help but be impressed with this method of entry, and he promised himself that he would get his hands on one of those tools soon.

Hawk was the first in through the window, seeming to flow like a liquid shadow into the darkened room beyond. Lucius gratefully accepted his hand as he crossed the threshold himself, to find they had entered what must be the main sitting room. In the fireplace on the far wall, glowing embers shed a soft orange light across leather-bound furniture as they both crouched next to a carved wooden desk. Pictures hung from all four walls and while Lucius could not discern any details, he guessed they would collectively be worth a small fortune. A shame, it crossed his mind, that they were here on business other than straightforward theft.

"Guard must have been nodding," Hawk whispered, before gesturing to a door on the wall to their right. "That'll lead to the hall, methinks. We need to get upstairs quickly. I doubt there will be mercenaries up there, and I'll feel a lot safer."

Nodding his assent, Lucius padded to the door, winding his way carefully past the settee and tall chairs. The door was ajar, and he opened it a little further, looking into the hall. Nothing stirred on the other side, and he saw a marbled floor leading to a grand staircase that split into two before turning back on itself to climb up to a balcony that overlooked the entire hall.

A low hiss caught his attention, and he looked up to see another thief had beaten them to the balcony. The dark shape motioned him to follow and, with a nod from Hawk, he stepped into the hall and padded up the stairs.

At the top the balcony backed onto a corridor that seemed to run the length of the house. He noticed that Hawk kept looking over the balcony to the marble below, and he realised the man was keeping an eye out for the mercenaries. The action unnerved him a little, for it was a reminder that though this mission had been quiet so far, the penalty for any mistake could be the death of them all.

The thief that had waved him up had continued down one side of the corridor to join his partner, who had started to open one of the many doors that lined the walls. A quick check inside, and then he moved to the next, evidently having not found the sleeping Brink. Hawk gestured to follow him down the other side of the corridor, and Lucius complied, acutely aware of the sound his boots made on the hard wooden floor, as light as his steps were.

Opening the first door they came to proved as fruitless as the other pair, and Lucius caught a glimpse of a study lined with shelves packed with books before Hawk moved on. They both gave a start as the next door opened just as they reached it, and they drew blades instinctively as a man stepped out, before realising it was Caradoc. He smiled back at them as he lowered his own sword, then jerked his head back towards the room he had just left. Inside, Lucius saw another thief binding the hands of a young girl behind her back as she lay flat on her stomach on her bed. No more than six or seven, she had already been gagged and she caught Lucius' eye, her expression one of sheer terror. The window of her bedroom was open, the route by which Caradoc had entered the house.

With Caradoc leading, they proceeded down the corridor, checking each room in turn as they hunted for the money lender. Blade still drawn, he motioned for Lucius to take a door on the left, while he went for its counterpart on the right.

The door opened easily at Lucius' touch and he crept inside as soon as he saw the young boy sleeping peacefully. Perhaps no more than a year or so older than his sister, he was blissfully unaware as Lucius padded across a soft rug, hand outstretched to throw across the boy's mouth in case he should wake.

From somewhere out in the corridor a bell tolled. It sounded almost mournful as it clanged with dutiful repetition, but it filled Lucius with alarm as he looked over his shoulder. He heard a commotion erupt from somewhere on the ground floor, quickly followed by shouts of surprise, then anger. A piercing cry froze him for an instant before he turned back to see the boy, sitting bolt upright in his bed, screaming at the sight of an armed and cloaked intruder in his bedroom, the very vision of a nightmare.

Lucius hesitated for a fraction longer then cursed under his breath. He retreated out of the room, knowing that whatever was happening outside was of far greater threat than a prepubescent boy.

Caradoc and Hawk were already ahead of him, running at full tilt down the corridor and as Lucius fell in behind them, he saw the lieutenant leap over a motionless form on the floor as they sprinted for the stairs; as Lucius passed over the same spot, he saw it was the body of Caradoc's partner, and he side-stepped the pool of blood in which the man lay.

"There he is!" Caradoc cried as he reached the balcony and pointed downwards with his sword. Lucius skidded to a halt next to him and looked down to see a man being bundled along like a sack of wheat by two armoured mercenaries.

Looking anxiously about, Lucius saw no sign of the other thieves that had also been upstairs and, thinking the money lender had appeared from one of the rooms they had been searching, feared the worst for them. Hawk was already leaping down the stairs, two at a time, but Caradoc climbed onto the railings of the balcony and, with just a second's pause, leapt down to crash among the three escapees.

Tumbling down the stairs in a ragged pile, they came to rest on the marble floor. The mercenaries scrambled for their weapons while Caradoc struggled to his feet, clearly hurt by the fall. The money lender was pushed aside by one of his men as they formed a barrier before Caradoc, their swords drawn as they began to advance. One swiped at Caradoc and he pushed the blow to one side before the other mercenary stabbed forward, forcing him to give ground.

Hawk reached the mercenaries and the area at the foot of the stairs began to turn into a general melee, the sound of metal smashing against metal ringing against the walls.

Having already determined that he would aid Hawk in dispatching the mercenary he faced, Lucius was dismayed as shouts reached his ears just before the main door leading to the front garden was thrown open, and more mercenaries rushed in. Two grabbed the money lender and carried him outside while three others strode into the battle, weapons swinging.

"He's getting away!" Caradoc cried out, and Lucius could not help but marvel at the lieutenant's single-mindedness in the midst of a fight that would very likely prove fatal. He had no idea how an alarm had been tripped — for he knew the thieves would have taken every precaution — but now they faced their worst fears; a fight in which they were outnumbered by skilled and disciplined warriors. It was a fight they could not win.

Hawk was the first to fall, pierced by a sword thrust to his chest as he faced two mercenaries. They had forced him further and further back until he was flat against a wall with no room to move. He collapsed to the ground just as Lucius swung his sword at the head of one enemy, only to have the blow turned by an iron helmet.

The mercenary reeled back under the blow, but his place was quickly taken by Hawk's two killers, and Lucius immediately found himself on the defensive as he fought next to Caradoc.

"This is no good," Caradoc said breathlessly. "You've got to get out of here. Go, I'll cover you."

Though he appreciated Caradoc's willingness to die in his place, Lucius could see there was no way out. The mercenaries pressed against them, forcing them back. When they were finally pushed against the wall, they would die as Hawk had done.

Cursing his luck, Lucius took a breath to steady his nerves, even as his sword arm rose and fell, beating back the blades of the mercenaries. He reached inside himself to find the strands of energy coursing and twisting as they always had done. During his time with the Night Hands, Lucius had resolutely refused to use his magic, partly because he was keen to learn the skills of the trade without taking shortcuts, but mostly because of the fear and suspicion the thieves would have for him if they knew just what he was capable of. Now, left with no choice, he released the magic once more and the familiar surge of arcane energies felt like an invigorating breeze, a cool shower after a voyage across the desert. He mentally pulled upon a particularly destructive strand and pooled its power, waiting for the moment to strike.

One mercenary stepped forward, intending to drive Lucius back another step or two, and his sword swung low. Lucius met the blow with the edge of his blade and pushed it up and to the side, leaving the man wide open. With his other hand he stretched forward, only releasing the power he had held when it was inches from the man's face.

A jet of fire exploded from his palm and smashed into the mercenary's skull and a bright flash lit the hall for the briefest of moments. The man was dead before he hit the floor, and the remaining mercenaries all took a step back in fear as they turned toward the source of the fire.

Caradoc, no less mystified, nevertheless saw his advantage. He thrust forward, disembowelling one of the men he faced, then raced for the door, crying for Lucius to follow him. The mercenaries did not take long to recover and as one turned to chase after Caradoc, the last two rounding on Lucius.

These men had fought together before, Lucius could see, as they worked in almost perfect unison, standing side-by-side as they kept their enemy off balance with repeated blows. The winding energies in his mind's eye separated for an instant, and Lucius drew one of them out, imagining its silver coiled force emanating from his heart to travel down his sword arm. He felt new strength coursing through him and, almost imperceptibly, his blade began to hum as it vibrated in tune with the magic.

Shouting a dreadful battle cry, Lucius stepped up to his attackers and stabbed with all the power he could muster, amplified by otherworldly energy. The mercenary tried to parry the blow, but Lucius' sword was irresistible as it sped forward to spear its point through his eye. The man screamed as Lucius yanked his blade free, then pushed him into his friend.

The bulk of the dying man checked the final mercenary's advance, giving Lucius time to release the last of the energies he had prepared. The shadows of the hall flared, spreading darkness in their wake. The mercenary cried out as he realised he was blinded while Lucius, following his memory of where the front door had been, carefully picked his way across the body strewn marble. When fresh air hit his face, he reached out to find the door frame, then propelled his way outside.

Seeming serene after the chaos of the hall, the front lawn was quiet, and it took Lucius a second to realise what had changed. One of the front gates lay open and, as Lucius dashed towards them, he spotted the body of another armoured mercenary lying still on the grass, the hilt of a dagger protruding from his back.

Grasping the open gate for support as he tried to catch his breath, Lucius saw Caradoc fighting a little further down the street. Evidently he had caught up with the money lender and his remaining guard. Brink was huddled up against a wall, abject terror on his face as he watched the two men fight over him, Caradoc had been wounded, and he clasped his thigh with a bloodied hand as he held his sword out in front of him, trying to keep the mercenary at bay.

Lucius cast an anxious look down both ends of the street, knowing that an open fight here could bring a patrol running with all speed. Violence was simply not tolerated in this part of Turnitia. Trying to control his breathing, Lucius gripped his sword firmly and started to pad up behind the mercenary.

As he closed the distance, he caught Caradoc's eye, who quickly saw his way out. Holding up a hand and dropping his sword, he smiled at the mercenary sweetly.

"My man, I surrender," he announced.

The mercenary took a step towards him, though whether it was to take Caradoc into custody or murder him in cold blood would remain a mystery, as Lucius' sword entered the back of his neck and drove downwards, killing him instantly.

Such was the force of the blow, pushing the sword half its length down into the man's body, Lucius had some trouble removing it. In the end, he had to position the guard on his side, then use both hands while putting a foot on the man's shoulder to pull it free. As he did so, Caradoc sheathed his sword and drew a knife, holding it at the money lender's throat.

"We're not unreasonable men, Brink," Lucius heard him say with a quiet, dreadful menace. "You pay on time, every time, and you'll see we take care of you."

He patted Brink on the shoulder as he smiled, though his knife never wavered from the man's neck.

"But if we ever hear you have declared for those tosspots in the Guild, we will pay you another visit," he continued. "We'll kill your family, we'll kill more of your very expensive guards and maybe, just maybe, we'll kill you too – after we have seen how many times we can wrap your guts around that grand house of yours. Do you understand me, Brink?"

The money lender was beyond words now, such was his raw fear, but he shakily nodded his head.

"That'll do him?" Lucius asked, anxious that a patrol would turn up at any time.

"That'll do him," Caradoc confirmed, as he pulled a scarf from his tunic and began wrapping it around his injured leg. "Well done lad, we'll have words when we get back to the guildhouse. Now, let's go before we catch the attention of the guard. Split up and make your own way back, usual drill."

Lucius hesitated, eyeing Caradoc's leg. Blood was oozing from what looked like a deep stab wound.

Caradoc waved him on. "Don't you worry about me, I've had worse than this. Now, be off with you!"

Jogging away, Lucius kept the shadows. He cast one last look back at the gates of Brink's place, watching as the money lender dragged himself, sobbing, back to his home. Lights were beginning to flicker on inside the house, and Lucius could hear sounds of activity as more mercenaries scoured the gardens and searched rooms for other intruders.

For a brief moment, he saw a figure silhouetted in one of the first floor windows, arms crossed as it stared down into the gardens. There was something familiar about the figure that tugged at Lucius' mind but, after just a few seconds, it turned and left his view.

CHAPTER 5

News of the evening's events had already reached the guildhouse by the time Lucius made his way into the common room. As he walked in, a ragged cheer went up from the gathered thieves, and a mug of ale was pressed into his hands. He smiled sheepishly and looked around for the others he had fought alongside. Picking out three, he dared to hope their losses had been much lighter than he had first feared. Each was surrounded by a small gaggle of their comrades, being pounded with questions and asked to recount, yet again, their exploits.

Lucius soon had his own audience, but he elaborated little on what he had seen, unsure of how free he should be with his speech, even here in the guildhouse. When he told them he had seen Hawk fall, and there had been at least one other death, a groan swept over all assembled. He felt the atmosphere of the common room become mixed, elation entwined with mourning for the loss of a respected talent. Mugs and glasses were raised, and he joined in with the toast to fallen comrades. Someone remarked that it was a better death than one might find in the Citadel, a fate all thieves strove to avoid. Ambrose, though, pointed out that no money lender was worth the life of a good thief, and this was greeted with murmurs of agreement.

Louder cheers were raised when Caradoc entered, limping while supporting the weight of another thief. Both smiled at the welcome, collapsed heavily into the two chairs brought to them, then accepted drinks. Caradoc waved a hand at the man he had helped to the guildhouse.

"Sarnol thought the best way out of the house was through the window – seems he forgot we were no longer on the ground floor!"

Sarnol smiled with embarrassment. "Ah, I didn't forget that," he said, before his expression suddenly turned serious. "Twisted my ankle when I hit the lawn. It was the only escape I had. I saw Kernne struck down by one of those damned mercs, and knew I was next."

"Kernne as well?" someone asked sorrowfully.

"It was a tough one," Caradoc said, scanning the crowed as he counted how many of his men had returned. "Hawk also – he died fighting by my side as we held off a veritable army of the bastards. And Lucius was with us too!"

Caradoc raised his glass to Lucius, who nodded in return. One man was inspecting Caradoc's wound, and it was apparent that he had lost a great deal of blood. The scarf was soaked through as the man removed it, and more blood flowed as the pressure was released.

"We best get you seen to," he said.

"Little more than a scratch," Caradoc insisted, though he shifted his weight as he attempted to stand.

"Yes, well, let others be the judge of that. Let's get you up stairs, Magnus wants to see you. Come with us Sarnol, we'll check you out too."

Several thieves moved to help the two injured men, bearing their weight as they filed out of the common room towards the back of the building.

As he watched them leave, Lucius found himself manoeuvred into a tall leather chair and was instantly surrounded by those who wanted to hear the story all over again, but from his perspective. Lucius gave them a quick rundown, crediting Hawk for keeping him out of trouble early on, much to their approval. He spoke of the desperate fight when the alarm had been triggered, of how he, Hawk and Caradoc had fought side by side, though he carefully neglected any mention of how his magic had swung the battle. Instead, he described how Hawk had sacrificed his life to save both Caradoc and himself, creating a diversion that allowed them to escape and continue pursuit of the money lender.

He lingered on the description of Caradoc's warning to the cringing money lender, and this too met with the approval of his audience. There was clearly nothing they liked better than a happy ending. After his tale, there were more questions, more ale, and as a soft haze began to envelop his brain. Lucius' descriptions of the night grew little by little, until it seemed as though there had been half an army stationed within the house. Not that those listening minded, for it simply made their guild seem all the more daring.

"So, the triumphant heroes return!" The voice that rose above the general hubbub of the common room was clear and confident, needing little raised volume to command attention. All the thieves rose to their feet, causing Lucius to look around in confusion before clumsily scrambling to his own.

A well-dressed man clothed in silk and cotton had entered the room, flanked by two others who strode in his wake. The man was middle-aged and greying, though he possessed an obvious vitality that the years had yet to touch. He smiled and Lucius immediately formed the impression of both confidence and trustworthiness. Of course, having spent time with any number of con artists and tricksters, he had learned to be on his guard when confronted by such people, but this man also had an obvious command of, and respect from, the other thieves present. His face was rounded and non-descript, except for his eyes which seemed to constantly sparkle with amusement.

The two men who flanked him were almost the complete opposite. Dressed in black leather with long knives at their belts, both exuded an aura of menace. Lucius thought, if there were such a thing as natural born killers, these two would be the definition.

It was not until the man was among the thieves and clamping a hand on the shoulder of one who had been on Caradoc's mission that Lucius heard someone thank him by name and understood who he was. So this was Magnus, the guildmaster of the Night Hands. Despite all the time Lucius had spent in the guildhouse recently, he had yet to meet the man, though he had heard plenty of stories about him. He recalled Ambrose once telling him that Magnus had been a lieutenant in the old Thieves Guild. When the guild had broken apart, it had been Magnus who had tried to centralise the scattered thieves into a new organisation, at great risk to his life from the guard and other, less pleasant forces. If half of what

Lucius had heard was true, then he thought this would be a very easy man to admire.

After shaking another thief by the hand, Magnus turned towards Lucius, and smiled.

"And this would be our newest recruit then. Lucius, isn't it?"

"Uh, yes sir," said Lucius, unsure of how to address the guildmaster.

Magnus waved the honorific away, though Lucius was acutely aware of the attention of his two bodyguards, who seemed to be itching for him to make one aggressive move.

"Just Magnus, please," he said. "You've done well tonight. Brink represents a significant account for us, and the return of his business is worthy of congratulations. I believe you are staying here now – eat and drink well tonight, you've earned it."

"Thank you, err, Magnus," Lucius said, as graciously as he could, though ale and discomfort vied to tie his tongue.

"Get some sleep too. Then come upstairs tomorrow, feel free to explore the place. Perhaps we'll speak further." One of his bodyguards whispered something into Magnus' ear that escaped Lucius hearing. Magnus sighed.

"Ah, that's right. I am afraid I must leave you all now." He looked back at Lucius with a smile. "Pressure of the job you know, they never let up. Welcome, Lucius, I have a feeling you will do well for us here."

As Magnus swept out of the room, the others clustered about Lucius, slapping him on the back and shaking his hand. Through their own celebrations, it took them a while to see that Lucius was thoroughly confused as to what was happening. It was Ambrose who took him to one side to explain.

"You've done well, lad," he said. "I knew you would."

"I don't follow."

"Caradoc must have given a glowing report of you while getting his leg mended. Only senior thieves, those who are full members of the Hands, are permitted beyond the ground floor. You, my friend, are now a true thief!"

Lucius smiled nervously as Ambrose thrust another mug into his hand before calling upon the entire common room to toast him. Raising his mug in return, Lucius thanked the thieves and, ignoring a wag calling for a speech, sank back into his chair, happy to listen to his peers talk business for the rest of the evening.

Morning came too soon for Lucius, and he awoke to find himself in the same chair he had collapsed in a few hours before. A few other thieves were also in the common room, lying insensible, though most seemed to have had the sense to retire earlier on. As Lucius sat up, the world swam for an instant, and he leaned forward, burying his face in his hands as he waited for the after effects of the ale to subside.

His mouth feeling dry and pitted, Lucius stayed in that position until he lost all sense of time. No one else stirred in the common room, though he heard someone snoring softly in a far corner. Shakily, he stood, and wandered out to find water, both to drink and to wash. Running into Ambrose as the veteran thief scoured the kitchen for breakfast, he was invited to take Magnus up on the offer of seeing what else the guildhouse had to offer.

He spent the rest of the morning exploring the two higher levels of the building, and it seemed as though his eyes grew wider at each new sight. It was only now, when he could see the guildhouse in its entirety as a functioning, well-oiled machine, that he understood just how sophisticated the Night Hands were as an organisation. And how much work it took to keep the guild running on a day to day basis.

Three rooms were dedicated to maps and charts, scattered over tables, pinned onto walls, and rolled up on shelves that reached to the ceiling, ready for inspection when a mission demanded. The patrol routes of the Vos guard were accurately timed and drawn on one map, allowing any thief to see exactly where blind spots would appear and when. Floor plans of many buildings in Turnitia were collected in the stacks, and Lucius watched another thief pour over one as he devised his next robbery. Information was collected on people as well as structures, and he learned that the libraries were considered to be living things, constantly added to as the guild learned more and more, for the benefit of all its members. A laboratory was present, allowing thieves to make all manner of concoctions, from smoke and sleeping powders, to deadly poisons that would ensure no enemy of the guild would survive for long. There was even a training room, suitably soundproofed with targets for shooting or knife practice, a ring for blade training and, round the edges of the over-sized chamber, a running course across which could be strewn a variety of different obstacles.

It seemed, too, as though Lucius had not been wholly wrong when he had imagined a guildhouse with links to the sewer system of Turnitia, for that is exactly what this building boasted. Near the underground vaults in which the greatest stolen treasures were kept, as well as the guild's own vast treasury, were several secret passages that took a winding path down into the sewers.

These were built to allow members to enter or leave the guildhouse freely, beyond prying eyes.

Lucius was later drawn back to the armoury, which lay next to the training room. Blades, spears, sections of armour and hundreds upon hundreds of various tools of the trade lay on shelves and in racks.

He saw a host of weapons of varying lethality and, having been told senior thieves were free to pick and choose from the armoury, started to inspect an incredibly well-crafted crossbow. Honed from a lamination of light but strong woods, a series of lenses in a wooden tube was mounted over the groove that took the bolt. Standing at a window, Lucius found he could adjust the lenses to bring far objects into focus. Fine wires within the tube marked exactly where a fired bolt would strike, should the target be within range. Other weapons soon revealed similar ingenuity, such as the sword whose pommel could be separated to draw a dagger from the hilt – useful if the main blade was ever broken.

However the weapons were the least of the treasure in this room and Lucius soon found himself exploring the vast cornucopia of tools, such as pots of swordblack used to dull a blade from reflections, dark silk bodysuits that could make even a clumsy thief silent, and the glass-cutting cups Hawk had used to break into Brink's house.

"There is just something about the mind of a thief that makes him fascinated by these toys," said a voice behind him. Lucius turned to see Caradoc leaning against the door frame.

"This was where I came as well, when I was brought into the guild proper," he continued. "Though there were far less toys back then."

"I am not sure I would call that a toy," said Lucius, indicating the crossbow.

Caradoc smiled. "You'll want to practice with it first. It is not as easy to use as you might think – you have to learn how to use the sights, or your shots will never land anywhere near your target. But I think you are quite wrong about these not being toys. All a good thief really needs is a decent blade, soft boots and his wits, the last being the most vital. It seems as if there is always someone trying to get an advantage, however they can. They come up with an idea, and try to build it. Some work. Some need constant revision, with many minds applying themselves to the problem over time. Which, really, is what this place is all about."

Lucius nodded in understanding. "How long have you been with the Hands?"

"Since the beginning. I knew Magnus from the old guild, and he brought me with him when he created the Hands."

"You are close friends, then?"

Caradoc paused and frowned. "We trust each other, certainly."

"You... don't always agree with what he does?" Lucius asked, wondering where the boundaries were in this conversation. For some reason, he knew he would never have been so direct with Magnus, though the guildmaster seemed far more personable than his lieutenant.

"You don't always have to agree with your leader," Caradoc shrugged. "He knows I'm not an automaton. The important thing is that he trusts me to follow his orders, and I trust him to do what is best for the Hands. That is what we have in common – a desire to make the Hands the best guild it can be."

"So what about the other? The Guild of Coin and Enterprise?"

For a moment, Caradoc looked as though he might spit in disgust, before he remembered where he was. "Well, that is where Magnus and I may differ. He believes we can reach an accord, dividing the city between us without bloodshed. He says it is the most profitable route for both organisations, and I guess I can see the sense of that."

"They don't seem very receptive to that idea," Lucius said.

"No. Once, maybe up to a year ago, we might have made an agreement. But something has changed within the Guild. They are too aggressive, pushing too hard." He sighed. "I fear a war is coming. This might not have been the best time for you to join us!"

"I can take care of myself."

"You proved that last night. Look..." Caradoc seemed self-conscious as he mustered his next words. "I wanted to thank you for stepping in yesterday. Those mercs were tough, and I am not sure I could have taken them all. You did well."

Lucius blushed and he felt as uncomfortable as Caradoc looked when confronted with this gratitude. "Anybody else would have done the same."

"Well, you were there and they weren't. Thanks anyway," Caradoc said, looking at the floor. "What was it, flash powder you used to distract them?"

Not trusting his voice to carry the lie, Lucius just nodded.

"Good move. Painful stuff too, when shoved in someone's face. Still, that bastard deserved what he got."

Not having anything more to add, Lucius simply smiled, and the expression was returned by Caradoc. Neither said anything more, and Lucius pretended to look over the crossbow again, doing anything to break the uncomfortable silence. He looked up again when Caradoc coughed.

"Anyway, there's a meeting going on. Magnus asked me to fetch you."

"Me?"

"Just routine business. Magnus thinks that it would be good for you to see how the guild operates."

"Well, if Magnus has asked... Who else will be there?"

"The most senior thieves of the Hands. These meetings are used to track business, spot opportunities, and generally ensure everything continues to run smoothly. Needless to say, your input won't be required. Just watch and learn."

Leading Lucius up to the third and highest level of the guildhouse, Caradoc took him to Magnus' own meeting hall. Lucius had to bite his tongue to stop from gasping at the sight of the room.

The walls were covered with carefully sculpted wooden panels, displaying exquisite craftsmanship in their varnish and carving. No rare paintings hid their natural beauty, and Lucius got the feeling that Magnus was, at heart, a man who enjoyed simpler things.

The room itself, however, was dominated by a long dark wood table, whose polished surface reflected perfectly the light of the oil lanterns standing on pedestals in each corner of the chamber. Around the table were eighteen tall-backed chairs, upon sixteen of which were seated an assortment of men and women. Some Lucius had seen before, passing through the common room, but he did not know any of their names. At the head of the table at the far end of the chamber sat Magnus, and he smiled as they entered.

"Here comes our hero Lucius – welcome to the Council," Magnus said grandly, and Lucius felt acutely discomforted as all eyes turned on him. Caradoc had taken his seat at the opposite end of the table to Magnus, indicating that Lucius should take the last free chair, halfway along the left edge.

Lucius was aware of the short woman seated to his right watching him as he sat, and he nodded in greeting. She was perhaps of a similar age to Magnus, but showed few signs of ageing. Her hair was dark and slicked back along her scalp, while her face was marred by a scar that split her lower lip. Feeling there was something disconcertingly serpentine in the way she looked at him, Lucius turned to glance at the man on his other side, but found he had already returned his attention to Magnus.

Seeing the new arrivals settled, Magnus waved at the group to continue their business. A young man opposite Lucius spoke up.

"We have started to move prostitutes from the docks to the merchant quarter during evening hours, and this has proved a profitable move. Traders far from home still look for home comforts, and our girls are very good at what they do."

Magnus grunted, and then sighed. "There is still something distasteful in this operation, I find myself thinking. To profit so directly from human trade – it seems a little too close to slavery for my liking."

The woman to Lucius' right raised her voice in response. "Better they are in our care than someone else's. Can you imagine how the Guild would treat them? With us, they earn good money, and do so in relative safety."

"Yes, yes," said Magnus, "as you said before, and that is why I have allowed it to continue thus far. Still, it is something I will keep a close eye on."

"It is also a mistake to think that all these girls have been forced into the work," the woman continued. "If you have an efficient organisation like ours behind you, there is good money in it – far better than common labour. I hear they even have their own guild in Allantia."

"You are just too old-fashioned, Magnus," another, younger, woman said, and a few laughs stirred round the table. Even Magnus gave a wry smile.

"Maybe," he said. "Nate, please continue."

The young man across from Lucius spoke again. "The Street of Dogs is quiet after Caradoc's mission last night. Brink hasn't shown up for work yet..."

There were a few more laughs round the table at this.

"... but I think it will be a while before anyone openly challenges us again."

"I disagree, and we must not be complacent," said the man to Lucius' left. "Most of us here profit in some way from the Street of Dogs, and I would not see us risk that. Brink could just be a prelude, and if we were to find that those mercenaries were funded by the Guild and not Brink himself, well... I would advocate more direct action against the Guild."

There were a few murmurs of agreement and Lucius flicked a look at Caradoc, but the lieutenant was staring fixedly at the table in front of him.

Magnus rapped on the table to regain everyone's attention and the murmurs stopped instantly. He opened his mouth to say something, then seemed to think better of it. After a moment's pause, he turned to look at Lucius.

"What do you think, young man?" he asked. "What would you do about the Guild, were you in our place?"

Once again, all eyes turned on Lucius, and he felt himself blush. "I... I wouldn't know, exactly," he stammered.

"Nonsense," Magnus said. "You are clearly an intelligent man, talented enough to be made a senior thief in a matter of weeks. You have your own mind. Speak!"

Lucius thought hard for a moment. It was, he realised, a good opportunity to play politics, to support the guildmaster, to start building up his own phalanx of friends and enemies on the Council. He instantly dismissed the idea as foolish and, frankly, beneath him. He did not know nearly enough about the thieves sitting round this table, and he had a feeling Magnus would see through any disingenuous arse kissing.

"So long as incidents can be contained, I think we should watch and wait. If we act, we cannot take anything back."

"You're timid, then," said Caradoc, and this burst of shrewishness surprised Lucius until he looked back at Magnus' measuring expression, and guessed this kind of prodding was a play between them, with Caradoc acting as the fall guy.

"Cautious, yes, not timid," Lucius said carefully. "It might be foolish to tip the scales if the possibility of another solution lies round the corner."

Lucius winced inwardly as he realised he had just called the opinions of at least some of the Council members foolish, but he continued onwards. "If my advice were sought, I would say we watch to see what the Guild does next, and do what we can to ensure they do not cross the line."

"Ah ha!" said Magnus. "And where exactly is that line?"

Smiling, Lucius held the guildmaster's eye steadily. "That, I believe, is what this Council will decide."

Magnus returned Lucius' smile, then laughed. "Well said."

The table fell silent for a moment, before the woman seated next to Lucius spoke again. "Are we seeing more pressure round the Five Markets?"

A hairy man next to Caradoc, who for all the world reminded Lucius of a badger, answered her. "We are still getting kids pressuring our teams. Some have taken to wearing blue scarves, round their heads or arms, though Kerberos alone knows why. Dead give away to the guard."

"Then they are obviously not worried about the guard. They are likely a warning to intimidate our kids – difficult to concentrate when you know you are being watched, and a collection of blue scarves would tend to stick out in the crowd." He looked up at Magnus. "I recommend we leave it in Ambrose's hands for now. He'll ask for support in the Five Markets if he needs it."

"Agreed," said Magnus. "Though I would be loathe to send thieves down there. The pickings will be far less than they are used to, and they'll see it as a step down."

"Perhaps some compensation from the vaults could be made, show we are taking their work seriously," Caradoc said.

"Perhaps," said Magnus. "I'll give that some thought. We can't open the vault every time we want to get something done. The point of a guild is that things work both ways, and sometimes members just have to get on with it. However, the Street of Dogs is the key. If something happens, it will happen there. Nate, you believe our hold there is solid for now?"

"More or less," the young man answered.

"Well, which is it?"

"No one is about to jump, but I am damn sure they'll be courted by the Guild. Maybe they'll spin a story about Brink that will make us look as if we took action against him for no good cause, and *that* was what made him move to the Guild."

"We'll set up watches then," said Magnus. "You pick out a half dozen of the shakiest clients, and we'll station thieves on them. Make sure they are not approached by the Guild and give them the frighteners if they are."

"That will be more revenue deducted from the Street of Dogs," remarked the short woman.

"Money well spent, I am sure," said Magnus. "And I believe we have our first volunteer. Lucius, are you inclined to give us a hand here?"

Lucius was again caught by surprise, and he kicked himself for not being more alert. He certainly should have known that Magnus would take the opportunity to test him, rather than simply allowing him to be a passive observer.

"Of course," he said, after taking a breath. "I was just starting to plan a few things of my own, but I can push them back –"

Magnus held up his hand. "No need! We'll get you working in shifts with someone."

When Lucius looked at him with confusion, Magnus explained. "We always reward personal initiative among the Hands, and if you are planning an operation of your own, I would be most fascinated to see what it is and how you get on with it. However, you must also learn to serve the guild's interests when necessary. So, we'll have you watch some merchant or shopkeeper by day, and give you free reign in the evening to plan and execute your grand larceny, whatever it may be."

Looking round the table, Magnus raised his eyebrows. "Any other business?" he asked.

As one of the senior thieves close to the guildmaster started to propose a tiered percentage of takings for the guild, based on seniority and wealth, Lucius glanced back down the table at Caradoc. The lieutenant gave a brief smile and nodded his compliments.

Lucius had made a good impression, and he knew it.

CHAPTER 6

Allowing the shadows to envelope him, Lucius held his breath as another patrol of Vos guards marched past his position, their red tabards appearing almost black in the half-light of Kerberos. With a second's concentration, he summoned the shadows of the alley to completely cloak him, but it was an unnecessary precaution, for the attention of the guards was fixed firmly across the Square of True Believers and the grand edifice that was nearing the last stages of completion.

When Vos had swept through Turnitia in its grand war of conquest which was intended to break the back of Pontaine, its arrival had been heralded by a rise in the Final Faith. It had started with preachers appearing on street corners, haranguing the crowds as to the fate of their souls. Soon enough, the Final Faith was using the support of converts, who were acting as a network of spies and scouts, marking those in power, officially or not, for the Vos captains to hunt down when their armies moved into the city. The capitulation of the city was therefore accomplished quickly and without many losses among the armies; the people of the city were the ones who suffered.

That the Faith was able to annihilate its rivals, the Brotherhood of the Divine Path, was more than a bonus for the Anointed Lord and her followers. It allowed them to start with a clean slate in the city, making their faith the official religion of Turnitia as much as it was in the rest of the Vos Empire.

In recognition of the efforts the Final Faith had extended during the occupation, the Empire had permitted the creation of the Square of True Believers, the site of a new church dedicated to the dominant religion. Though most of the resources used in the reconstruction of Turnitia were swallowed by the Citadel and its expansion, the followers of the Final Faith had taken what they could from the authorities and then tackled a great deal of the work themselves. They pulled down the houses that stood where their church would rise, excavating the foundations and then piling stone upon stone to create their place of worship.

It was said the square was wide enough to accommodate the entire population of the city, for the conversion of all was the Final Faith's stated aim. The church itself was not yet completed, and scaffolding would surround its southern tower for another year or two at the least. However, the nave was complete and, as far as the priesthood was concerned, that made the church open for business.

Far from alienating itself from the population after the riots it had started before the Empire arrived in force, the Final Faith had worked hard to ingratiate itself within the city. The people of Turnitia had traditionally carried their own beliefs lightly, as befitted a free city, but instead of being a hindrance to conversion it had meant there were no doctrinal barriers for the priests to break down. Once established, the Final Faith had dispensed food and money to the poor, offered shelter to those forced from their homes by the armies and, most of all, created a sense of community centred on the Square of True Believers.

While the people of Turnitia would never become fanatics, in the way those of Scholten were often described, living in the shadow of the Faith's great cathedral, most would now describe themselves as followers, even if they did not observe every holy day on the calendar. As a result, the money started to flow into the coffers of the new church from those seeking to help those less fortunate or those wishing an easy path into the afterlife. This was the reason that Lucius was now staking out the square.

As the patrol moved past his hiding place, Lucius recalled some of the lessons his father had tried to teach him of the Brotherhood and its beliefs. He had never really embraced religion in his youth, and his father had never forced it upon him, believing instead that his son should find his own path in life, and for that Lucius was grateful.

The Brotherhood, Lucius learned, had splintered from the Faith a century earlier, a dispute arising between two factions over the excesses one saw in the other. However, the schism was rooted in just one difference of interpretation of ancient texts. The Faith believed mankind had to be led on a tight and narrow path towards complete unity, in order to achieve salvation of all and ascendance to the next plane of existence. To this end, the priesthood was known to play politics at the highest levels, influencing cities and nations in an attempt to bind the peninsula into one cohesive organism.

Indeed, it was said that the Faith was the prime motivator behind the last war, seeking to make the Empire of Vos dominant over its old rival, Pontaine. That past Anointed Lords had tried to make Pontaine ascendant over Vos did not seem to strike any true believer as contradictory.

The Brotherhood believed Mankind was already on this path, and merely had to suffer war, bloodshed and terror as part of the process it was already fated to follow. The rituals and observances differed between the two religions, of course, but this was the centre of their dispute, the one difference responsible for so many deaths over the past hundred years.

Scanning the square, Lucius saw another patrol on the far side, and began to time their approach. Just gaining entry to the church would be problematic, he realised, for the priests clearly had enough friends within the Citadel to ensure the square was watched at all times.

He was confident that a man of his... abilities could do it but he suspected only the most accomplished of thieves would succeed, and they would likely not be interested in the risk/reward ratio of breaking into the church, the ultimate calculation every good thief lived by. Once inside, the pillars, statues and altars, along with the shadows they created, would be his allies, but everything rested upon crossing the open square without catching the attention of the guard. He began to look upwards at the roofs of the nearest buildings, wondering if a more vertical approach would be appropriate, though the closest structure lay over a hundred yards away from the church, which seemed an impossible chasm to cross.

"So, you are running with the Hands now."

The female voice behind him made Lucius start with a

fright, and he was ashamed to find that all the excuses he had rehearsed for the event of getting caught by a patrol momentarily fled his thoughts. He caught himself and turned round, his mind working once more as it recognised the voice.

"Aidy, you are forever creeping up on me," he whispered.

Her eyes, dark on the brightest of days and virtually invisible in the shadows, looked at him with what he guessed was utter contempt.

"There is no need to keep your voice low," she said, and he thought something approaching loathing was in her words. "The guards cannot hear us."

Lucius tilted his head to one side as he concentrated on the flow of magic he now realised filled the alley. Adrianna was using her mastery of stealth to ensure a passer by would neither see nor hear them. He finally nodded in understanding.

"Your training has all but deserted you," she said scornfully.

Not wanting to engage in another verbal duel, Lucius tried to change the subject. "How did you find me?" His question drew a hiss of frustration.

"I told you before, you are like a beacon to me. I can feel your presence from half a city away."

Becoming irritated at her superior manner, Lucius snapped back. "So, what do you want?"

She took a step closer, looking straight into his eyes. Of matching height, he could feel anger radiating from her in waves, and he fought to return her stare without blinking.

"You have caused me no end of problems lately. Do you consider yourself a thief now?"

"I *am* a thief, Aidy."

"So far the mighty fall," she said.

It was his turn to show anger. "I told you before why I had come back to the city. I'm doing alright at the moment, and I'll thank you to stay out of my business. You'll just have to endure my presence a little longer, then I'll be gone."

"Unless, of course, you make yourself too comfortable where you are," she pointed out, then seemed to change tact. "And as it happens, you are not doing me the courtesy of staying out of *my* business."

"What do you mean?"

"I'm working a contract with the Guild of Coin and Enterprise."

Things suddenly clicked for Lucius. "It *was* you there that night. In Brink's house. How can you be working for those bastards, Aidy? Do you have any idea what they are doing?"

"Don't be such a bloody idiot. People like you and I have greater allegiances than the petty concerns of thieves. Or, at least, we should. They are but a means to an end, Lucius."

"They are my friends."

"A man like you has no friends," she said caustically.

Once again, anger flared in him. "You don't know a damn thing about me now, Aidy. Whatever you thought of me before was wrong, and you are no closer to the truth now. People died in that house, and I am willing to bet you were in a position to stop that happening."

"I raised the alarm, nothing more. I had thought the mercenaries we had brought in would be able to handle a bunch of rouges with few problems. They probably would have, had a Shadowmage not been among them."

"Well, you could have done something about that, surely," he said. "You are clearly greater than I, so why not just kill me and let the mercenaries deal with the rest of us?"

She looked at him as though he were being particularly stupid, an expression he was beginning to resent a great deal. "Are you deaf, or just wilfully ignoring what I tell you?"

"Was there something you wanted, Aidy, or did you just come here to torment me?"

Adrianna stopped for a moment, then sighed heavily. When she spoke, it sounded as though she were almost spitting the words.

"If you are going to continue working in the city, there are going to have to be some rules."

"Damned if there will be!"

Her hand shot out of the darkness to close, painfully, around his arm. "Listen to me, idiot! I don't want this conversation any more than you do but, as I have been trying to tell you, there are larger things at work here. Now, shut up and follow me!"

Saying that, she spun on her heel and stalked into the depths of the alley, disappearing from sight almost immediately. Casting a last look back at the church, Lucius groaned inwardly and raced to follow her. The Final Faith would have to wait at least another day.

Lucius had visited the docks earlier, and this time his ears became accustomed to the crashing sea far quicker. The noise was relentless, with immense waves breaking against the grey stone defences that rose from the water like monoliths.

Before men had laid the foundations of Turnitia, the sea had already carved a wide bay from the cliffs, hacking away at the land over aeons. The origins of the architects of the defences that were built across the mouth of the bay were lost in antiquity. Merchants and dockmasters, certainly, couldn't care less about the effort that must have gone into building the immense structures, and scholars had long since moved on to investigating the mysteries of the Sardenne and the world's Ridge Mountains, explaining the construction away as the product of ancient magic and, therefore, unknowable. Some tales suggested the barriers were older than the race of men, though Lucius put little credence in children's tales.

Standing on the edge of the cliffs, he looked down as the water surged against the granite harbour. A complex array of winches, lifts and ropes were fixed to the sheer wall of rock, allowing goods brought in from the sea to be brought up to the city, where they could be traded in the merchants quarter and, finally, the Five Markets. A dozen ships lay in the bay, heaving constantly as the water surged beneath them. They remained in relative safety, so long as their anchors and the ropes that bound them to the harbour did not break their grip and send the vessels crashing into the barriers or cliffs. After gold had changed hands with one of the dockmasters, Lucius had learned earlier that the captains were waiting for the sea to subside a few degrees before risking an egress that would take them beyond the barriers and into the violent waves. Few risked such voyages, preferring the safety of travel over land. But for those willing to risk the churning waters, rogue waves and, so tales went, immense serpents, the rewards could be great.

Looking out to sea, Lucius wondered what life must be like in that hostile wilderness, trusting chance as much as personal skill. The seamen of Allantia were renowned for their ability to master the waves, as were the barbaric savages of the Sarcre Islands, but there were few truly civilised men who were adept at reading the ebb and flow of the sea, and thus have a chance of making their destinations safely. Even the best captains kept close to shore, and no one knew for certain what lay beyond the horizon.

Adrianna had sped through the city to reach this place, and Lucius had been pushed hard to match her long, determined stride. They had not spoken further, and resentment once again began to flow through him as he realised she was dangling him on the end of a rope, possibly for her own amusement.

She stood, back straight and arms folded, as Lucius had seen her in the window of Brink's house. Not looking at him, she too stared out to sea, though he thought her mind was elsewhere. After a few minutes, his boredom got the better of him.

"Well?" he asked, not without a little sarcasm.

"Wait," she said.

Lucius sighed and turned to walk slowly along the cliff. The immediate area was filled with cranes that leaned over the edge and a wide road that served as a loading area for wagons and carts, separating the cliffs from the row upon row of warehouses. He began to wonder whether his father's warehouses were close by – and who owned them now – when a pungent and heady odour filled his nostrils.

It reminded him of the scent that hung in the air after a storm but, looking back at Adrianna, he saw she had either not sensed it or was ignoring it. A low crackle reached his ears, and it seemed to come from all around. Looking around he tried to locate the source of the sound, but it proved elusive.

A brilliant blue-white flash in front of his eyes made him react, taking a step back. The dull light from Kerberos seemed to dim further for a moment, then another flash followed, this time from the side of one of the nearby warehouses. Lightning crackled around the walls of one of the buildings, shards of light playing across the wood and stone with a sizzling of high energy. With a low rumble of thunder, the electrical discharges coalesced into a tightly packed ball a yard from the ground.

Holding a hand over his eyes to shield himself from the glare, Lucius saw something move within the dancing light, a dark shape stepping through the flashes and sparks. He saw the form of a man walking down to the ground as if on a short flight of stairs. As he placed a foot on the cobbles, the lightning disappeared with the pop of air rushing into a vacant space.

The man was in his later years and wore a tightly-trimmed beard shot through with grey streaks but was otherwise completely bald. Dressed in the jacket and pantaloons of a wealthy merchant, he walked with a limp, leaning on a cane as he crossed the road to face Lucius. Still looking out to sea, Adrianna introduced the newcomer.

"Lucius, this is the Master of Shadows, Forbeck Torquelle."

Eyeing the man warily, Lucius nodded slowly in greeting, but his suspicion seemed to bounce off the man.

"My dear boy," the man said, extending an hand. "I am so very pleased to meet you. Adrianna has told me a great deal about you."

"I'll bet," Lucius said cautiously as he accepted the man's hand and shook it. The Master's voice had the distinct ring of a Pontaine accent, which Lucius found attractive in women, but slightly effeminate in men. Despite the man's careful politeness, Lucius could sense the underlying power in his demeanour. This was someone who was used to getting what he wanted, smothering his iron hard will with a veneer of courtesy.

"I hope you will forgive my showy entrance," Forbeck said apologetically. "I normally reserve such things for weak-minded and superstitious fools, but I wanted there to be no doubt in your mind as to who I am and why I asked for this meeting."

"And why is that?"

"We all felt your presence when you came back to the city, Mr Kane. We didn't know what was happening or what portent it held, until Adrianna first tracked you down. But once we discovered the truth, we just had to make contact."

"We?"

Adrianna turned back to face Lucius. "There is a new guild in the city. The Shadowmages are returning, and are slowly regaining both their numbers and their power."

Lucius smiled at this and began to shake his head, raising a hand to forestall any argument. "I'm sorry to have wasted your time –"

Forbeck overrode Lucius, speaking quietly but firmly. "This is a new guild, Mr Kane, with a new attitude. We have been reforged from the disaster of Vos conquering this city and wiping out our old infrastructure. Not to mention many of the original members."

"I already belong to a guild," Lucius said.

"Yes, I know that. But ours is the only one of its type in the entire peninsula. Please, Mr Kane, walk with us for a moment."

Forbeck turned and there was something in his voice that commanded Lucius to obey, despite his better judgement.

As they walked along the cliff top, deviating only to avoid cranes or piles of empty boxes, Lucius heard

Adrianna's measured footsteps behind him as he kept pace with Forbeck.

"You see, Mr Kane, Shadowmages are unique individuals, having not only the very aptitude for stealth and secrecy that has lead you to find a place within the Night Hands, but also a natural affinity for magic. And I mean natural – it takes many men years and years of study and practice to harness the most basic of spells, if they are even capable of it in the first place. Men like you and I – and, sorry Adrianna, ladies too – can control the magic as easily as we breathe." He laughed. "Well, perhaps with a little more effort than that, but you do take my point."

"I do," said Lucius, wondering where this was going. He knew an offer to join the guild was looming, but he was perplexed as to why. He had already made his case for solitude to Adrianna, and he could not imagine for one moment that she had spoken up for him.

"The combination of stealth and magic is a powerful one, as our predecessors realised, but they never understood its potential. Mr Kane, a Shadowmage, properly trained and in full control of his abilities makes for an excellent – no, he makes for the very best – scout, infiltrator, thief, spy... assassin. The Empire of Vos fears us precisely because of this. That was why they worked so hard to eradicate our kind."

"Well, I have those abilities now, plus the support of a decent guild."

Forbeck shook his head. "The Hands are decent enough, far easier to deal with than those rogues from the Guild of Coin and Enterprise, as Adrianna has recently discovered. But you are quite wrong in thinking you are anywhere near as good as you can be."

He stopped suddenly, catching Lucius by surprise. His

gaze was one of passionate intensity as he spoke. "I see such potential in you, Mr Kane. I can feel the power and possibilities emanating from you as you stand there now. You have no idea of what you are really capable of."

Coughing, Forbeck looked down at the ground briefly before raising his head again to Lucius. "This is the purpose of the guild, you see. We need no guildhouse, membership roll, or shady deals to survive. Our magic and other abilities compensate for all of that, in one way or another. But we can work together for a common cause, and that, Mr Kane, is why you should be with us."

"And just what is the common cause?" Lucius asked.

"That we share information on the practices of stealth and magic both, and through the accumulated wisdom of our members, we become an institution valued and respected. Imagine, Mr Kane, no more disguising the fact that you are more than a mere thief. Think of the lords and nobles who will line up to hire one of our number to engage in the most secret of commissions. Whether it is riches or arcane knowledge that motivates you, you will find it among fellow Shadowmages, not thieves."

"I am not sure I would like serving two masters – remember, I already belong to the Hands."

"Oh, you misunderstand me," Forbeck said, brushing aside the argument with a hand. "Stay with the Hands, you could not do better. I am sure you will learn many techniques in their service that will be of great interest to other Shadowmages. We have no dues to pay, and no chores to fulfil, Mr Kane. Our organisation is one of common accord, nothing more. We only have one ultimate directive."

"Which is?"

"One Shadowmage may never strike at another directly, even if they find themselves on opposing sides of a contract. We have suffered too much in recent years, and to fight among ourselves is folly of the highest order." At this, Lucius noticed Forbeck throw a quick glance at Adrianna. "The consequences of such an attack must, by necessity, be dire. We take an oath to that effect."

Lucius was silent for a moment, thoughts churning through his head. He was fairly sure he did not need another level of complication in his life, particularly one that involved the bitter Adrianna. He had continued to think that his stay in the city would be brief, that he would make his money, and then leave to continue his adventures elsewhere. Yet, he had made himself comfortable among the Night Hands and, if he was utterly truthful with himself, he had made no plans to leave in the near future. There was also that hard edge behind Forbeck's calm exterior that troubled him, and he decided to test his theory.

"You are not going to let me simply walk away, are you?"

Forbeck gave him a grim smile. "You are very perceptive, Mr Kane. We cannot have a rogue Shadowmage at work in this city, risking everything we have worked for so far. Imagine a loose wheel on a wagon – sooner or later, it is going to fall off and bring everything crashing to the ground around it. That's you."

"So my choices are what, join you or die?"

"We are not completely cold-blooded, Mr Kane, and we find it repugnant to be forced to attack one of our own. Think of yourself as a troublesome child who would have to be forced out into the wider world for both your safety and our own."

"Join you or leave then," Lucius said flatly.

"Please, do not think of it in those terms," Forbeck said. "Think of what we can offer you. Support when you most need it, friendship beyond that of thieves. But most of all, training to bring your full potential to light. I was not merely playing you before, Mr Kane. You do have something within you that could be most magnificent. I do not know quite what it is yet, but it will be a fascinating journey of discovery for both of us, I am sure."

Sighing, Lucius shook his head. "You leave me with little choice. How will this work then?"

"After taking the Oath of the Shadowmages to never strike directly at another, you will enter my tutelage immediately."

Beside Lucius, Adrianna gasped in shock. "You cannot be serious!"

"Adrianna –" Forbeck began.

"You don't know this man, Master," she said, her voice dark and loaded with menace. "He cannot be trusted – he has already betrayed the guild once!"

"I would remind you that was the former guild," Forbeck said, before turning back to Lucius. "You must forgive Adrianna. By allowing me to restart your training, you will also be ensuring that you two see a great deal more of one another."

Lucius caught Adrianna muttering something about seeing him first, but ignored it. He took a breath, wondering what fate he was sealing for himself, and whether he would soon be fighting someone else's battles.

"Do I have to call you master?" he asked.

Forbeck smiled back wolfishly. "When you feel ready to, Mr Kane. When you feel ready."

CHAPTER 7

The Hands were present in force during the next round of collections from the Street of Dogs. What would normally have been accomplished over a few lazy afternoons by lower ranking members who had bought their way in to the protection franchise was now being planned and executed with military precision.

Lucius found himself playing watchman, pacing the street as if he had no cares in the world. In reality, he was keeping a sharp eye out for the two thieves who had just entered a tanner's workshop to collect the dues owed to the Hands for another week of relative peace. Three others were also on the street keeping watch and, fifty yards up the hill, the operation was being repeated by another team. The intent, Magnus had explained to them all before they had been dispatched from the guildhouse, was to demonstrate a show of force, both to the shopkeepers and any spies from the Guild of

Coin and Enterprise who would no doubt be looking for a sign of weakness in any territory that belonged to the Hands.

Thus the morning had passed without event. It was the same routine every time; the collectors went into a shop, storehouse or tavern, took their money and listened to the proprietor's complaints, then exited, giving those watching a brief nod to announce the visit had gone according to plan. Then they would move on to the next stop. After every dozen collections, the team would leapfrog the one further up the hill and begin the process again. The use of two teams had been suggested by Caradoc, and it served a dual purpose. First, it was a show of force to the Guild, an announcement of the manpower the Hands could field. However, it also would give those under protection less warning that the collection was about to arrive.

As predicted by the Council, the takings for those not directly linked to the franchise, Lucius included, were slim, but most accepted the duty without complaint, realising that this was a time for unity, not argument. It was also an easy role to play, Lucius realised as he stopped briefly outside a wine merchant to casually view the more expensive casks and bottles on display. All part of the act.

For his part, Lucius was grateful for the respite, though not for the early start. He was still considering his meeting earlier in the week with Adrianna and her Master – his now as well, he realised. His relationship with Aidy had clearly soured further when she had learned he was to be taught alongside her, and her venomous looks, split equally between him and Forbeck, made it apparent that she was not going to make life easy for either.

Having taken the oath not to directly harm another Shadowmage, which gave some small comfort in itself considering Adrianna's disposition, Forbeck had talked briefly with him about his past, his time in the old guild, his family, his reasons for leaving Turnitia, and what he had seen on his travels beyond the city.

After that, Forbeck had disappeared, promising that Lucius would be contacted soon to begin his training. He did not reveal how or when the message would be delivered, and Adrianna had been in no hurry to educate him further. So, it was back to the Hands and a thief's work.

The two collectors, junior members of the franchise but, on this operation, very much Lucius' superiors, left the tanners and gave the nod before moving next door to a dressmakers he knew was run by an elderly spinster. From what he had heard in the common room, the collectors would get little real trouble there, but would be forced to endure a lecture that encompassed everything that was wrong with the city, and how the Hands should go about fixing it. He reflected that with such clients on the books, the greater share the collectors were earning today would be well earned. Keeping pace with them, Lucius moved his attention to the window of a potter's shop front, looking over the decoratively painted clay mugs, plates and bowls while trying not to look bored.

He was eventually distracted by movement down the hill. One of the other watchmen lifted a finger in signal, but Lucius had already clocked the danger. The collectors had not yet left the spinster and coming towards the team now was a group of perhaps twenty men. It was the tightness of their gathering that first alerted Lucius, for while friends may travel so closely together, no one walked in such a large group unless they had distinct purpose.

Eyeing the men without looking at them directly, he spotted a few cudgels carried openly, while others sported suspicious looking bulges under their tunics that suggested concealed knives and clubs. He glanced at one of the other watchmen, a young man called Swinherd, who returned the look with a shrug, clearly not knowing how to respond.

It was unlikely that the proprietors of the Street of Dogs had banded together to raise a small army in order to dissuade the Hands from collecting their dues, as the tax was mild enough and Magnus had made sure there was always some tangible benefit to paying; burglaries in the Street of Dogs were quite rare. The Vos guard, if they deigned to get involved in a benign protection racket, would send armoured and uniformed men. That just left the Guild of Coin and Enterprise, and that meant trouble.

While Lucius had yet to learn all the intricacies of the unique sign language used by the Hands, he knew enough to get his general meaning across, and a casual crossing of his hands told the other watchmen to stand ready and make no overt moves. He was gratified to see their assent, and they continued watching as the men approached.

As they moved closer, Lucius realised that they were paying him no attention, but one burly man at their centre nudged another and pointed directly at Swinherd, obviously recognising him as a Hand. As one, the men altered their course and steered directly for him.

To his credit, Swinherd stood his ground, raising his head in acknowledgement as they gathered around him in a semicircle. The first words exchanged were quiet and beyond Lucius' range of hearing. One of the other watchmen sent a discrete signal, suggesting they move in to support Swinherd, but Lucius shook his head. He guessed that at least some of his fellow thieves had not been recognised either, and while they remained invisible to the Guild men, they retained an advantage, as badly outnumbered as they were. Lucius found himself anxious to move closer, to hear what was being said, but he steeled himself to remain passive and await an outcome.

It all seemed rather amiable, Lucius thought, as he kept a watch out of the corner of his eye, the potter's wares now completely forgotten. The burly man leading the Guild men kept his hands in plain view as he spoke, and Swinherd was nodding and shrugging as if he were chatting to an old acquaintance. Then things became heated.

The burly man pointed a finger back down the hill, as if ordering Swinherd to leave the street, at which point the young man shook his head in refusal and took a step back. They followed him and men on the flanks began to crowd round, hiding Swinherd from sight as he raised his hands, trying to appease them. Knowing he was about to witness a beating in broad daylight, Lucius gave a quick signal to the other watchers and trotted across the street.

"Swinherd!" he said in greeting as he pushed his way through the tight press of men. Keeping his voice jovial, he also completely ignored the baleful stares that were now being directed his way, and he hoped the other thieves had taken his lead and were just a few paces behind. "We've been looking for you. Come we've got work to do, no time to stand and chat with old friends."

"We're no friends of that this toe-rag," growled someone in the crowd.

Lucius kept his eyes fixed firmly on Swinherd, whose gratitude at being rescued was palpable. "Well, that's unfortunate."

A bearded man took a step to stand directly before Lucius. He held a club low down one leg. "You spineless dog," he said in a low voice.

"We've got no argument with you," said Lucius, trying hard to put an edge in his voice while ignoring the hostile gazes from the assembled men. "It would be best for all if we went our separate ways."

The burly man jabbed a finger hard into Swinherd's chest, though his words were directed at Lucius. "Your time here is over. This street belongs to the Guild now, and we'll be taking over the collections today."

"You don't want to do this," Lucius said. "This is a fight no one can win."

He was, of course, referring to a wider war between the two thieves guilds, but he belatedly realised that such grander thoughts of strategy were likely beyond the men who had been sent to scare them off.

"There's more of us," the bearded man piped up again. "I'm thinking we can win this easy."

"Understand this," the burly man cut over him. "The Hands are finished. There can only be one Guild in this city, and that's us. You'll either join us, or spend the rest of your lives as cripples. Those are your only choices."

Lucius and Swinherd quickly exchanged glances, and the young man nodded in understanding of what was about to happen. Lucius stared straight into the eyes of the burly man.

"If you don't leave now, I promise, you won't walk away from this," he said, his voice even.

Someone near the back of the crowd laughed. The burly man smiled and nodded at him in a mock salute. He then grabbed the club from the bearded man and swung it hard at Swinherd.

Lucius had been ready for the first attack. He dove between Swinherd and weapon, catching the man's arms as the club started to descend.

"Run!" Lucius shouted over his shoulder and Swinherd, needing no prompting, turned and fled. Raising his knee Lucius rammed it into the crotch of the burly man, who exhaled noisily before staggering to the ground. Reacting a great deal slower than Lucius, the others began to draw knives and daggers as he turned and ran as well.

The collectors had chosen that moment to leave the spinster, and their faces were almost comical, eyes wide in astonishment as they saw their watchmen running at full tilt down the street, pursued by an angry and cursing mob. They took their cue from their friends and started to sprint away, goaded on by Lucius' shouts.

Casting a look behind him as he ran, Lucius saw the Hands had scattered, diving into alleyways, vaulting over walls, splitting up to ensure at least some would escape unharmed. He decided to continue running directly up the centre of the street in order to provide the most visible target, but the Guild men were not co-operating.

Swinherd had rocketed past the collectors, then dived into an alley that stretched alongside the long wall of a tavern proclaiming itself to be the Grateful Rest. With no real co-ordination on their part, the Guild men had zeroed in on their original target and were pounding just a few steps behind the young man, who was clearly in fear of his life.

Coming to a stop, Lucius turned back and shouted a challenge at the pursuing men, calling out the bearded man in the lead.

"Hey, pig!" he bellowed. "Was your mother wedded to a hog, or was she a sow whore putting it to every merchant in the city?"

He was answered by an angry, inarticulate cry, and the mob surged up towards him. Smiling, Lucius bolted. It never failed.

Hearing the clatter of leather on cobbles gaining ground on him, Lucius tried to measure his breathing as he sought the strands of energy that were never far from his grasp. Control of his magic was difficult while sprinting, but he was only attempting rudimentary control. He caught the needed thread, feeling its power flush through his entire body. Feeling a new wave of strength, he banished all thought of fatigue and ignored his aching legs as he gained in speed, pulling away from the mob.

Within seconds, Lucius was in the territory of the second collection team, and he saw the surprised looks of their watchmen.

"Guild men!" he shouted, jabbing a finger over his shoulder. They reacted instantly, one diving into a shop front to retrieve his collectors while the others melted away into side streets. Lucius grinned, satisfied that the other thieves were retreating to places of safety. It took just one more glance over his shoulder to remind him that he was still in great danger himself. The expressions on the faces of the mob left no doubt as to his fate should he be caught.

Deciding that the chase had gone on long enough, he darted right, vaulting over a fence that ran round a small townhouse. Hitting the ground in a roll, he found himself in an unkempt garden, full of uncut thigh-high grass and weeds. He bolted across the small patch of wilderness and swung his legs over the low wall on the other side. Behind, the Guild's men were cursing as they became entangled in the undergrowth, but enough were making good headway to convince Lucius not to slow down.

Over the wall, Lucius found himself in a smaller street, its buildings a mixture of shabby houses and shops whose owners were unable to afford the prices commanded on the Street of Dogs. He ran a short distance past the nearest buildings, then jerked left into a narrow alley, intending to lose the men in the network of twisting turns and junctions that were common in these districts of Turnitia.

After a few more minutes, Lucius felt safe enough to stop and catch his breath, leaning against the brickwork of an abandoned house. The magic that had propelled him this far and this fast was now ebbing, and a deep fatigue spread through his body. The complaints his bones made at having been pushed so hard were finally heard. Crouching down as he drew in painful gasps of air, he rubbed his ankles for some relief, but he stopped when he heard new cries coming from a short distance away. They were just one or two streets over from where he stood.

Fearing one of his fellow thieves had been caught, Lucius forced himself to his feet, shoving the weariness away. He retraced his steps cautiously, heading down a short road that led back toward the Street of Dogs. More calls echoed off the walls of the nearby buildings, and he dove into a doorway as three Guild men ran out of an alleyway a few yards ahead of him, coming to a stop in the middle of the road as they looked about them.

Pressing himself against the door, Lucius carefully tilted his head to watch them. They were obviously having a disagreement as to which way they should run next, which was finally resolved by one returning the way they had come, while the other two dashed up towards the Street of Dogs.

Lucius released a breath he'd not realised he had been holding, then caught it again as the door behind him opened, which forced him to grab onto the frame to stop himself stumbling. Turning around, he saw a small girl in a dirty shirt looking up at him expectantly. Winking at her and smiling, he fished out a silver tenth from his pouch and flipped it to her, before running across the road into another alley.

Finding himself between two rows of houses, Lucius saw alleys criss-crossing every thirty yards or so and he skidded to a halt at every junction, checking each intersection. Another shout of anger, and the clash of metal on metal from up ahead spurred him on, and he rounded a corner in time to see Swinherd pull a knife from the belly of a Guild man, who collapsed, sobbing, onto the hard ground. Another watcher who had been on Lucius' team stepped out from another alley and, on seeing what had happened, patted Swinherd on the back. Lucius, dismayed, ran towards them.

"What have you done?" he said in a harsh whisper. "What have you done?"

"Bastard tried to jump me," Swinherd said, kicking the man as he groaned and clasped his hands to his stomach in a fruitless attempt to stem the flow of blood.

"Why didn't you just keep on running? You should have just ran!"

Swinherd shrugged. "I was trying to hook up with you guys again. I had to defend myself!"

"Yeah, back off a moment," said the watchman, who seemed to take greater offence at Lucius' interruption that Swinherd had.

"So we have a dead Guild man on our hands. So what? One less suits us just fine, I say." The watchman bent down to look the dying man in the face. "You hear that, you worthless bastard? You're going to die soon."

"You fools!" said Lucius, trying to keep both his temper and voice low. He could not see why these two did not understand what was at stake. "Up to now, we have just had a few beatings here and there. This is the first time a Hand has killed someone in the Guild."

When they just looked at him blankly, he sighed and continued, speaking a little slower so his meaning would not be lost. "They are going to be after our blood now."

The watchman looked at Swinherd, then at the dying man, then back at Lucius. "Well... we could hide the body."

Lucius rolled his eyes. "Where? You planning on hoisting it over one of these walls? One way or another, the Guild will find the body, and even if they don't they'll guess what has happened when he doesn't show up at their guildhouse."

"So what do we do?" Swinherd asked, now suddenly less elated at his victory.

Thinking hard, Lucius scratched the back of his head. "We've got to get back to Magnus, tell him what has happened."

"You going to tell him it was me?" Swinherd said in a quiet voice.

"Believe me, he is going to have far greater things to worry about than punishing you."

They split up again, after bearing a lecture from Lucius

as to how they would *not* go looking for more Guild men. They were to take their separate paths back to the guildhouse and get there as quickly as possible.

He just hoped Magnus would have the wisdom to see a way through this, and perhaps make some compensation towards the Guild. The alternative was too terrible to contemplate.

CHAPTER 8

Lucius cursed as the small ball of fire ignited another roll of paper. For the third time in a row. Behind him, he heard Adrianna quietly clack her tongue, though whether it was in amusement or impatience, he could not decide.

Moving quickly for an older man, Forbeck kicked it to one side and stamped out the flames, before replacing it with another roll.

"Try again, Mr Kane."

As the sun descended beyond the western horizon, Lucius had felt a curious itch in the back of his mind. A prickling on the nape of his neck. Unable to shake the sensation, he had left the guildhouse and the turmoil it had fallen into, and quickly realised the feeling grew stronger as he headed north, but weaker when he turned aside from the path.

Arriving at an abandoned warehouse, the itching growing ever more insistent, he discovered this was

Forbeck's way of summoning him to their first lesson. Lucius was at first irritated at having been called in this manner, but quickly found himself curious as to the measure of subtle control needed for such magic. Knowing the master had managed to pick him out of the entire population of the city, then plant the urge to follow the signal was impressive, and it left him wanting to know exactly how it was achieved. Forbeck, however, had other plans for that evening, and Adrianna was her usual implacable self.

Within the empty confines of the dusty and cobweb-strewn warehouse, Forbeck had devised a simple test to measure Lucius' control of his talent. Having quickly divined that Lucius was capable of conjuring fire at will, six rolls of paper had been placed in a row, and Lucius had been asked to summon a small ball of flame, and weave it in and out of the spaces while leaving the papers intact.

It was not an easy test, and Lucius was growing more frustrated with each attempt.

He had thought it a simple challenge when Forbeck had initially spelled it out and, ignoring Adrianna's knowing look, Lucius' first try had blasted the first three rolls into cinders. By the third attempt, he had managed to guide the fireball around the first roll, but had watched helplessly as it wobbled into the second. The trial seemed to be going nowhere fast.

The problem was that Lucius had never, since he had first realised his gift with magic, tried to exercise such precise control for anything more than influencing tumbling dice for a split second. Calling upon the power to blast an enemy with a jet of flame, sending him reeling to the ground with the force of the strike even as the fire consumed him, was relatively easy. Aside from the shaping of the necessary energies, it required very little control whatsoever. Just creating and maintaining a small globe of swirling flames for more than a few seconds was enough to make Lucius break into a sweat. Guiding it with precision was seemingly impossible, though Forbeck had earlier demonstrated a successful attempt at the exercise to prove it was not.

"Remember, all it takes is practice," Forbeck said, as he watched Lucius frown in concentration.

Kneeling, Lucius opened his right hand as a bright spark ignited upon his palm. Growing into a sphere of rolling fire half the size of his fist, he placed his hand on the stone floor and willed the flames to tumble forwards. The fire bounced once and, before he could arrest its momentum, bumped gently into the first roll of paper, lighting it immediately.

"Practice makes perfect," Lucius muttered. "I'm getting worse!"

"Did you really think you would come here, accomplish everything laid before you with so little effort and then leave, smug in the knowledge that there is nothing you cannot do?" Adrianna said.

Lucius bit his tongue to forestall the first retort that came to mind. "That was not my first thought, no," he finally said.

A rap echoed across the rafters and walls of the warehouse as Forbeck struck his cane on the hard stone, silencing the argument brewing between his students.

"I wish I could tell you there was an easy way through this part, Mr Kane," he said, replacing the burnt roll. "I wish there was some secret meditative technique, or command word, that would allow you to control your magic as I have asked. But I am afraid there is not. The only route to success lies in practice, practice, practice.

Master your frustration at failure, and direct your energies to trying again."

Narrowing his eyes and laying his palm flat once more, Lucius called upon his magic to bring another fire globe into existence, but this one just fizzled away after the first few sparks.

He sighed. "I am not sure I am in the best frame of mind for this today."

"Have you ever had trouble making your talent do what you want before?" Forbeck asked.

Lucius thought for a moment. "No. Not since the early days anyway."

"I would guess that is because you have only ever used your magic when your life was in peril, or perhaps occasionally for your own amusement. You have never had to influence with such delicate control before."

"Taking the path of least resistance," Adrianna said, but they both ignored her.

"Please, try again," Forbeck said. "Forget the distractions of your ordinary life and fill your mind with the magic. There should be nothing else."

Taking a deep breath, Lucius looked at the line of paper rolls before him. The truth was that distractions *were* intruding on his thoughts. Marching back to the guildhouse earlier that day, Lucius had been filled with dread. He knew they had failed utterly in their mission on the Street of Dogs; the disruption to the collections could be excused – but the death of the Guild man in the skirmish after could not.

They had confronted Magnus, all twelve thieves assigned to the task and, upon hearing what Swinherd had done, the guildmaster had fought visibly to control his anger. The shadow across his face had subsided quickly, but he had told them all how very disappointed he was in them. That seemed worse somehow. Though they all knew that it was Swinherd that bore the brunt of blame, they also all felt in some measure responsible. It had after all, happened on their watch.

Ordering the rest of the Hands to keep a low profile in the city over the next few days, he clearly hoped there would be no direct retaliation, that the Guild would see the senselessness of direct action and chalk the death down to over exuberance on the part of some of its members. It was, after all, what he would be inclined to do in their place. However, Lucius was not so sure. There was a dark feeling in the pit of his stomach that refused to be silenced, and it had been troubling him all day, as if they were now just waiting for the hammer to fall. It was certainly affecting his concentration now.

Lucius aimed the next fireball to the side of the first paper roll, thinking that he could at least bypass the obstacle with little effort on his part. As the globe slowly bounced past the paper, he half-closed his eyes as he tried to imagine an invisible thread between it and himself. Gently, he pulled on the connection, willing it to veer to the left and therefore bounce between the first two rolls.

The fiery globe seemed to hesitate just a few inches above the floor then, with infinite slowness it seemed to Lucius, curved a lazy arc between the rolls. It was not a neat line, but the globe now bobbed on the other side of the rolls, close to the second. He could feel the connection between himself and the fire grow complicated and tenuous, but he took a breath and willed it forward just a little, then started a new curve to the right, to take it past the second roll and onto the third.

As the fire globe slowly drifted in the new direction, he allowed himself a smile of satisfaction. The break in his thoughts was enough to sever the link he had so far maintained, and the ball suddenly picked up speed, veered left and right randomly, then headed straight for the third roll, blasting it to cinders.

"Damn it!" he shouted, frustration getting the better of him.

"Easy, my boy," Forbeck said, placing the end of his cane on Lucius' shoulder, as if to restrain his anger. It caused him to turn round to face the other two Shadowmages.

"You may not believe me, but you are doing well to get so far so quickly," Forbeck continued. "We have been here little more than an hour, and you are showing the ability to influence your magic beyond the point of egress, to maintain a physical form for several seconds, and to guide it with growing precision. I do not know if I recall seeing someone with so much ready aptitude."

Lucius noticed Adrianna's eyes narrow suspiciously at this, but he said nothing. Scoring cheap points against her was not the way to an easy life, he had long ago realised. Forbeck fell silent with his own thoughts for a moment, then focussed back on Lucius.

"Let's try another tact," he said, pacing a half circle round Lucius before leaning on his cane with both hands. "Tell me how you see your magic. What do you imagine when you call upon the power?"

"The same as you, I would think," Lucius said.

"Indulge an old man," Forbeck said, smiling. "What do you *see*?"

"Well... It's always there, to one degree or another. You kind of get used to it. It's like I can see many different lines, strands, umm... threads, I suppose. Not see them for real, but they are in my head somewhere. They all wrap around one another as they go off into the distance, spinning round and round, crossing one another's path. I sort of reach in and pick out the one I need, and I feel it right here," he said, putting a hand on his chest. "After that, I can direct and shape the energy into what I need it to do."

"Fascinating," Forbeck muttered. Lucius noticed he glanced briefly at Adrianna, who raised her eyebrows in an expression that seemed to suggest she had won an argument between them.

"And what, exactly, are you able to do with these threads?" Forbeck asked. "How can you manifest your power? What can you *do*?"

Lucius shrugged. "Create fire, as you can see, though normally I only use that to start a camp fire – or catch an enemy off guard. I can increase my strength and speed for a short time, send a stone flying through the air, cloak myself in shadows, bend the branches of a tree, umm... well, whatever I need, really."

He purposefully did not mention the darker aspects of his talent, the powers he knew were at his call but had always seemed black, ruinous... evil. He saw Forbeck was eyeing him with a calculating look, seeming to measure him by the ounce.

"You may be a truly remarkable individual, Mr Kane," Forbeck said quietly.

This puzzled Lucius, for he had expected some ridicule, especially from Adrianna, for how little his abilities had progressed over the years. The test with the rolls of paper was clearly an exercise in humiliation for him.

"What do you mean?" he asked.

Forbeck paused again as he marshalled his thoughts. When he finally spoke, his voice was slow and measured. "Every Shadowmage visualises their power in a different way. However, there are common themes. Most see it as a centralised concentration of power." Seeing Lucius frown at that, Forbeck tried to quantify his remark. "They see something like a large cloud, a lake, or maybe a river. They fuel their magic by metaphorically reaching into that source, scooping out the gas or water, and then forming it into what they need."

"I don't see anything like that," Lucius said.

"No. And that is what makes you at least a little different. Tell me, Mr Kane, what you know about the fundamental properties of magic. What is it do you think, that guides what a practitioner, be they Shadowmage, wizard, witch or priest, and limits what he can ultimately achieve?"

"I am not sure I know," Lucius said doubtfully. "Practice, I suppose, as you said."

He saw immediately from Forbeck's expression that it was the wrong answer.

"Do you think you could move a mountain, Mr Kane?" Forbeck asked.

"Well, no."

"So, there are clearly limits to what can be done. However, there are other boundaries that confine a practitioner to certain tasks that he can accomplish with magic. Do you understand what I mean?"

"Not really," Lucius said.

"Well, we have been watching you create your little balls of fire this evening. Would it surprise you to learn that Adrianna is completely unable to ignite so much as a spark, let alone sustain a fire through its own energy alone?"

Lucius blinked. Yes, he was surprised that Adrianna could not accomplish something he found so easy. She was, after all, far more accomplished as a Shadowmage than he. However, as he cast his mind back, he suddenly realised that, for all the time they had spent together in the past learning under Master Roe, he had never seen her use fire in her magic.

"Why is that?" he asked, completely perplexed.

"There are different types of magic, Mr Kane," Forbeck said. "Or rather, different sources. I am not sure anyone knows them all, but the important thing is that the vast majority of practitioners in this world only ever master one. Just one, Mr Kane. Now, all Shadowmages have an aptitude for magic involving stealth and secrecy; that is one of the aspects of our practice that sets us apart – the other is that we can manipulate magic so easily, almost instinctively, while others require years of study, practice and ritual. However, the very best of us also gain mastery of another source. Do you follow me?"

Looking blank, Lucius just waited for him to continue.

"For example, I can create the same fire you do, but Adrianna cannot. She can greatly influence parts of the natural world – weather, animals, plants and so forth. But I cannot. We share an affinity for stealth and secrets, for we are Shadowmages, but otherwise we are very different.

"When I see the source of my magic, Mr Kane, I see two clouds. One is still and dark, and is where I reach when I want to clothe myself in shadows or walk silently past an alert watchman. The other is turbulent and frightening, a tempest of power that I often struggle to harness. But reaching for that cloud is what allows me to create fire, animate water, or suck the air from the lungs of an enemy. Most Shadowmages are confined to the magic of stealth, which is where we earned our name. Only the best, those destined to become masters of the guild, can add another weapon to their magical arsenal. And then we have you."

"Me?"

"You are clearly not bound to one, or even two sources of power in your magical endeavours, Mr Kane. Adrianna tried to tell me this earlier, but I did not believe it. And yet when you, just now, described what you can achieve with your magic, you told us of things that would ordinarily take half a dozen Shadowmages to accomplish."

Lucius was quiet for a moment, and the silence of the empty warehouse began to press upon him as he struggled to find something to say.

"So... what does mean?" he asked.

"I am not sure," Forbeck said. "That you have access to formidable powers was obvious to me before we even met. Every Shadowmage in the city felt something when you arrived. But it is also clear you have access to perhaps an unlimited number of arcane sources of power. It will be fascinating to watch what you can ultimately achieve and, because of this, I implore you to continue your training. You can be so much, Mr Kane, and I just hope I can help set you on the right path. There is something about you that sets you apart from not only other Shadowmages, but perhaps every practitioner of magic in this world. It would be a crime to allow that to simply fade away."

"That is a lot to think about," Lucius said.

"I know, and both Adrianna and I will do all we can to guide you through these early stages. I cannot promise you anything, Mr Kane, and I cannot foretell the future. But I very much want to train you, for your own sake, as well as that of our guild."

"Then, in that case," Lucius replied, "I think I will stay around. For at least a little while longer."

"Thank you, Mr Kane," said Forbeck, and Lucius sensed his relief. "I think we have covered enough – more than enough – this evening. Carry on with your practice when you can, try to exercise finer control. That will be key to your later studies. When we meet again, we will see how far you have come. I look forward to that time."

With a slight bow, Forbeck spun on his heels and walked out of the warehouse, the sound of his cane ringing on the stone with each step.

Lucius stared down at the line of paper rolls in front of him, sensing Adrianna's eyes fixed on the back of his head.

"You put a word in for me, then?" he asked.

When she did not answer immediately, he turned back to face her, seeing a dark expression bearing down upon him.

"You are a rogue and a scoundrel," she said accusingly. "But you do have power. That, I have always sensed."

She stalked past him to follow Forbeck, her voice floating back to him as it echoed around the warehouse. "Learn from Master Torquelle, and you will find a home among the Shadowmages, Lucius. Betray us again and, I swear, I will finish you myself."

His mind now full of magic, as well as the struggle between thieves, Lucius nevertheless felt as though some burden had been lifted from his shoulders. What passed for an olive branch in Adrianna's mind had been offered to him, and he clearly had an ally, if not yet a friend, in Forbeck. For the first time in many years, he had a sense of purpose, of a greater goal to be achieved, rather than aimless wandering. He had to admit, it felt good. There were troubles to be faced by the Night Hands but, he now believed they could eventually be solved and, maybe, he would have a part in that.

When Lucius returned to the guildhouse, after walking the twilight streets of Turnitia for an hour or more, he found that nothing would be solved easily, and that greater dangers now hung above all the thieves.

The sombre mood in the common room was palpable when he entered, for no one spoke above a whisper. Clumped together in their regular groups, the thieves simply nursed their ale or wine, and avoided looking directly at him or one another. Sensing something had gone very wrong, Lucius dashed upstairs, seeking Ambrose or Caradoc, finally finding the latter in the council chamber with two others that Lucius had seen earlier.

"You can't be here," Caradoc warned him. "The Council is gathering to discuss the attack."

"What attack?" Lucius asked, suddenly anxious.

"Where have you been? One of the pickpocket teams was found in the afternoon, stabbed to death and thrown into Drake's Alley in the Five Markets."

"They were only kids," said one of the Council members, a bitter note in her voice.

Suddenly downcast, Lucius turned to leave, before a thought struck him. "Which team was it?"

"Just been put together," Caradoc said. "Some young lad called Tucker, only joined us this week. He was with two experienced kids; Markel and Treal, brother and sister, I think."

Lucius sagged against the doorframe, trying hard not to picture the children, their bodies lying in a deserted alley among the dirt and filth, blood pouring from open wounds in their chests. They must have been so scared, he thought, and cursed himself for not being there to save them.

He barely heard when Caradoc spoke again. "It will be war now, you mark my words. There is no way Magnus can back down from this. It will be war."

CHAPTER 9

The guildhouse was alive with activity, rumour and gossip. From the first light of day, thieves had been gathered in small groups, and conversation had stealthily made its way through the common room, armoury, kitchens and corridors; the Guild of Coin and Enterprise were coming.

It had been later in the afternoon when Lucius had been summoned to the council chamber, its polished wooden walls seeming to reflect the mixed emotions of excitement and dread that had permeated the entire guildhouse by now. He had already that heard there had been a noisy dispute among the Council – particularly between Magnus and Caradoc – but the guildmaster had made his wishes clear, vetoing all other proposals. Seeing where violence between the two guilds would inevitably lead, Magnus had called for a summit between them, inviting the leadership of the Guild into his most secret lair as a sign of trust and concession.

That had been the rumour, but as Lucius passed Caradoc in the hall and saw his haunted expression, he came to believe all he had heard. They were waiting for him in the council chamber, the table turned so it stood at right angles to its normal facing, with the most senior thieves hunched together on the far side facing a row of empty seats across an assembly of wine urns and cups. Magnus sat in the centre with Caradoc's empty place to his left, while behind him stood his two bodyguards; Lucius had learned they were brothers, Taene and Narsell, and they had terrible reputations for cruel brutality, but served the guildmaster with complete fidelity.

A smattering of other high-ranking thieves stood against the wall behind the assembled Council, and Lucius was directed to join them. He had no idea why he had been summoned to this meeting, other than it had been at Magnus' direct request, as he knew the others would be present to act not only as witnesses, but also as advisors and counsellors, should information be needed during the discussions. What he had to offer, Lucius could not say, but he was grateful indeed that he would see what happened here first hand, and not have to rely on the guildhouse's own, not always accurate, grapevine.

"Are we certain they will show?" one of the Council members asked, a young man whom Lucius recalled was called Nate.

"The offer caused quite a stir within the Guild," another man answered, "or so our spies have told me. I wouldn't be surprised if they were still arguing about what to do."

"They will show," Magnus said confidently. He noticed a few doubtful looks about the table and continued. "The Guild has as much to gain and lose as we do. Though we have very different ideas about how to run this city, Loredo is not a stupid man."

"He also risks a great deal by coming here, to our home ground," Nate said. "If the situation was reversed, I would be worried about an ambush."

"True," Magnus agreed. "But we risk a similar amount by inviting him here. Look at it this way. If the situation were indeed reversed, would you not be swayed by the chance to see your enemy's stronghold?"

The Council considered that, and Lucius saw a few heads nodding round the table as Magnus' reasoning became apparent.

"More important is what happens after the initial greetings," he said. "I confess, I am not entirely sure what the Guild will be after, nor how aggressively they will negotiate. They must be willing to consider compromises, or we would not have been able to arrange this meeting. However, we must be ready to cede ground if it first gains us territory elsewhere and, second, ensures peace between us. I will not have war among thieves, not while I am guildmaster."

Conversation then turned to the operations and territories the Council wanted to keep and which they might consider for trade. As they spoke, Lucius' head began to swim with information; he had no idea of the complexity or number of the operations the Hands had an interest in. There was far more than just theft at stake.

The growing prostitute rings were clearly an important element for some of the Council, for while new to the Hands and still small, it showed much promise. They fought against the advocates of smugglers and blackmailers. Lucius learned of a city-wide counterfeit ring that traded in false documents, coin and art. It was confirmed that the Hands did indeed have a burgeoning trade in assassinations, whose franchise owners were considered among the most skilled in all the guild. As

well as the pickpockets, protection rackets and general
burglaries, the Council spoke of narcotics from the Sarcre
Islands, trade of arcane artefacts from ruins in the darkest
parts of the Sardenne, and an underground network
that could spirit Pontaine agents too and from Turnitia
throughout the year.

Lucius began to wonder just how wealthy the Night
Hands were, when all their operations were stacked up
and accounted for. He thought of the vaults built into
the foundations of the guildhouse, and thought of how
they must be nearly overflowing with coin and valuables.
Not for the first time, he could see the organisation he
had chosen to join as a whole, that it was not simply
a gathering of those who worked outside the law, but
a business, run as tightly and efficiently as that of the
richest merchants. Fundamentally, it was all about the
money.

A short thief poked his head round the open door of
the meeting room. "They're here," he said, before ducking
back out of sight.

The mood in the room changed immediately. Council
members sat straighter in their seats, while Magnus'
bodyguards, Taene and Narsell, shifted their weight ever
so slightly, moving their hands a fraction of an inch
along their belts to where their blades lay. For his part,
Lucius folded his arms and squared his shoulders as he
waited for the Guild's delegation to arrive.

They heard quiet voices talking amiably from down
the hall, accompanied by footsteps. Everyone in the
meeting room seemed to draw in breath at the same time
as Caradoc appeared at the door, standing to one side as
he politely waved his guests through.

Though Lucius had never seen the leader of the Guild
of Coin and Enterprise before, he recognised the man

immediately by his bearing and demeanour. He looked exactly like a guildmaster should.

So did Magnus, of course, but Lucius had always seen him as a natural guildmaster because of his authority, leadership and wisdom, all of which became apparent after talking to him for just a few minutes. Loredo Foss was different in just about every way. Lithe and graceful, he was dressed in a black leather jerkin lined with dark red thread. His hair was black and slicked back, while his beard was small and pointed, barely covering his chin. This man was a natural guildmaster, Lucius thought, because he was a master thief, among the very best in his game. That would make him a very dangerous enemy, and Lucius began to appreciate some of the risks Magnus had accepted in opposing himself to the Guild.

Loredo was followed only by one other, which was a statement in itself, considering they had entered the lair of *their* enemy. It was Caradoc's counterpart, Loredo's own lieutenant and trusted confidante, a woman Lucius had heard of but had never seen.

She stalked into the meeting room behind her guildmaster as if she were the leader of all thieves, not he. Her boots, whose hard leather clattered on the floor of the meeting room, ran past her knees, and Lucius could not help but think of all the weapons that might be hidden within them, even though they had been told to divest themselves of any offensive items before entering the guildhouse.

Named Jewel, she had a reputation among the Hands for being utterly lethal, for it was rumoured she was more assassin than thief. Her narrow eyes regarded everyone suspiciously and though she was not at all unattractive, the hardness of her features, which promised quick and silent retribution to anyone who would cross her, seemed to sap any desire.

It was a brave move bringing only one bodyguard to a meeting between thieves of this level, but Lucius thought that, between them, Loredo and Jewel might account for many Hands before they were slain, should the summit take an ill turn.

Magnus stood up to greet his guests, and the action was quickly copied among the rest of the seated Council.

"Loredo, Miss Jewel," he acknowledged as he extended a hand across the table. "I bid you a warm welcome to our humble home, and hope your journey here will prove a fruitful one."

Accepting Magnus' hand with a firm shake and brief nod, Loredo replied. "You show great wisdom in calling this meeting, Magnus. I, too, hope for an outcome beneficial to the both of us."

The Council returned to their seats as Loredo sat down, followed by Jewel. The woman said nothing but eyed each of the Hands methodically, as if judging the threat they might pose to her master. As her eyes swept over Lucius, he drew an involuntary breath, and fought to keep his own gaze even. He had the unlikely notion that Jewel had just given him a number that placed him in the order of people in the room she would like to kill.

As Caradoc joined Magnus' side, the guildmaster remained standing as he took a wine urn and poured four cups. He placed the cups in a row and looked across at Loredo, who smiled. He selected two and passed one to Jewel. Magnus scooped up one of the cups that had been left and drained it, before setting it back on the table with a loud clack. Caradoc followed suit, before reaching for the urn once more and refilling Magnus' cup, then his own.

"I thank you for that show of honesty, Magnus," Loredo said. "But I would think that if you wanted me dead, you would not stoop to poison, nor would you go to the trouble of arranging this meeting."

"Merely demonstrating my willingness to be open here," Magnus said, as he watched Loredo take a sip from his cup. Jewel's cup remained untouched on the table before her.

The two guildmasters regarded one another briefly before Magnus spoke again. "Loredo, you and I have a problem. I run a guild of thieves, and have an interest in making money. You run a guild of thieves and have an interest in making money. Of late, these interests have clashed too many times. If we allow this to escalate, we risk a war that could destroy both of us."

"I have no interest in a thieves war," Loredo said. "It would prove messy and bring the Vos guard crashing down on us. If you have an easy solution, I would gladly hear it."

"We could perhaps divide the city in two," Magnus said, a hint of sarcasm in his voice. "We could take the west while you have the east, or perhaps we control the north while you take the south."

"Giving you, in the first instance, the docks, and in the second, the Five Markets," Loredo said.

"As we can all see, there is no easy solution," Magnus concluded, and Loredo nodded once in agreement.

"I suggest we make the division based on territory and trade," Magnus said. "If we give something up, you make a concession in return. We will ensure there is parity between us, and that every one of our members understands there are some areas they simply do not work in."

"That, I feel, would be the most equitable solution," Loredo said. "So, where would you begin?"

"Let us start with the disputed territories that have led us here. The Street of Dogs and the Five Markets."

For the first hour, Lucius listened with rapt attention as the two guildmasters spoke, proposing and counter-proposing over and again, as they vied for each advantage. Never once was a voice raised in anger, but each retained a hard edge that served to reign the other in when a demand grew too insistent. After the second and third hours, Lucius' legs began to grow numb, and he noticed others shifting their weight or fidgeting.

Magnus made a point in asking various members of his Council or one of the senior thieves to clarify a point, to list earnings over a given period, or give a rundown on recent activities. By contrast, Loredo never asked Jewel for anything, and he seemed to have the uncanny knack for knowing exactly what Magnus was talking about, citing figures and statistics without fail.

Lucius was startled when Magnus asked him a question, briefly wanting to know the average takings for the pickpocket team that had been slain by the Guild. Lucius answered automatically, but he found his mind drifting back to the brother and sister team he had known, Markel and Treal, and the brutal way in which they had died. It was so very hard not to regard the two thieves on either side of the table as mortal enemies, and yet the meeting was being conducted with both respect and courtesy. He began to wonder if it had been Jewel who had sanctioned the murders, or even had performed the act herself; she seemed just the sort of woman who could cold-bloodily kill a child.

Throughout the meeting, Jewel only spoke once, while Magnus had been proposing an exchange of trades. The pickpockets in the Five Markets had been placed on the table, and they were considered a valuable operation;

while they generated comparatively little money, whoever held the children of the pick-pocketing teams would have a ready source of new blood for recruitment as thieves proper. Loredo was proving intractable over the Hands control over the Five Markets, and so Magnus raised the possibility of allowing the Guild to take the pickpockets, if in return the Hands could claim complete dominance over all assassinations in the city.

"No." Jewel only said the one word, and when she spoke it was as if ice had been dashed in the faces of the Council. Loredo, ignoring the effects of her input, went on to say that assassinations were a specialised field that had highly specialised agents. The idea of one guild holding them all was simply not feasible.

As hours four and five went by, it seemed as though a little progress was being made, but the guildmasters still proved relentless, neither wishing to show weakness by calling for a break in the meeting first.

Assassinations, it was decided, would be regarded as being outside of the discussion, with a view to perhaps creating a separate assassins' guild in the future. Magnus was able to retain control of the Five Markets, in part because he allowed the Guild free use of his smuggling routes.

An argument brewed between Caradoc and Loredo as the matter of compensation for the deaths of those who had been involved in the earlier 'skirmishes,' as they were euphemistically called, between the guilds. Loredo had demanded the princely sum of a thousand gold coin for the death of his Street of Dogs man, which would be an extortionate amount for a rich merchant's ransom. When the subject of the murdered children was raised by Caradoc, Loredo flatly denied any compensation, reminding him that the earning potential of one so young was negligible. Seeing his lieutenant clearly struggling with his temper, Magnus stepped in before voices were raised, announcing that he would not only relinquish any interest in compensation for pickpockets, but that he would agree to the thousand gold blood price for Loredo's man – but he also made sure the Street of Dogs came down firmly in the Hands' territory because of this.

Scams in the merchant quarter went to the Guild, while the Hands retained the docks. This was an arrangement that suited neither guildmaster well, but both realised something valuable would have to be sacrificed in the meeting. Lucius, for his part, was happy at this decision, for he had been planning his own operation in the docks, and was now favouring it over his plans for the raid on the church of the Final Faith; bothering religious fanatics could prove distinctly unhealthy, he had eventually decided, and he doubted the priests would go anywhere soon, whereas the ship he had been watching was scheduled to depart later in the week.

After seven hours, a weary Council stood as the guildmasters shook hands and toasted one another's success. An accord had been reached. There would be no war among the thieves.

The following days seemed almost like an anti-climax to Lucius, and he formed the impression that many others among the Hands felt the same. The common room was filled with complaints from those who'd had their franchises pulled, the operations now passing to the Guild of Coin and Enterprise, but there was an equal amount of relief, felt in the quiet conversations of others. Everyone had been expecting the worst, with strangled or stabbed bodies strewn throughout the alleyways of

Turnitia. Instead, there had been nothing. If anything, business was picking up.

Those who had been present at the meeting between guildmasters had been forbidden to speak of what they had seen and heard, for Magnus wanted the changes to the Hand's operations to come from him alone, speaking to each franchise holder in turn and informing them of whether they still had a regular source of income or not. It was not until two days later that Lucius had the chance to discuss the meeting, and that was with Magnus himself.

He had literally run into the guildmaster as he was leaving the training chamber, wiping the sweat from his face with a ragged cloth.

"Ah, Lucius, my boy," Magnus greeted him. Once he realised who was talking to him, Lucius threw the cloth back into the chamber and smiled hesitantly.

"Magnus," he acknowledged with a nod.

"Preparing for your first operation? You are going into action this week, are you not?"

"Tomorrow, all going well," Lucius said. "Still need to find a few more volunteers though."

"You'll get them. Many may not sign on until the last minute, but I think enough trust you now." He gestured up the corridor. "Come, walk with me for a moment."

The request caught Lucius off guard, and he had to stride quickly to catch up with Magnus.

"You opted for the docks in the end, then?" Magnus asked.

"Yes. I had a plan for the church of the Faith, but there were a few impracticalities."

"Indeed. The priesthood would have been straight on to the Vos guard, demanding the entire city be closed down and every thief hung from the cliffs. If you had not scrapped the mission yourself, the Council might have been forced to step in. You demonstrate both ambition and good judgement, two qualities that do not always go hand-in-hand among thieves."

Not knowing quite what to say, Lucius just nodded. He had walked with Magnus past the meeting room, and he glanced into the open door to see if any of the Council were present, but it was empty. Magnus began asking about his training, and Lucius did not realise where they were headed until the guildmaster halted outside a plain wooden door and produced a key. Behind the door was a small flight of stairs, spiralling upwards. With a wave of the hand, Lucius was ushered up, but he hesitated.

Though he had not been in this part of the guildhouse before, it was fairly common knowledge that Magnus kept his own set of chambers on the highest floor. Few were invited into his personal living space, and Lucius wondered why he was being accorded the honour.

"Come along, boy," Magnus prompted. "I have much to do – a guild does not just run itself!"

With Magnus close behind, Lucius ascended the stairs as they rose in a tight spiral.

They emerged into a small study, spartan in appearance with few nods to luxury. A desk lay below a single skylight, strewn with papers, maps and a single oil lantern. A leather bound chair sat behind it, while in front, three austere wooden seats, of the sort that might be expected in a commoner's kitchen. These were the only items of furniture in the study, and all rested on a tired-looking threadbare rug. Two doors faced one another to Lucius' left and right, and a quick glance told him they were both very thick, with intricate locks holding them fast.

Magnus manoeuvred himself behind the desk and nodded to Lucius to take a chair while he sat. Leaning back casually, Magnus released a sigh, as if happy to have come to the study, and he leaned back in his chair, legs straight out, hands steepled across his stomach.

"As you can see," Magnus said, indicating the piled papers on his desk with a wave, "the business of the Hands is never ending. There is always something!"

Not knowing why he was here or what he was expected to say, Lucius just smiled as if he understood just how much work Magnus was required to handle. In truth, he had little idea.

"It is the *Allantian Voyager* that you are planning to strike, isn't it?"

"Yes," Lucius said. "One of the dockmasters told Elaine that it was taking on silk from Pontaine. When she heard I was scouting out the docks, she suggested I run the operation."

"And her take?"

"Twenty per cent of the gross."

Magnus pursed his lips. "That could be a lot, considering she is taking none of the risks."

"It is my first job, so I thought it fair," Lucius shrugged. "And if I do well on this haul, she will be all the more ready to let me know when the next valuable cargo comes in. I have to pay my dues first, after all."

"You do," Magnus said, smiling. "You seem to be learning the franchise system well, though I would be concerned that there may not be much left for yourself, after you have shared out the profits among everyone you gather to help you – those silks will need a lot of manpower, and any fence is likely to charge a large commission on such a sizeable haul."

"I thought about that. If I am generous on the first job, recruitment for my second will not be so hard."

"But your next volunteers may become greedy."

"I'll always be up front about payment. Everyone will know where they stand."

"That is well. I think you are beginning to understand, Lucius, that when working alongside those who thieve and swindle for a living, the only guarantee one has is mutual self-interest."

Lucius became aware that Magnus was eyeing him closely, and he shifted under this gaze uncomfortably, becoming acutely aware that the hard wooden chair he had taken was beginning to numb his backside.

"I like you," Magnus said at last. "I have been taken in by nobles who promise the earth in the past, and the less said about my romantic attachments to women, the better. But I know thieves, Lucius. I have grown able to spot, very quickly, those who were born to the life, and those who merely pretend. And I see in you the makings of a great thief."

The praise was completely unexpected. "Well... thank you."

"No need for thanks, Lucius, you got here on your own strengths. All learned from your time in the Anclas Territories, were they?"

"Mostly," Lucius said, evasively, but Magnus seemed to either not notice or not care.

"Caradoc recognises your talent too, though he finds it shameful to admit you saved his life."

"Any one of us would have done the same."

"Maybe. You must remember that, despite us all belonging to the Night Hands, some here really are rogues of the highest order. But you will learn that truth soon enough," Magnus said, then suddenly changed the subject. "What did you make of Loredo and his woman during our summit?"

Lucius paused, marshalling his thoughts. "Very capable and very deadly. That woman, Jewel, in particular gave me the shivers."

"A natural killer. Of all the assassins in Turnitia, she probably commands the highest fees. She is very good at what she does."

"But I don't think they can be trusted."

Magnus raised an eyebrow. "You think, perhaps, I was wrong to call the summit and make the deal?"

"Hardly matters what I think, guildmaster," Lucius said, hoping his use of Magnus' title was respectful enough.

"Of course what you think matters. You are one of the Hands, you have a stake in what we do here, that decision affected you directly," Magnus said, then he gave Lucius a sly look. "Of course, your *opinion* may not always count for much, but I would still hear it."

"The summit was important, as it forced both sides to put their cards on the table. And, if nothing else, it has created at least a couple of days of peace."

"True," Magnus nodded. "Anything else?"

When Lucius frowned in thought, Magnus prompted him.

"Why, for example, would I risk inviting them here, into our own guildhouse?"

"A show of trust, as you said," Lucius began, then a flash of inspiration took him. "And to get both Loredo and his woman close – you wanted to watch them, see how they would take the proposals."

"Very good, Lucius," Magnus said. "Loredo I knew before, but the years can change a man. Jewel, I know only by reputation, and most of the tales told of her are likely exaggerated. Or maybe not. I like to know who I am dealing with. And you are right – they cannot be trusted."

"So, what have we gained?"

"Well, time, as you said. Even a moment of peace is infinitely preferable to the immediate onset of war. There are those, of course, who think a good, bloody war would straighten the city out and set things right, but we cannot guarantee we would be on the winning side, can we? At least, not yet."

Thinking Magnus' words over, Lucius looked up at the guildmaster.

"While I appreciate the trust, why are you telling me this?" he asked.

Magnus sat up straight, abandoning his leisurely posture to clasp his hands together as he leaned over the desk.

"Several reasons," he began. "I meant what I said about liking you. It's an instinct. You are going to do well for us here, Lucius, if you work hard and do not cheat us."

"I wouldn't –" Lucius began, but Magnus waved his objection away.

"It occurs to every thief at some time. A few coins here, a few valuables there, before anything reaches our fences. Just... just be warned that we have our own methods for discovering and tracking down those who embezzle from us. However, the one point of real contention between the Hands and the Guild are the docks and outlying merchant quarter. The Five Markets are what attract citizen and visitor both, but the money all flows from the ships and wagons of the merchants. Not having both the docks and the merchant quarter in the possession of either guild makes lasting peace between us impossible."

"You think they will try moving against us so soon," Lucius asked, thinking of his own operation about to go into action.

"Probably not," Magnus said. "It is probably just me worrying too much about every little thing the Hands get up to. But promise me this, Lucius. If you get the merest hint that the Guild are getting ready to hit us, the slightest suspicion that everything is not quite right when you make your raid, pull out. Don't risk the lives of the men who volunteer to go with you. They may escape only with their skins that evening rather than the goods they hoped for, but that is good enough if danger threatens. Do you understand?"

"Of course."

"I'm serious, Lucius. Whether it is this week, next month or next year, the Guild will be coming for us. I don't want any of us caught in the firing line when they do."

CHAPTER 10

Lucius cast a wry glance up at Kerberos as the blue-grey giant leered down upon the docks. He had heard the sphere called Thief's Friend, on account of the twilight it cast during the late hours, creating shadows throughout the city in which a rogue could readily hide. Only rarely did it dip completely below the horizon and so shroud the world in the pitch black of night. He ruefully thought he might have liked such a night, with darkness completely clothing both himself and his allies as they surrounded their target.

The *Allantian Voyager* was berthed just a few dozen yards ahead of him, its three masts rising into the faintly star-speckled sky. With its hull heavily reinforced to withstand the battering it would face on its travels across the churning sea, it was a squat and unlovely vessel, but one eminently suited to the journeys it would face. Typical of Allantian designs, the *Voyager* was the largest ship in the harbour, with others from Vosburg and the Sarcre Islands much smaller by comparison, designed to ride the huge waves they would face rather than plough a course through the maelstrom. Such ships would inevitably be smashed to splinters within a year or two, having encountered one natural disaster too many. It was said the best Allantian ships could last for more than a century of continuous travel.

A small flash of light made Lucius look upwards to the cliffs rising behind him. He nodded to himself, knowing the wagon party was now ready. Having commandeered a massive crane, they now awaited the haul of silk to be loaded onto its platform, which they would then raise and transfer onto the wagon they had acquired. From there, the silk would be taken to one of the Hands' affiliated fences to be sold; job done.

The light flashed again as one of the thieves high above lifted his cloak slightly to reveal the hooded lantern he held close to his body, then dropped it, his signal complete. The first part of their task was done. Now they had to wait for the other thieves to board the *Voyager* and make off with its goods before their turn in the heavy lifting began.

In all, Lucius had managed to raise a score of thieves to join him in his expedition, most signing on at the last minute. Quickly briefing them on the plan, and noticing some of the older thieves suppressing smiles as they watched him draw out positions on the many different maps he had prepared, Lucius had led them to the docks and delegated positions. He was, at least, gratified to see Ambrose with them, a familiar face on his first planned mission.

A few members of the party were simply serving as lookouts, though no serious trouble from the Vos guard was expected. The few men of the wagon party were now ready, but the bulk of his strength was in the harbour itself, stalking the *Voyager*, watching for overly curious crew, and getting ready to engage in the toil of heaving bundles of silk from ship to crane.

Crouched behind a large coil of rope, Lucius raised his hand, the signal that started the next part of the process; the approach to the *Voyager* itself.

As the sign was passed from thief to thief, each within eyesight of another in the gloom, Lucius saw dark shapes detach themselves from the shadows, keeping low and taking advantage of any available cover. A single sentry on the deck of the *Voyager* had already been sighted, and the role of silencing him passed to a veteran of such missions.

Lucius broke cover too, a slight manipulation of arcane energies allowing him to bring some of the darkness of his hiding place with him; just enough to give him a little extra protection from prying eyes, and not too much that would alert his fellow thieves to anything unusual.

The ship grew closer and, as he approached, Lucius only just began to realise just how large it really was. There were entire warehouses in Turnitia that were not as long or broad, and he wondered whether they would easily find the silk they were seeking to rob from its hold.

He saw some thieves gaining access to the ship's deck by the ropes that moored it tightly to the dock, clambering hand-over-hand as they swarmed up. Though they had plenty of skill in the use of ropes, he could see even the best of them were having some trouble, as the ship constantly lurched up and down, the ropes binding it creaking with the strain of holding it in place against the constant, surging waves that flooded past the barriers and into the harbour.

Joining a small group of thieves near the bottom of a ramp that led straight up onto the *Voyager's* deck, he crouched and waited with them, ready to charge forwards at the call of the next signal. He did not have to wait long as a low thump and groan issued from the deck, quickly followed by a quiet whistle; the ship's sentry had been dealt with.

Leading the rush, Lucius sprinted up the ramp, still keeping his body low as the thieves behind him followed suit. His first time on the deck of a ship, Lucius quickly looked around to get his bearings. Seeing the wheelhouse, three masts and prow allowed him to picture the deck plans of the ship in his mind, but the reality was entirely more confusing. It seemed as if nowhere was free of stores, debris and rope; lots and lots of rope. Only having the vaguest idea of why a ship needed so much rigging, or why it so often needed replacing, he trotted over to the space between the centre mast and the one ahead of it, knowing the hatch to the forward hold must lie there.

Several thieves, including Ambrose, were quicker and got there ahead of him, already lifting the massive double hatch to reveal a black maw that descended into the bowels of the ship.

"This is it," one whispered. "I'm going down, there'll be a second hatch down there. Someone look about, there'll be a winch round here somewhere."

Another thief was already rigging a winch and pulley to a metal pole jutting from the main mast, lashing it to a square platform, not unlike those used by the cranes on the cliff. Lucius could see each thief attending to his assigned role, and was pleased with how quickly and efficiently they worked together. He was less happy with the noise being generated, and though they had been near silent as they boarded the *Voyager*, the harder work of preparing to lift bales of silk out of the hold inevitably stole their stealth. Casting an anxious eye around the quieter areas of the deck towards the stern, Lucius could not help but think they were being watched.

Clapping Ambrose on the shoulder to let him know he should continue as planned, Lucius padded softly away as the other thieves started descending into the darkness below the deck. Drawing his sword from his back, he kept his body low and stayed to the shadows as he crept away.

Passing the thick masts, Lucius picked his way stealthily along the deck, nodding briefly to another thief who was coming from the opposite direction.

"All clear," the thief whispered, and Lucius gestured for him to proceed helping with the unloading of silk. With the haul the dockmaster had promised lay on board, they would need all the hands they could muster to make their theft before any of the remaining crew on board were wise to their presence. However, Lucius could not shake the ominous feeling he had and, cursing Magnus for putting doubts into his head in the first place, he approached the poop deck.

Raised above the level of the deck, the poop was accessible by two ladders, one on either side of the ship, and flanking a simple wooden door that Lucius knew gave access to the lower decks and the captain's own quarters. Mounting the first two rungs of a ladder, he poked his head over the lip of the poop, and scanned the area.

The wheel lay before him, lashed tightly as part of the precautions to keep the *Voyager* steady while berthed in the dangerous harbour. Two large siege crossbows were mounted to either side behind large purpose-built shields, perhaps intended to keep the ship safe from the pirates and corsairs Lucius had heard roamed the straits between the peninsula and the Sarcre Islands. He could also just make out a slumped form behind one of the crossbows, the bound and gagged sentry, now oblivious to the presence of the intruders.

Seeing nothing out of the ordinary, Lucius hopped back down to the main deck and crept to the door. He had not wanted to risk exploring the rest of the ship but, while his men were busy with their haul, he reasoned that it was better to be safe than very, very sorry. He tried the handle, resolving himself to simply blocking the exit with a barrel or something similar if it were locked, in order to stop any attempt by the crew to storm the main deck, and was faintly surprised to find the door swung easily open. The interior was pitch black and he cast a quick look over his shoulder, suddenly apprehensive. He could see the shadowy shapes of thieves at work at the far end of the ship in the half-light of Kerberos and, seeing nothing more amiss, steeled himself to take a look inside.

Stretching a hand outwards, Lucius summoned a small flame, its purple light flickering crazily. Inside, a small corridor extended ahead. At its end was a stout door lined with metal bands – leading to the captain's quarters, Lucius presumed. To his left was another closed door and to his right, a small set of stairs descended into darkness.

Creeping forward as quietly as he could, Lucius ducked his head down the stairs briefly. He had no desire to pace his way through sleeping crew. Just wanting to ensure no one was awake, he peered into the gloom and was greeted with a rank smell that made him retch until he buried his face into his cloak. He had never smelled anything like it; the stench of a body left in the sun too long, mixed with the pungent aroma of salt and dead fish. It was not pleasant like the scent of a fresh catch being unloaded dockside from a fisherman's boat, but something altogether more sickening. Shaking his head at the hygiene of Allantian sailors, Lucius turned away to approach the door to the captain's quarters.

There was no sound of movement behind the door and for that, he was grateful. Not quite knowing what to do, Lucius eventually settled on snuffing out his flame to call upon a reflection of the same thread of power. Reaching towards the lock, he felt a chill sweep through him as the magic surged in his body. His hand becoming the focus, he concentrated until a stream of cold air blasted forward to envelope the lock's mechanism, softly whistling as ice began to form.

Hoping that would be sufficient to at least delay the captain should he awake to the noise of the thieves working at the far end of the ship, Lucius started to retrace his steps.

He froze as he heard a strangled cry ahead. Though the door to the deck was open before him, he could not see any of the other thieves, and he at first thought they were either hidden by the masts or else working in the hold. That did not make any sense though, for the unloading of silk should have begun by now. A heavy thump seemed to resonate through the ship, as if something very large had been dropped, and this was followed by a shout of warning.

Startled now, and worried by what might have stirred the thieves into breaking their silence, Lucius started to run to the main deck, but was halted by the sound of movement from the stairs leading to the lower deck. The crew of the ship would have been awoken by the thieves on board, and Lucius crouched, sword drawn, ready to skewer whoever came up the stairs first.

Seeing a shadow move, the stench he had smelled before suddenly strengthened and he realised someone was approaching. He felt the comfort of the threads of magic spin in his mind's eye, ready to be unleashed if his sword alone proved insufficient. Stepping forward, blade ready, Lucius prepared to thrust his weapon into the chest of whoever emerged and then sprint out to see what danger the rest of his team faced.

A loud cry of fear and alarm rang out, resounding in the confined space. Dimly, Lucius realised it was he that had screamed. The figure before him climbed up the stairs inexorably, but he was rooted to the spot, unable to move as he watched the horror approach.

Two shiny, black eyes – each the size of his fist – looked back at him unblinking. They were mounted in a bulbous, scaly head, its wide maw filled with rows of razor-sharp teeth. It was naked, but its skin was completely cloaked in the same foul green scales that covered its head. Spines rose from the top of its skull and continued down its back, and they flattened menacingly as it spoke a language he did not recognise, a base slurping and lapping sound that no human could imitate.

Slime covered its hideous body but it was not until it raised a hand, its nails stretching out into wicked inch-long webbed claws, that Lucius was finally galvanised into action, his instinct for survival overriding his conscious mind.

Screaming again, he flailed out with his sword, but it was swatted away with a metallic chink by one of the claws. Reeling backwards from the blow, he knew the creature was immensely strong, and that he was about to die, torn apart by those talons, and then savaged and consumed by those fangs.

Reaching a hand up in defence, his fear and anger mingled, and he was distantly aware of two threads of power smashing together to form one continuous bolt of energy that whipped through his body violently. Crying out in pain now, Lucius sought to unleash the magic building up inside before it burned him to a cinder and he focussed it forward, straight into the creature.

Lightning erupted from his hand and struck the creature in the centre of its chest with a massive impact, sending it flying back down the stairs with an inhuman wail. Standing, Lucius continued to direct the flow of magic, sending bolts of white hot light down into the lower deck where they smashed into the corpse of the creature, incinerating it, before blasting through the floor into the darkest regions of the ship. The flickering light illuminated the lower deck, and he saw more of the creatures caught in the explosion, shielding their large dark eyes from the glare as they pulled themselves in through open portholes in the ship's hull.

Shouting out obscenities, Lucius directed the pulsing magical energy to wherever he saw movement, striking down one monster after another, their scales sizzling in the blinding heat. Without warning, the magic waned and he felt the two threads separate. The lightning stopped and he staggered back, suddenly weary, before collapsing to the floor.

Breathing heavily from the exertion, Lucius clumsily raised his sword to ward off a sudden rush of the creatures up the stairs, but none came. He had either destroyed them all or at least scared them off, and he sobbed for a moment, overcome by the horror of what he had faced and the sheer exhaustion of focussing so much magic at once.

More cries from the main deck cleared his fogged mind, and he clambered back on his feet. He rushed to the door shakily, and braced himself on its frame as he looked out.

The creatures covered the deck, loping along with a strange gait that seemed unsuited for dry land. Clambering over the sides of the ship, their claws digging into the wood to give purchase, dozens more were rushing away from him – and towards the thieves.

He saw men battling them, but they were completely overwhelmed by the strength and numbers of the horrors. One thief, armed with two knives, circled one of the creatures to find an opening, but – with frightening speed – it whirled round and he screamed as its claws raked his face and tore out his eyes. The creature's mouth closed upon his skull, and Lucius heard the wet crack as his head was torn apart.

Elsewhere arms were torn from sockets and bodies were hurled in great arcs through the twilight air into the sea, where their desperate cries were quickly silenced. One thief had tried to escape the carnage by climbing the mainmast, but he was quickly overtaken by two of the creatures who, using their claws, were able to scramble up the smooth wood with ease. He was cast back down to the deck, his stomach torn open with one vicious swipe.

Panicked, Lucius stalled for a moment, realising the creatures were unaware of his presence as they rejoiced in the slaughter. He saw Ambrose bravely face one creature that had its claws deep in the chest of a younger thief, and was spurred into action.

Trying to summon a wave of fire that would sweep the deck clear of those creatures closest to him, Lucius was alarmed to find the magic stutter and disappear, his concentration too muddied with fear to manipulate the threads. Desperate now, Lucius ran down the length of the ship, closing in on the nearest creature. It was alerted to his presence an instant before he struck, and began to turn just as he thrust his sword forward. The movement was sufficient to turn the blade, its edge skidding across the scales on its back. Keeping his momentum going, Lucius crashed bodily into the creature, knocking it off its feet.

Well aware of the teeth and claws that were eagerly reaching for his flesh, Lucius rolled off the beast then brought the point of his sword down into its chest. Throwing his full weight onto the weapon, he was amazed at the resistance the creature's scales gave before the blade pierced them and slid into its body.

Wailing, the creature slobbered as it died, but as Lucius stared into its large black eyes, he saw no change, no glazing of its stare as its body stopped twitching. Its eyes remained as fixed in death as they had in life.

Jumping back to his feet, he saw his attack had not gone unnoticed. Some embattled thieves cried out for help, while three of the creatures turned to avenge their fallen comrade.

"Lucius, there are too many of them!" It was Ambrose's voice that reached him, from somewhere near the prow.

He knew he could not save them all. Wherever these things had come from, they were strong, fast and deadly, and thieves were no match for them.

"Run!" he shouted. "Save yourselves!"

He saw Ambrose rally a few thieves and they began

fighting as a unit, attempting to cut their way to the ramp; after having seen the fate of some of their friends, no man wanted to risk jumping into the sea.

Lucius was closer to the ramp, but his way was blocked by three of the creatures and as they loped towards him he was forced to back away. A bright burst of light illuminated the deck for a brief second, and the nearest creatures to the blast wailed as they turned away from the glare, shaking their heads in pain. Someone had used flash powder, and Lucius cursed for not taking some himself from the armoury. The distraction was enough to give the thieves room to manoeuvre, but the creatures were quick to return to the fight, dragging down the thief that had thrown the powder, as well as the man who rushed into the melee in an attempt to save him. Their strangled death cries made Lucius shudder as he reached down to draw a dagger from his boot.

Taking quick aim as the creatures approached, he threw the dagger at the leftmost of the three, and grinned as the blade sank deep into its eye, the size of the black orb making it an east target. It wailed, its inhuman voice cutting into the nerves of every man on board as it dropped to the deck and thrashed in pain, trying to remove the blade.

Seeing the opening, Lucius rushed the two remaining creatures, and they opened their arms wide, claws ready to tear him apart. He feinted to the right, and the creatures followed his movement, crouching as they prepared to leap and drag him down, but as they began to move, he quickly jinked left and leapt onto the railings lining the side of the ship.

He saw more shapes on the dockside moving in the characteristic gait of the creatures, and he inwardly groaned as he realised they would have to fight their way clear of the entire harbour, not just the ship. The railings were smooth but not wet, and Lucius hopped past the creatures on the balls of his feet before lightly dropping down behind them. He raised his sword high above his head before bringing it down on the skull of the nearest creature with all his strength. It staggered under the blow and a deep gash streamed dark blood as it sank to the deck.

The remaining creature hissed and burbled something in its mongrel language as it spun round, a claw whipping through the air. Lucius was forced to take a step back and he felt the creature's talon cut through his tunic as it sliced across his mail beneath. The links in his armour buckled under the attack, but held.

Dropping low Lucius threw out a booted foot, which crashed into its knee. This caused the creature to spit something unintelligible at him, the sound of a jellyfish being thrown against a rock, and he fancied it was a curse of some kind. However, whereas his boot would have shattered the knee of a man, it merely seemed to slow the creature down slightly. Seeing it recover, Lucius jumped to his feet and ran.

Men lay strewn across the deck, a few moaning in pain as they died from hideous wounds, but most were still in death. Ambrose and his cohorts had managed to fight their way clear to the ramp and were starting to run down it at full speed, though they were leaving many of their original number behind.

Lucius ran to join them, the creature behind in hot pursuit, but another reared up before him, just yards away from the ramp. The last thief of Ambrose's group turned as he jumped on to the ramp, and threw something at the creature's feet. Knowing what was coming next, Lucius closed his eyes as he ran and heard the muffled crump of flash powder igniting. Opening his eyes again, he saw the creature clasping its claws over its face, writhing in pain.

The thief grinned at Lucius and held out a hand for him. Lucius smiled back before gasping in horror as another creature sailed through the air, the result of a huge leap. He watched, feeling the creature was moving with agonising slowness, yet he could do nothing to alter its course. It ploughed into the back of the grinning thief, knocking him off the ramp and carrying him down to the hard stone of the dock where they landed heavily.

Lucius screamed in protest and rushed down the ramp, all too aware of the creatures swarming behind him. Something whipped through the air past his head as he ran and he glanced quickly over his shoulder to see an arrow jutting out the chest of the beast nearest him. It had stopped running, and seemed to be looking curiously at the shaft which jutted from its body.

Lucius leapt from the ramp, planting both feet on the back of the skull of one of the monsters, before they both sprawled onto the dock. As he stood, he saw that the creature was groggy from the attack, stumbling on all fours as it tried to pick itself up. Lucius sank his blade into its neck. The creature shuddered for a moment and was still.

Another shout arrested his attention and Lucius saw Ambrose waving to him. Sprinting away from the ship, he saw that the *Voyager* was swarming with the monsters. Others on the docks were closing in on either side, pursuing Ambrose and his remaining men. They caught one, and the man was dragged down, screaming as he thrashed about with his club. The weapon just bounced off the scales of the creature, and his cries turned to a burbled moan as it tore his throat out.

Running, Lucius passed the creatures as they began to feast on the man's body. He launched a kick at one, sending it sprawling, but carried on sprinting, knowing he could do no more for the comrade.

"To the crane!" Lucius shouted to Ambrose and the thieves ahead, and they turned as one, glad to have an order to follow, a direction to head in amongst all the chaos. Lucius looked behind once more and saw that, while the creatures were still following, they seemed to be moving slower than they had earlier. Thanking God for small mercies, he began to hope that the nightmare would soon be over.

As Lucius raced along the docks to the cliff face, he spied the waiting platform. Ambrose waved him over, and he increased his speed, ignoring his complaining muscles. A hand clapped him on the shoulder as he reached the group.

"You made it!" someone said.

Lucius looked around and saw only two other men stood with Ambrose, who was now frantically pulling on the ropes, the signal to tell the thieves working the crane to start raising the platform.

"This is all?" Lucius asked, and was answered only by mute nods.

"Look!" cried one of the thieves, pointing out into the darkness of the docks.

The creatures had massed, and were approaching the platform, fanning out to surround the thieves.

"In the name of all that's Holy, come on!" Ambrose screamed, lifting himself off his feet in the effort of jerking the rope, desperately hoping to get the attention of the wagon team above.

The creatures started to move closer, the ring drawing tighter around the men. One of the thieves unlimbered a bow and sent an arrow into the mass, but aside from drawing a hiss out of the creature it struck, it had little effect. He notched another arrow and sent it flying.

"Have they got to the men on top of the cliff too?" someone asked.

Lucius didn't see how but, seeing no movement from the crane, he jumped off the platform, sword drawn. He did not know what he was going to do, only that he hoped he could buy enough time for them to start the ascent.

One creature broke from the pack and swiped at Lucius with its claws. He parried the blow, and took a step back to avoid a second. He heard movement behind him and another creature slobbered at his back. A low whistle punctuated the air and he heard a dull thud as an arrow hit home.

Hearing an angry wail and hoping the creature behind had been taken out of the fight, Lucius stepped to one side, looking to create an opening. The creature in front followed his movements and, as it raised a claw to strike at him again, Lucius swung his sword in a wide arc, catching the creature's arm.

He felt the sword bite deep, and wondered if the creature's scales were not as thick on some parts of its body as others. It shrieked in pain, and scrambled backwards, cradling its injured arm which was hanging at an odd angle, bone sheared by the impact of Lucius' sword.

Apparently not liking the way the combat was going, the massed creatures hissed, the sound undulating eerily, sending a shiver down Lucius' back. He held his sword out in front of him as they began to advance, their movements a little halted and slow. He made a couple of feints towards the closest creatures, hoping to force them to draw back, wishing he could scare them into at least re-considering their actions. They were relentless, however, and ignored the flashes of his sword. It was not as if he were able to stop them all.

He heard a creaking behind him, and knew the strain had been taken on the ropes of the platform.

"Lucius, come on!" Ambrose cried, but he needed no prompting.

The platform was beginning to rise with agonising slowness and Lucius hurled himself up onto its wooden surface. Hands steadied him as he turned round to look down at the creatures.

Seeing their quarry beginning to escape, they hissed in frustration and some shambled forward. Lucius saw their movements were becoming more exaggerated, slow and awkward. Even so, they did not have much ground to cover and they crashed into the platform, causing it to swing alarmingly. Ambrose was thrown to one side and he clutched wildly at the rope to stop himself from toppling into the snarling mass below. Claws whipped over the edges of the platform as it continued to rise above their heads. Lucius carefully grabbed a rope to steady himself before moving to the edge and stamping down hard into a scaly face.

The scrabbling sound of claws gouging chunks from the underside of the platform caused one thief to moan in terror. He screamed as one of the creatures launched itself from below to grab onto the side of the platform, beginning to pull itself on board. Its claws dug deep into the wood, giving it all the leverage it needed. Lucius kicked out again as they all lurched crazily, but the creature ignored the blow, intent on its prey.

It reached out and dug a claw into the boot of one of the thieves. The man cried out in pain as the claw drove through leather and bone, pinning him to the wood. Another thief tried to help him but lost his grip on the rope and fell into the dark, ferocious mass now twenty yards below, the sounds of flesh being ripped apart soon cutting off his cries.

Curling an arm around the rope as he tried to gain his footing on the tilting platform, Lucius hacked down with his sword at the arm of the monster, trying to sever its hand to free the thief, but he could not gain enough purchase to put any real strength into the blow. Blood seeped from the wounds he had caused, but the creature just hissed malevolently.

"Hold on!" Lucius shouted, and the thieves gripped the ropes they were holding more firmly when they saw what he intended to do.

Strapping his sword to his back, he reached into a boot to draw his last dagger. Frantically sawing at the rope he was holding, Lucius steeled himself, closing his other hand around it in a death grip. He knew that if he were to let go, he would fall into the claws and fangs of the creatures below. The threads of the rope sprang open, one by one, until with a final lurch it broke.

Men screamed as one side of the platform gave way completely, leaving them dangling in the air by the ropes they clung to. The creature's grasp was wrenched away by the sudden movement, and the man it had pinned shrieked as the claw was ripped out with brutal force.

Lucius caught a glimpse of the creature as it fell, its shining black eyes reflecting what little light there was, before they disappeared into the churning swarm of the horde below. The crane continued to raise the tattered remains of the platform, leaving the three remaining men to look at one another with the wild eyes of those who have confronted their worst demons.

"What were those things?" Ambrose asked.

No one had an answer for him.

CHAPTER 11

Hunched over the long table in the council chamber, Lucius flicked his gaze over to Ambrose, who sat straight, arms wrapped around himself as he shuddered. The veteran thief looked shaken to his core, and Lucius could not blame him, for the events of the evening weighed heavily on his mind.

It had been his operation, *his* plan. The thieves who had volunteered knew there were risks involved but that did not excuse what had happened. His big ideas had cost thirteen men their lives, unless by some miracle, a few had managed to evade those hideous creatures and were, even now, making their way back to the guildhouse. Lucius now had to explain himself to Magnus and tell him exactly why his operation had gone so tragically wrong. In part, he resented the deaths. Up to now, Lucius had never been responsible for anyone, and this was an excellent illustration as to why he had avoided it so long.

He wondered how the Hands had managed to sucker him in, made him feel part of their guild and accept the accountability he now faced. At the same time, he knew it was a childish regret, that the lives of good men — thieves though they may be — was an order of magnitude above his own petty concerns. He had no idea what he would say to Magnus. He still did not understand what had happened.

Of the three who had survived boarding the ship, Lucius was to answer for the tragedy, as would Ambrose, being the only senior thief to emerge unscathed from the *Voyager*. The only other thief to make it out alive, Sandtrist, had been excused on account of his injuries; Lucius had already heard that he was likely to lose his foot, and what use would the Hands have for a one-footed thief? In his own way, Sandtrist had been lost that evening as well.

Footsteps sounded from outside the room, and Lucius braced himself for the confrontation, though he still had little idea of what he would say. Ambrose seemed not to have noticed the sound, and he did not look up when Magnus entered and stood, watching the two thieves.

Since he had known the guildmaster, Lucius had thought him wise, extremely competent and utterly benevolent to those in his charge. But as he looked at the man's face, he could see a terrible hardness in his eyes, an iron will he had always suspected must lie within Magnus, but had never seen. The guildmaster smouldered with barely contained rage, and Lucius swallowed, awaiting the onslaught.

"Would you like to tell me," Magnus said, starting quietly but gradually allowing his anger to take control until he shouted the last words: "Just why thirteen of my thieves are *dead*?"

"Ambush –" Lucius began, but his voice was too quiet.

Striding over to the table, Magnus hammered a fist down, the sudden violent sound jerking Lucius back. It even seemed to rouse Ambrose.

"What?" Magnus said in a deafening tone that promised quick punishment to anyone who would chance a wrong answer.

Lucius cleared his throat and started again. "We were ambushed, Magnus, there was no warning, I –"

Magnus' fist crashed down on the table again. "What happened to your plans? Where were the sentries? Why did no one see them approach? Why are my men dead, Lucius?"

"They weren't human, Magnus."

"Who weren't? What are you talking about?"

"They just swarmed all over the ship while we were unloading. I swear to you, we scouted the area, silenced the sentry, and only then started the haul. But they were on us in seconds, too many of them. They started killing..." Lucius broke off at that, seeing again in his mind's eye the terrible carnage on the deck of the ship.

"So who was it?" Magnus demanded.

"I... I think they came from the sea."

Magnus looked utterly confused. "As an excuse, this is a poor one, Lucius," he said dangerously.

"He's telling the truth," Ambrose said, and they both looked at him in surprise. "On my mother's grave, Magnus, he's telling the truth."

Magnus sighed and, drawing out a seat, sat down with them.

"You better tell me what happened, from start to finish. Leave nothing out," he said.

So Lucius explained, with Ambrose adding comments where he could. He told Magnus how he had begun preparations for the operation, using the Hand's resources to learn about the ship and its cargo. He outlined the different teams involved, who was part of each, and what their expected roles were. He told how they had boarded the ship, located the silk, and then started offloading it.

Then he began telling Magnus of the appearance of the first creature, describing how it looked, its strength and deadly, murderous intent. Intentionally leaving out the use of his magical talents, he went on to tell of the slaughter that had followed, of the sheer number of the creatures that had boarded the ship after them, and how men had died. Their desperate escape from the *Voyager* followed, along with the pursuit across the docks and the final, terrifying assault on the platform as they fled the scene. When he finished, Lucius was shaking, the retelling of the events forcing him to relive them once more.

Magnus' anger had subsided, but he shook his head in disbelief.

"I have never heard of such things," he said simply.

"On my *mother's* grave, Magnus," Ambrose said again, and the seriousness of his expression seemed to give Magnus pause.

"You think they came from the sea?" he asked.

Lucius shrugged helplessly. "They seemed... adapted to it," he said, remembering the foul sea stench, the webbed claws and scaled skin. "And they moved slower once they had been out of the water for a few minutes."

"I noticed that," Ambrose said.

"Well do you have any idea why they were there?" Magnus asked. "Who sent them?"

They both shook their heads.

"I would dearly like to blame the Guild for this," Lucius said. "But I saw nothing to suggest their involvement."

"Then there are three possibilities that come to mind," Magnus said. "First, the Guild has new allies. Second, we have inadvertently wandered into some dispute between the Allantians and these... sea demons."

"And third?" Lucius prompted.

"Third, there is a new power in the city." He raised a hand in a helpless gesture. "But none of those seem very likely to me. What would sea demons want with a city on land? Why have we heard nothing about them before? None of this makes sense."

He prompted Lucius to retell the story again, searching for any information that had been missed the first time, anything that could give him a clue as to what his thieves had faced that night. No matter how many times he quizzed Lucius over particular points, however, they seemed no closer to the truth. Magnus was about to ask Lucius to describe the attack on the *Voyager* again, when shouts and excited cries reached them from the open door. When someone shouted for the guildmaster, panic evident in his voice, they all started.

Leading the way, Magnus rushed from the meeting room and vaulted down the stairs, Lucius and Ambrose in tow, where another thief directed him to one of the rooms used as sleeping quarters. Trotting behind Magnus, Lucius entered the room and gasped.

Tiny though the room was a dozen thieves were gathered in a tightly packed mass that they had to push their way through, some only relinquishing their place when they saw it was Magnus who had entered. Lying on the bed, its sheets already soaked through with his blood, was Caradoc. Helmut, a thief from Vosburg who was versed in some of the arts of healing, was tending to him, fussing over a crossbow bolt that jutted from the lieutenant's shoulder. Writhing in pain, Caradoc looked up at Magnus as he entered.

"Caught me on Ring Street," he gasped. "Tried to kill me."

"Would have done too, but for another three inches to the left," Helmut muttered to no one in particular.

"Who?" Magnus said, leaning over the bed to catch Caradoc's words.

"Didn't see," he said. "Too dark. But... Guild. Has to be... the Guild. They've broken the truce."

Magnus frowned at that, then laid a hand on Helmut's shoulder. "Can you help him?"

The Vos man looked at his patient as he thought. "We need to remove that bolt, and that won't be pleasant. But if he makes it through this evening, I think he will be just fine. So long as no poison was used, of course."

"We'll take care of it," Magnus said quietly to Caradoc. "We'll find who did this."

"Guild..." Caradoc started to say again, but Magnus hushed him.

"We'll find them," he promised again.

As Magnus left the small, overcrowded room, he pulled Lucius to one side.

"You think it was the Guild?" Lucius asked when they were out of earshot of the others.

"What I am thinking is whether there is a connection between the attack on Caradoc and what happened with you down at the docks." Magnus said, rubbing his chin in thought. "The timing is... too much of a coincidence."

"But if we assume that, then we have to also assume the Guild have new allies in these creatures."

"And that, Lucius, is what really worries me. It is just too incredible to believe. Damn it! We need answers, we cannot carry on operating blind like this. We need to reach out to our contacts outside of the Hands. I have a few ideas on who we can talk to, but it will take time to set things up. You are Turnitia born and bred – do you have anyone on the outside who can help us?"

The image of Adrianna and Forbeck flashed through his mind.

"There may be someone," Lucius said. "I'll see what I can find out."

Standing in the centre of the warehouse that had been used for his training, Lucius eyed the scorch marks on the floor ruefully, the evidence of another session that had ended in failure. He had not been able to practice the steering of the flame globes as much as Forbeck had wished for, and he had been chided for it. The Master of Shadows had insisted he try the exercise himself in his own time, but with the events within the Hands of late, that had not been possible.

A tickling at the back of his mind signalled a presence behind him and he whirled round to see Adrianna stalking out of the shadows, her pace measured and confident.

"Well, your training is having at least some effect I see," she said. "You can now sense the presence of another Shadowmage within, oh, at least twenty yards."

"At least you came."

"It is not often I receive a summons, least of all from you. I was mildly curious."

"I'm glad to see it worked," he said. Lucius had been curious as to Forbeck's ability to sound an alarm in his mind from half way across the city, and had tried to do the same for Adrianna, concentrating on her disdainful face and willing her to him through the threads of power.

"It was faint, but I sensed it. You need improvement."

Her remark was no surprise to Lucius, for he never expected an easy compliment from her.

"As it happens, I wanted to see you as well," she continued.

"Oh?"

"I have a contract, one that may bring us into conflict. By the terms of the Shadowmage charter, I must inform you of this and find a resolution between us."

He rolled his eyes. "Which, I presume, is Shadowmage language for 'stay out of my way'?"

"As you say," she shrugged.

Sighing, Lucius shook his head, then a thought struck him.

"You've been contracted by the Guild of Coin and Enterprise, haven't you?"

"My employers are making some aggressive moves in the city, and you are within their chief target. I recommend you leave the Night Hands and find a more stable contract. Forbeck can help you out there. I might be able to put a word in with my current employers too, if necessary."

"It's not going to be that easy, Aidy," Lucius said, a smile beginning to flicker on his lips. "Your current employers are scum, and I will do everything I can to bring them down."

"I cannot force you to do one thing or another," Adrianna said. "But I would advise you to remember the oath you took."

"I'm not going to attack you, Aidy."

"It is likely that our current employers will force the issue, one way or another."

Adrianna's inhuman attitude was beginning to grate on his nerves once again, and he marvelled at how little time was needed in her presence before anger flared. He briefly wondered whether he was alone in his constant head-butting with her, or if it was common in everyone she met.

"It was the Guild who drew first blood, Aidy," he said, letting himself ride the wave of anger she had sparked. "There was a truce between us, the city had been carved up – there was an agreement."

She shook her head carelessly. "That is not my concern. The accord has been broken, and my specific role is to ensure my employer is victorious in the struggle ahead."

"And your contract is all you care about? There are good men within the Hands, Aidy, they don't deserve this. The Guild is full of cold-blooded killers."

"While the thieves of the Hands are entirely honourable? Don't kid yourself."

"The Hands are not the ones allying themselves to devils from the sea."

That checked her, Lucius saw, and her scorn was replaced by a puzzled expression.

"What do you mean?"

"You're telling me you weren't there at the docks? Yesterday evening?"

Adrianna frowned, and Lucius was at least gratified to see her stumble when someone was accusing her for a change.

"Lucius, I swear to you, I have not been directly involved in any of the Guild's operations around the docks. I know they want to take that territory away from the Hands, and I know they planned an ambush there last night, but I had nothing to do with it. I am contracted for specific... duties, no more."

"It was my operation they ambushed."

She looked him up and down briefly. "You seem to have survived."

"Oh, I did, but many of the men I took with me didn't. Do you have any idea who the Guild is dealing with these days? I'm telling you, they have an alliance with something truly evil."

"I'm sure you are exaggerating."

"Really?" he said, moving onto the attack. "Scales, bulging eyes, webbed claws. Hordes of them, Aidy, coming from the sea to tear us apart – and I mean, *tear* us apart. They killed most of us within minutes, and damn well nearly got me."

Her next words were slow in coming, as she chose them carefully. "Assuming you are not making this up, I have no idea what you are talking about – truly. That the Guild was planning to disrupt the operations of the Hands on the docks as a prelude to taking them over is all I am aware of. I... I can talk to Master Forbeck, perhaps he knows what you are speaking of."

"Well, that's something," Lucius muttered.

"But if you are right, Lucius, you need to be careful. The Guild is not messing around this time, they want the Hands gone. Smashed, broken, the members either dead, fleeing from the city, or on their side. And they can do it. They have the power and the determination. That is not something you want to be caught in the middle of."

He suppressed a smile. "Well, at least you can spare a thought for me."

Adrianna closed the distance between them in a single long stride and jabbed a finger, painfully, into his chest.

"What I want, Lucius, is for you to go," she said adamantly. "To leave this city, to disappear. What I want to avoid is breaking my oath to the Shadowmages. I will be on the frontline in this fight, and woe betide anyone who stands between me and the completion of the contract."

Spinning on a heel, she stalked away, their meeting clearly at an end.

"Well, just ask yourself this, Aidy," Lucius shouted at her retreating back. "If the Guild are capable enough to hire a Shadowmage when most people haven't even heard of us, who or what else have they employed, eh? Do you even know what you are fighting for? Just which one of us is the mercenary here?"

His voice still echoing through the empty warehouse, Lucius cursed the shadows into which Adrianna had disappeared. He had known he would not find a friend in her stern glare, but had hoped to discover at least an ally.

CHAPTER 12

There were no smiles among the Council or the senior thieves surrounding the table in the meeting room. Too many deaths had taken place within the Night Hands, and more than a few were thinking about Caradoc. After all, if someone could strike at the lieutenant of the Hands, how safe were the rest of them when they left the guildhouse?

Various theories had been put forward by Council members as to what was happening and who was responsible, but while few doubted the Guild's involvement, Magnus kept demanding proof. With none of the Council able to provide anything more than rumour, he turned to Lucius.

Lucius was acutely aware that all eyes in the room were now focussed on him, and that not all were waiting for his explanation. He was still, officially, a low-ranking thief within the Hands, and though he had not yet been made a senior, many had taken note of Magnus' obvious favouritism toward him. It was breeding jealousy, he knew, and Lucius was distinctly conscious of being part of an organisation whose members, while overtly supporting one another, were just as likely to settle a difference or imagined slight with a knife in the back.

He cleared his throat as he marshalled his thoughts.

"The Council is correct – the truce has been broken," Lucius said to them all. He hoped that by affirming the Council's thoughts, he might find a friend amongst them or, at least, make it look as though he were paying his proper respects and not trying to subvert anyone's position. It was a small gesture, but he knew that when the danger to the Hands was over, differences would be settled one way or another.

"Our operation on the docks was disrupted at the Guild's instigation," he continued. "And they orchestrated the attack on Caradoc, though I have no information on who exactly was responsible."

"So it could just be a few troublemakers in the Guild?" asked Nate.

"It hardly matters," said Elaine, a tall middle-aged woman who controlled the Hand's concerns around the docks. It had been she who had provided Lucius with information on the *Allantian Voyager* from her paid contacts among the dockmasters. "Whether it is just a few or the whole Guild, we are still under attack and we must defend ourselves."

This raised some murmurs of assent from the table.

"Where did you get this information, Lucius?" asked Nate.

Lucius hesitated. "I cannot say," and inwardly winced as a collective look of contempt swept the table, but it was halted by Magnus' raised hand.

"He does not need to say. Lucius, for now, has my trust," he said. *That* would create a few enemies, Lucius thought.

"Could he be mistaken?" Elaine asked. "There is always the possibility of another player coming into the city, and starting a war between the existing powers is a good way of getting a foothold. Divide and conquer."

"We use the information we have," Magnus said. "I won't have us jumping at shadows."

"Could it be the work of an insider?" asked a tanned man whose face looked more like that of a weather-beaten sailor than a thief. "After all, it was you, Elaine, who provided the lead for Lucius' disastrous operation at the docks."

"You dare accuse me!" Elaine spat.

A hand slapped the table, bringing all attention to Magnus. "I will not have us fighting each other!" he said, eyes flashing dangerously, challenging anyone to make another charge of treason. For a few seconds, the Council was quiet.

"Then we must hit back," Nate said. "And hit back hard. We cannot just roll over and let them take our operations from us. If they tried to take out Caradoc, Magnus, they are deadly serious. Striking at a lieutenant is unheard of! Who will be next? One of us? You?"

"There will be blood in the streets," someone muttered.

The Council broke down into bickering parties, some wanting to wipe out the Guild in a single night of violence, others supporting the idea of another parley in an attempt to discern the Guild's true intentions.

Clearing his throat, Magnus brought the arguments to a halt. "Reluctant as I am to admit it, Nate has the truth of it. Right now, we are just waiting for another arrow from the dark to strike one of us down, and who knows what our foot soldiers will face on the streets as they go about their work. We *do* need to demonstrate that we will not roll over. More than that, we must show the Guild that we can strike them where it hurts the most."

"We go for Jewel?" Nate asked, a little doubtfully, and Lucius understood his hesitation. He was not sure which of the Hands would be capable of accomplishing that goal.

"We go for the merchant's quarter," Elaine said flatly. "Disrupt their protection rackets, squeeze their main source of revenue. Starve them of gold."

Magnus nodded in appreciation. "Your strategy does you credit, Elaine," he said. "That is how we start. If they are trying to take the docks from us, we will flood the merchant's quarter with our own men, making it impossible for them to operate."

"If I may?" Lucius asked. Feeling a little foolish, he ploughed on. "If we go in mob-handed, someone, perhaps a great many, will die. It will be the start of an all out war."

"Well, that is what we are discussing here," Nate said, a little contemptuous.

"Let him speak," Magnus said, raising a hand.

"We can be smarter than that," Lucius said. "We rough up their collectors – giving our men strict instructions to spill no blood – we fire a few warehouses, maybe plunder a few. Turn the merchants against the Guild by showing they cannot be protected, and make it impossible for the Guild men to fulfil their obligations. Then we pull out, quickly and quietly, and do the same thing the next day."

The Council was silent as they digested this. It was Nate who spoke first.

"Will it make us look weak, a half-cooked response to the start of a war?"

Magnus rubbed his chin in thought. "It *is* appealing. We have a chance to make the Guild back down, without doing anything irreversible. A chance to avoid all-out war."

"And we can always turn up the heat later, if it does not seem to work," Elaine said, adding her support to the idea.

"Right, we give it a try then," Magnus said, nodding. "We send six teams in, men we can trust not to let their passions get the better of them. Lucius, you will head one of the teams, seeing as this was your idea. You get to share the risks."

Lucius bowed his head once to show his acceptance. He knew this was a chance to shine. He just hoped they did not meet anything unexpected, for a second disaster that cost the lives of thieves might well put him on the hit list of their friends.

Squeezing through the stacks of large wooden crates marked with a Vos brand proclaiming they were filled with Malmkrug liquor, Lucius nodded at Lihou, who was laying a trail of oil on the warehouse floor. The young thief, like him, had recently been elevated from the ranks of the pickpockets, and he had the unnerving feeling the lad looked up to him.

The warehouse belonged to one Dietrich Schon, a merchant known to have extensive business interests in Turnitia and who was a fully paid up member for protection from the Guild. This evening, Lucius intended to show him that the gold handed over for a quiet life of business and profit was only so much waste.

As they made their way back to the warehouse's loading bay, Lucius and Lihou were joined by other members of their small team — Ashmore, Teton, and Judi — all trailing their own line of oil from other stacks. Looking up at the wooden pillars, supports and rafters of the building, Lucius could not help smiling. Most of the warehouses in the merchant quarter were new constructions, many of the originals having been destroyed by Vos when the army had entered the city as part of its reign of terror. These new buildings were designed to be large, cheap and quick to construct, so the Vos merchants who had all but paid for the invasion could start business as soon as Turnitia was pacified. This meant they had been built entirely of wood — this fire was going to be huge.

The team continued to pour oil from their leather flasks, joining their lines just outside the wide door that led to a street lined with other warehouses. *Phase one of the plan complete*, thought Lucius. Now he just had to wait.

Across the merchant quarter other Night Hands were at work in their teams. At least one other was firing warehouses, though no glow on the skyline had yet made itself visible. Others were paying personal visits to merchants staying in way houses or taverns, encouraging them to do business elsewhere or otherwise be forced to pay protection money to the Hands. Another team armed with clubs and saps was actively hunting down collectors from the Guild, intending to convince them they were working in dangerous territory.

Lucius had thought he could kill two birds with one stone, and so he and his team waited until their final member, Banff, appeared, with three Guild collectors in tow. Banff had been brought up from the pickpockets at the same time as Lihou, and Lucius had taken advantage of this, gambling that no one in the Guild would recognise him as a Hand. It had clearly worked.

The Guild collectors were clearly taken aback when they realised they were outnumbered, but bravado carried their leader forward.

"This is private property," he said, eyeing them warily. "Be off with you!"

"This property is under our care now," Lucius said, adopting a polite tone to mock the collectors. "We have a message for you to take back to your masters in the Guild. The first part is this; your time here is over. This quarter now belongs to the Hands."

"Arrogant son of a whore," muttered one of the collectors.

"The second part of the message is this," Lihou said, striking his tinderbox and igniting a rag whose end had been doused in oil.

Lihou glanced back at the collectors, then grinned as he threw the burning rag into the pool that had formed from the joint trails of oil that ran through the warehouse.

"Oops," he said, smiling.

The flame guttered for a moment, then flashed as it greedily consumed the oil. Fire swept out in four lines that shot straight into the warehouse. The look on the faces of the collectors was almost comical as they realised, finally, what was going on.

"You fools!" said the leader. "You have no idea who you have just messed with! They're going to be coming after you for this."

"I wouldn't worry," said Lucius, keeping his voice calm. "We are pretty sure we know what we are doing. However, there is a third part of the message we would like you to deliver."

The leader frowned, puzzled, until Lucius clicked his fingers and the rest of his team moved forward, eager for violence. As one, the collectors turned and ran, but they were brought down within a few yards by Lucius' team, who proceeded to pummel them senseless.

A dull crump from behind told him that the first crate of liquor had been burst open by the flames, which would now be spreading voraciously throughout the furs, spices and other goods of luxury stored in the warehouse. He watched his team go to work on the collectors and, though they were clearly enjoying the job, happy to be able to hand something back to the Guild after having been put on the back foot of late, he was pleased to see their discipline remained. He had warned them to use fists and feet only, unless one of the collectors drew a weapon. The point of the exercise was to frighten them and deliver a clear message. Not kill them in the street.

He had to conclude, though, after watching Judi hiss and spit and curse as she dug her boot into a man's groin — causing him to curl up and start sobbing — that perhaps the use of a dagger might have been more humane.

Seeing the collectors had taken enough punishment or, at least, understood the message, Lucius gave a low whistle. His thieves stood up from their task, all breathing heavily from the exertion. As they hurried down the street, leaving the scene, the open doors of the warehouse began to glow with the orange light of the flames inside as they took hold. It would be a few more minutes before the fire swept through the rafters and became visible to the whole city, but Lucius knew the place was already doomed. Even if a Vos patrol happened by now, it was too late; the only question was whether they would be able to save the warehouses either side.

"What's next, Sir?" Lihou asked as he trotted alongside.

Lucius smiled as he drew a rolled parchment from under his tunic. "No need to call me Sir, just Lucius will do." Consulting the parchment he nodded. "The Three Springs tavern. That is where our merchant, Mr Schon, is staying for the next week as he tries to sell what remains of his stock."

"There's not much profit in ashes," Judi said.

"True. And less in doing business with the Guild, as we shall prove tonight."

The Three Springs lay just a few streets over from the warehouse and was one of several establishments devoted to visiting merchants who could not bear to be far from their goods. No one else would visit a tavern nestled deep within the warehouses, so such places also formed a natural forum for negotiations and deal making, where traders could talk shop without being disturbed. There were also other pleasures available to those rich enough, even some that could technically be described as illegal in other parts of Turnitia. It was all part of a specialised service.

As they approached the small building, its two floors and narrow frontage looking faintly ridiculous as it nestled between two giant warehouses, Lucius spotted Gunnison and his team coming from the opposite direction. Gunnison, waved anxiously at them, and then dove into a narrow alley that lay between two warehouses.

Motioning his team to follow, Lucius trailed the veteran thief. Short, wiry and with a pointed face some might describe as rat-like, he had always thought Gunnison the archetypal rogue. The image most people saw in their mind when thinking of a burglar or pickpocket.

Gunnison gestured him to come closer as he crouched. Joining him, Lucius gave a quizzical look.

"Thought we might find you here," Gunnison said, his eyes constantly darting back to the street they had left.

"What's wrong?"

"The Guild has reacted far quicker than we thought. They've got men on the streets hunting for us."

"Yeah, we saw them," Lihou said cockily. "Gave them a right kicking, we did!"

Ignoring him, Gunnison spoke only to Lucius. "Armed men. We saw Wade's guys get hit. He got away, but left two of his men – killed or captured, I don't know."

Lucius sighed. "We should pull out, abandon this evening's operations."

"That's what I was thinking," Gunnison agreed.

"What? We can handle them, Sir," Lihou said. "There's more of us here, I'll bet."

"We are not set up for this," Lucius said, grabbing his arm. "We've already lost two men because we were not prepared for this kind of response. It is too dangerous to continue."

"Besides, if we have running battles in the streets, the guard would be on top of all of us before you could sneeze," Gunnison said. "Keep your team together Lucius, but we'll make our own way back to the guildhouse. Magnus will know what to do."

Nodding in agreement, he watched Gunnison and his men leave. Before he disappeared into the twilight gloom, Gunnison turned back to Lucius and said "Looks like the Guild means business after all."

Leading his team down the opposite end of the alley, Lucius poked his head out into the next street, carefully looking up and down the quiet warehouses to make sure the way was clear.

"Come on," he said. "If you see any trouble, run back to the guildhouse. I don't want any heroics tonight."

They padded up the street, moving slower than Lucius would have wished, but staying within the shadows of the tall buildings as they went, all but invisible. A patrol of Vos guards marched from an adjoining road, causing them to double back a short distance, and skip between two warehouses to take a parallel street out of the merchant quarter.

Lucius heard shouts in the distance as the burning warehouses dotted around the quarter began to be noted and men rushed to douse the flames. He became more confident then, as he knew the Vos guard would be drawn to the disturbances, likely giving his team a free run all the way back to the guildhouse.

He heard Judi hiss a warning, and looked over his shoulder to see they were being followed. A half dozen men, armed with clubs and short swords were calmly walking up the centre of the street as if they owned it, not bothering to keep to the shadows.

"Get ready to run," he whispered to his team. "Split up if you must and find your own way back to the guildhouse. Tell Magnus what happened. When I give the word, mind. I'll watch your backs."

"Lucius..." Lihou said in a quiet voice, as they saw a half dozen more men detach themselves from shadowy doorways, alleys and from behind resting wagons ahead of them. They, too, were obviously armed, and Lucius felt a sinking feeling in his stomach.

"Right..." he said. "Go! Now!"

As one, his team scattered, dashing for the narrow passages that lay between the nearest warehouses. As one, the men before and behind them scattered as well, matching their movements as they sought to cut the escaping thieves off.

Only two remained on the street, and Lucius made to draw his sword as they approached then, thinking better, reached down for a dagger with his left hand. Knowing his team would need his support in all haste, he resolved to dispatch the men quickly.

He saw immediately that they were barely trained to use the blades they carried, and he spun to dodge one overhead slash, while catching the other with his dagger. He thrust with his weapon, feeling it enter the belly of his opponent then, kicked out with his boot to push the man back to the ground.

If the second man was aware his friend was already dead, he did not show it as he screamed an inarticulate cry, while swinging his sword at Lucius' midriff. Taking a step back, Lucius avoided the blow, and shook his head in astonishment. The man was using his sword as one would a club. His next swing was easy to counter, and Lucius turned it aside before taking a step forward and driving his dagger into the man's throat. Gargling as blood swept down his chest, the man sank to the ground, a look of incomprehension in his eyes.

More shouts, much closer this time, spurred Lucius into action. Taking a guess, he tore across the street and raced down a narrow alley to follow the sounds. He emerged onto a wide road, one of the main thoroughfares of the merchant quarter, and saw Lihou and Judi running together, their feet barely touching the cobbled surface as four men chased them. Racing after them, he watched as they dived into an alley on the far side, hoping to shake their pursuers off in the network that ran between the warehouses. Panting heavily now, he cursed with painful breaths as he saw they were, out of obvious fear, sticking together and not splitting up.

Shouting a challenge, he gained the attention of one man, who turned aside from the chase to face Lucius with a club. Lucius did not bother to confront him, ducking instead down another alley he hoped would continue to run parallel to the one Lihou and Judi had taken, intending to outpace them to the other side.

Now with his own pursuer, he sheathed his dagger and sought the threads of power, summoning a flame to his left hand. Holding it as one might hold an apple, he stopped and turned, concentrating for a second to bind more energy to his bidding, then threw it at the man. Sizzling through the air, the lavender flames struck the man in the chest with the force of a hammer. He tried to scream, but fire sucked the air out of his lungs as it consumed his flesh. Knowing the man would be dead before he hit the ground, Lucius hurried on.

Racing out into the next street, Lucius looked to his left and saw Judi, standing at the entrance to an alley from which she had just emerged. He tore towards her, seeing the shock and fear on her face.

"They got him," she cried, pointing into the alley where Lucius could see three men kicking at someone curled up on the ground.

"Get out of here now!" he shouted at her. "Back to the guildhouse. I'll look after Lihou!"

He grabbed at her arm and bodily pushed her up the street away from him. Stumbling, Judi found her feet and began to run.

Drawing his dagger, Lucius padded quickly down the dark alley, closing fast on the men who were, so far, unaware of his presence. The first died without knowing what hit him, Lucius' dagger planted firmly between his shoulder blades, and the second had barely started to raise his sword as Lucius' own blade slashed across his face, leaving it a screaming ruin.

The last of the thugs held a hand up as he backed away, and Lucius snarled at him. Casting a last look at his bawling companion who was clasping bloodied hands to his face, he turned and ran.

Lucius silenced the screaming man with a quick thrust, as much to save his ears from the anguished cries as stopping him from bringing the guard down on their heads. He reached down to the huddled mass on the ground, and found Lihou, battered and bruised but alive. The lad's nose was clearly broken, and his whole face was a puffed up mass of injured flesh. As he tried to pick Lihou up, the boy moaned in pain, and Lucius went down on his knees to support him.

"Judi," Lihou muttered. "Tried to save her. Not running fast enough."

"You did fine," Lucius said, checking Lihou's body for other injuries, his hand came away sticky with blood. Running a hand across Lihou's tunic, he was shocked to find a mass of stab wounds.

"She got away," Lucius said, not knowing what else to say. "You showed real courage."

"Knew... I wouldn't amount to much," Lihou mumbled past broken lips.

As Lucius searched for another platitude, he felt Lihou tense suddenly, then relax. A last breath escaped the lad and he was still.

Silent anger boiled within Lucius as he carefully laid Lihou's body on the ground. He had seen plenty of people die in the past, many of them at his own hand, but he felt something different this time. Like the men who had died on the Allantian ship, Lihou had been under his leadership, had been his responsibility. It was not a feeling Lucius welcomed, and he cursed himself for accepting the roles Magnus had placed upon him but, most of all, he felt the need to bring down the men who had caused so much death. The Guild had to be brought to task.

Lucius sprang up and rejoined the main thoroughfare. As he trotted up the street, he kept alert, straining his senses to penetrate the twilight for any sign of Hands in trouble, or the Guild men after them.

More cries, including one prolonged and agonised wail which could only mark a man's death, guided him across a junction and into a side road. Rounding a small lean-to built against a warehouse, he saw a pitched battle in the middle of the street.

Men were clumped in groups, the fight scattered across the entire street. As one combatant sank to the ground, overcome by a deadly sword thrust or clout to the back of the head with a club, those fighting him moved to another victim. Closing in on the melee, Lucius found that he had trouble recognising who was on which side, though he spotted a couple of Hands he had spoken to in the common room on previous days, and rushed to aid them.

Ashmore was there, and Lucius gave him an angry sideways look for having got caught in the fight rather than making his way back to the guildhouse as instructed. To his credit, the thief seemed almost sheepish as he buried his small knife into the kidney of a man attacking another Hand.

"The guard!" someone cried, and Lucius ducked under a club swung at his skull, before rolling away. He glanced down the street in the direction of the cry and saw a patrol of six Vos guard — their eagle-faced tabards menacing in Kerberos' half light — approaching at a trot, with their swords drawn and mail chinking with each footfall.

The club swung down towards him again and, caught on the ground, Lucius barely had time to raise his sword to catch the blow. The blade dug deep into the wood, locking the two weapons together, and while the man attacking him strained to release them, Lucius hacked down with his dagger, driving it through the man's foot.

Reeling back in agony, the man collapsed to the floor, clutching his injured foot, while Lucius stood on the club and pulled, jerking his sword free. With one thrust, he ended the man's pain.

Hitting the fray like a bolt of lightning, men started to go down as soon as the guard entered the melee. Lucius shouted for the Hands to follow him, to escape, but some were already in a deadly fight with the armoured guard, and others were reluctant to leave them. Hoping it would not be the last decision he made, Lucius charged forward, catching a guard in the side and bowling him over, he stabbed down, but his sword was turned aside by the guard's thick mail.

Another guardsman, seeing his comrade in distress, rushed into the fight and was about to decapitate one of the thieves when he started shouting "Red diamond! Red diamond!" Lucius was amazed to see the guard turn from the man and march resolutely toward him. Lucius ran.

Shouting again for them to follow, other Hands gradually got the message and they scattered into the alleys, desperately trying to put ground between them and the guard. Instead, they found more guardsmen waiting for them.

Pulling one man out of an alley that another patrol of guard had started to close upon, Lucius ran with him down the street, this being the only clear path he could see. But as he approached the junction, yet another patrol appeared, trotting round the corner, weapons drawn. Seeing an alley to his left, Lucius shoved the man into it ahead of him and together they sprinted down the cobbles, only for Lucius to run into his comrade as the man suddenly stopped.

Blood pumping in fear as much as excitement now, Lucius looked at what had caused the man to halt in his tracks. The two warehouses that formed the alley had been joined together by a new connecting structure that towered above them, blocking their exit. One glance at the smooth planks that formed the soaring wall told Lucius that even Hawk would have found it difficult to scale.

"We've got to get out of here now," he said to the other Hand, and grabbed his shoulder to propel him back up the alley. A Guild man appeared at its entrance, and pointed towards them.

"Red diamond!" Lucius heard him say as the Vos guard appeared next to him. The guard sergeant nodded in understanding, then led his patrol down the alley toward them.

Lucius heard the man standing next to him curse, then throw down his sword. The guard approached two abreast, those marching behind them training crossbows on Lucius' chest.

With an angry cry of frustration, Lucius turned and kicked the wooden wall of the warehouse, having nothing else to take his fury out on. He then hurled his weapons to the ground and stared ruefully at the guardsmen, his hands splayed out to either side in surrender.

CHAPTER 13

The army of Vos was renowned throughout the peninsula for its efficiency, be it at grinding down the defences of an enemy city or calculating the food and supplies a force would need on a long march and ensuring it would receive them in good order.

That same efficiency was apparent here, in the depths of the Citadel. Lucius cast a rueful eye around his cell, illuminated only by the torchlight flickering through the barred window narrow in the single, stout oaken door. The flagstones were spotless, with any evidence of the previous occupants of the cell removed before he set foot inside himself. The manacles that bound his hands and feet to wall and floor were well-oiled with secure locks intended to foil the best efforts of any thief who managed to not only get a hand free, but smuggle a pick in with him.

He shared the cell with Luber, the thief arrested alongside him. He was a Vos-born rogue who had sought the freedoms of Turnitia only to find his old empire sweep over his new home with ease. He was well aware of Vos efficiency, and had spent much of his time bemoaning their fate, regaling Lucius with unwelcome tales of torture and mutilation before exhaustion finally overwhelmed him.

Ignoring the man's gentle snores, Lucius cast his eyes around the cell, debating exactly what to do next. The manacles, and even the cell door, posed no problem for him. There were any number of ways he could call the magic to his aid to find freedom, from the freezing of the chains so they would shatter with a sharp strike, to allowing the energy to increase his own strength enough to force the door open. There were few prisons that could hold an accomplished Shadowmage for long.

No, his problem would be with whatever happened next. Lucius was aware of guards passing by his cell door at semi-regular intervals, and he had already begun to count the minutes to the next arrival in order to determine the changing patterns. Assuming he could leave the cell without alerting them, he would then find himself in the heart of an enemy stronghold that had gained a reputation for absolute security. It was the home of every Vos soldier in Turnitia, and he did not relish the idea of providing them all with sword and crossbow practice. They were already too good.

Nor could he await the justice, such as it was, of Vos. Arrested thieves could expect the briefest of trials, followed by a stripping of their possessions (his sword and mail were not much, but they were his and he valued them) and, likely as not, the loss of a hand or foot in order to remind the citizens of the city that while Vos brought many economic benefits, disobedience would not be tolerated.

There was also something larger taking place, Lucius now realised. He thought back to the skirmishes in the merchant quarter, and the arrival of the guard – and the passwords that the Guild men had uttered. If the Guild of Coin and Enterprise had bought the guard... as unthinkable – not to mention unlikely – as it was, it spelt nothing but trouble for the Hands. They may as well try to fight the entire city.

Thoughts buzzing around his head like angry hornets, Lucius jerked himself back into alertness when he heard the now familiar heavy footsteps and chink of mail that signalled the arrival of another pair of guards. He frowned, and gave an angry sigh. The guard, it seemed, were intentionally varying the regularity of their patrols past the cells in order to throw the senses and timing of the inmates. However, there had to be an underlying order to their patrols (they were Vos, after all), and Lucius had begun to think he had discovered it. This patrol threw his calculations right out the non-existent window, however.

A jangle of keys on a chain and the sliding of several locks in the door heralded the arrival of three armed men. The first two stood either side of the cell's entrance, hands on sword hilts but in a casual stance that suggested they expected no real trouble. The third man to enter caught Lucius' attention immediately, for his tight, moustachioed face and narrow, suspicious eyes exuded both menace and authority. His presence seemed to fill the cell, making it seem that much smaller. Wearing a black leather waistcoat studded with metal plates, he might have looked like many of the thieves Lucius knew, were it not for the obvious expense and elegance of his armour. A long red cloak swept behind him, pinned to his waistcoat with elaborate gold brooches, and the hilt of his longsword was similarly well decorated.

"Good evening," he said, and Lucius saw he almost clicked his heels as he bent his head in mock salute. "I am Baron Ernst von Minterheim, Commander of the Citadel, Colonel of the Vos Empire and Master of the Guard."

He smiled briefly at his two prisoners. "I want to know the location of your guildhouse, its defences and a roll of all its members. As Commander of the Citadel, it is within my discretion as to the best methods to obtain this information so, in a way, it is up to you how this will go. We'll start with you."

The commander gestured at Luber, and the two guards sprang into action. One pulled the man to his feet, while the other busied himself with the locks round Luber's ankles and wrists. As he was carried out, Luber flashed a worried look at Lucius, who was paying more attention to the movements of the guards, watching for any opportunity to spring a bid for freedom. For he knew he would be next.

It came quicker than he thought. As the guards dragged Luber out of the cell, another pair stepped around the Commander to haul Lucius to his feet. He felt the manacles release his limbs from their pinching grasp, only to be replaced by an iron-like grip that drew his arms behind his back in a well-practised move. Propelled out of the cell, he was dragged bodily along a corridor and down a set of steps that descended further into the fortress. His mind churned as his feet slid along the flagstones, determined not to aid the guards in their labours in any way.

Any thieves captured by the guard would be in for a hellish evening, Lucius knew, but it would be the morning before anything more permanent would take place. Lucius was betting on this, if the Guild had any say on events in the Citadel, and the Vos guard liked a public display to stamp their authority on the citizens of Turnitia. A good hanging or maiming always drew a decent crowd, regardless of who was suffering.

That gave him some time, at least. He guessed the Vos guard and their commander would be inventive during their questioning, but Lucius had taken a beating before and believed he could face up to another one. His worry was how many other thieves had been caught, and how many of them would be quickly broken.

As they stepped out of the staircase and entered another level, Lucius noted that the environment seemed darker, and it took him a few seconds to realise that the torches down here were spaced further apart, creating more shadows; and a far more foreboding atmosphere. All part of the Vos game he decided, an attempt to convince those brought down here that hope was as far away as the day-lit world. The cries and moans from the cells they passed served to add to the atmosphere of impending defeat, a promise of what any prisoner would inevitably face. Lucius guessed that perhaps a dozen men and women were being questioned, though he had no way of knowing whether they were all thieves caught that night.

A painful crack, followed by sustained sobbing caught Lucius' attention as he was dragged past one such cell, and it was followed by a rumble of laughter from within.

Lucius was thrown onto the floor of a nearby cell, this one even smaller than his previous residence. He struck the ground and rolled, but was instantly grabbed again and shoved into the single wooden chair that was bolted to the flagstones. A heavy hand forced him back into the uncomfortable seat while others grabbed at his hands and feet, securing them to iron clasps, holding him immobile. One guard left the cell, while the other stationed himself behind Lucius, out of view but his presence menacingly obvious.

Taking a breath to compose himself, Lucius began to take in his surroundings, inspecting the clasps holding him to his chair, the thickness of the cell door, the space he might have to manoeuvre, should he break free and be forced to fight. His calculations were interrupted by the cell door opening again and another guard entered, followed by Commander Ernst von Minterheim.

"I have little time and less patience," he announced casually, almost seeming bored by this duty. "We already have much of the information we require, and your fellow thieves caught this evening have been most co-operative. I merely require you to confirm some of what they have told us. If your tales support one another, you can all go free come morning. Lie to me, and you will all hang."

Lucius looked up at him with a rueful expression. "I will not co-operate."

The commander gave a nod, and Lucius felt strong hands press down on his shoulders from behind. The guard who had entered the cell with the Commander stepped up and backhanded him with a mailed fist.

His head whipping round with the blow, Lucius gasped with the sudden pain, and he worked his jaw to ensure it was not broken. He glanced back at the Commander, this time with a baleful expression.

"That was just the start of what could be a very long evening for you," von Minterheim said. "Now, what is your name?"

Lucius stared back, saying nothing. Another mailed swipe set his teeth ringing.

"How long have you been with the Hands?"

This time Lucius' silence was met with a blow straight to his face. He felt something in his nose crack under the fist, and his eyes watered.

"Who are the current members of your Council?"

Lucius did not see the next strike coming, and he jerked against the clasps of the chair as the side of his head exploded in pain, causing the whole world to reel, then spin. A hand grasped him under the chin to hold his head upright before another backhanded blow blasted across his face. Hanging his head low, Lucius spat blood down his chest.

"I don't have time for another tight-lipped thief," he heard von Minterheim say, as if from a great distance. "Carry on with him. Let me know if he decides to loosen his tongue."

As light slowly flooded back into Lucius' world, he felt pain. His face felt like it had swollen to twice its normal size and, as he roused himself awake, the movement sent sharp bolts that lanced through his stomach and chest. Duller was the ache from his wrists and ankles, where they had been bruised from the clasps of the chair. Opening his eyes a fraction, he saw that his limbs were bound once again by chained manacles, and he guessed he was back in his cell.

Low voices made him aware he was not alone and, glancing at his cell mates, he saw he was somewhere else entirely. This cell was much larger, and held more than a dozen other thieves, all bound by hand and foot to the walls and floor as was he. Luber was to his right, and the man looked a wreck, with blackened, puffed up eyes and a dried slick of blood running down his chin. Guessing he looked no better himself, Lucius glanced round the other captives, tuning in to their low, hushed conversations.

"It'll be suicide," said one in a hiss.

"Better that than hang," answered another, a thin, reedy man about the same age as Lucius. "I heard von Minterheim say it himself; anyone not making a deal with them is strung up in the courtyard this morning."

"So, which of us made a deal?" a woman's voice asked, her tone one of guarded suspicion.

"Not me," said the thin man, who Lucius now recognised as a counterfeiter called Aeron. "Can't imagine anyone would."

"Oh, come on. There's, what, fourteen, fifteen..." she said, counting the bodies surrounding her. "Sixteen thieves here. You certain *no one* spoke?"

"Not really a problem for us right now," Lucius heard himself mumble.

"Hey, Lucius is awake," the original voice said. "What was that you said?"

Lucius worked his mouth for a few seconds, trying to find some moisture while ignoring the pain of moving his lips.

"Whether one or more of us answered any of the guard's questions is rather academic," he said. "It does us no good or harm while we are locked up here – and if we hang this morning, it won't matter to us either way."

A mumble of agreement spread round the cell. Aeron spoke up again.

"There are some who think an escape attempt is pointless, that we'll just be caught and killed that much quicker."

Seeing one man lower his head to avoid Aeron's pointed stare, Lucius tried to give a confident smile, but his lips only partially co-operated. "Would anyone here rather they met their end at the end of a noose than while fighting for their lives?"

He was met with silence.

"Thought not."

"So, it just remains for us to get ourselves free," said the woman. Lucius gave her a quick look but while he thought he had seen her in the guildhouse from time to time, he could not remember her name. As battered and bruised as the rest of them, he was impressed that her eyes still shone with the light of defiance.

Rattling her chains, the woman nodded to her manacles. "Anyone manage to get themselves free of these?"

Inwardly, Lucius sighed. He was not ready to unleash his magic with all the thieves as witnesses, however simple it might be for him. Even with the Hands under assault from both the Vos guard and the Guild, it was too dangerous. Looking around the cell for an answer, he was conscious of Luber moaning next to him, and was surprised to realise that the man was chuckling. Others watched the man as he gave a bloodied grin then produced a small hooked bar of metal from his swollen lips. A lockpick.

"Nice going, Luber," the woman said. "But how are you going to reach your chains?"

"Well, Natalia," he said. "There's a little trick I learned growing up in Vosburg. You might want to look away..."

Lucius saw her sneer at that, then followed her gaze as her eyes widened in shock. Next to him, Luber's face had turned into a grimace as he strained his right hand against the manacles that clasped his wrist. He watched as the man flattened his fingers, then brought his thumb down into his palm, before he pulled, shuddering with the effort.

The thieves winced collectively as a dull, wet snap reached their ears, and Luber grunted from the pain. Incredulously, Lucius stared as Luber simply drew his hand back through the manacles. Gingerly, he took the lockpick from his mouth and began prodding at the restraint around his left hand.

Waiting with baited breath, the thieves watched as Luber, with obvious pain and difficulty, probed the locking mechanism of the manacles, the action made harder tenfold with the broken joint of his thumb. He twisted the pick, and they all strained to hear the click of the mechanism unlocking, but instead heard Luber grunt again in pain as his hand spasmed slightly, and the pick fell from the lock, dangling only by a fraction of an inch of its hooked end. Lucius saw the woman jerk against her chains involuntarily, perhaps thinking she could catch the pick from across the cell, but Luber's reactions were up to the task. Giving a pained but wry smile at his audience, he scooped the pick up, and re-seated it back in the lock.

"God's teeth, Luber," someone muttered. "Could do this quicker myself."

"And could you break your own wrist first?" the woman asked caustically, only to be met with silence.

Moving slower and more deliberately this time, Luber continued his probing, then gave another grunt.

"Got it," he whispered, and hushed words of encouragement swept around the cell as they all heard a tiny click. With a shrugging motion, Luber discarded the open manacles and set to work on those chaining his feet.

Eyes began to flicker towards the cell door, as the thieves collectively prayed that the guard would not return before Luber's work was done, but luck remained on their side. He quickly disposed of the restraints tying his feet and then, shakily, stood, grinning in his new found freedom. A quiet cough brought him back to the job in hand, and he set to work on another man Lucius recognised as his partner. Once another set of manacles lay useless on the floor, the newly freed thief produced his own lockpick from inside a boot, and together he and Luber shuffled around the cell, releasing their comrades.

Even before the last thief was released, Lucius was by the cell door, inspecting its lock. He was joined by the woman.

"No craftsmanship here," she said. Noting Lucius' quizzical gaze, she gestured at the lock. "Why build a cell whose door gives access to the lock on the inside? Especially one designed to hold thieves. All that money from Vos to build the Citadel, but no finesse in its application."

"Lucky for us," he said. "I'm Lucius."

She took his extended hand. "Grayling. I've seen you around. Rumour has it you can fight." In response, he shrugged. "There'll be plenty of fighting soon," she continued. "Let's hope you are as good as your reputation. Luber, you finished there? We need this door open."

It was Luber's partner who answered her summons and, as he went to work, Grayling ordered the thieves into pairs, and Lucius was faintly surprised at the ease at which they accepted her leadership.

"When you leave, take your chances to go left or right down the corridor – either is as good as the other, and it will mean we are not all cooped up in one place if the guard see us. Find weapons if you can, but don't take risks. The goal is to get out of this cursed place. Go for the roof or the ground floor, as you like. Find a route out of this tower and then past the walls – that will be the difficult bit. Better to go over than through, but if some of us are found, it may cause enough distraction for the others. Once out..." here she paused, as the enormity of what they were attempting struck home. "Split up and make your way back to the guildhouse. Standard procedures. Make sure you are not followed, and make wide detours. Understood?"

She was answered by nods and grunts.

"Lucius, you come with me," she said, barely looking him in the eye.

A loud click froze the thieves as the lock of the cell door was forced by Luber's partner. He looked back at Grayling who nodded. Pulling Lucius to one side, she opened the door open a crack and, seeing no movement, swung it open fully. She darted her head outside, looking up and down the open corridor.

"You two," she said, gesturing at a pair of thieves. "Go!"

The two men sprang up and, with just a second's hesitation, darted left. The next pair called by Grayling went right. As the thieves funnelled out, Lucius began to fidget, feeling that the guards could return any moment, trapping him in the cell while the other thieves made their bid for freedom. As the last pair left, Grayling looked up at him.

"Ready?"

Without waiting for a reply, she peered out of the corridor once more, then trotted left, her soft boots making no noise on the flagstones. They passed other cells, and Lucius briefly entertained the idea of releasing all the prisoners held in this tower, but realised that such a mob would as likely get themselves killed as escape, and that the odds were stacked against the thieves as it was.

At the first junction, Grayling cocked her head, then pointed right, and as they made their way down shadowy, torch-lit passages, they caught the occasional snatch of raised voices and the unmistakable clash of metal on metal. Some of the thieves had already been found, and were now fighting for their lives.

An alcove revealed a spiral stone staircase leading both up and down, and Grayling began to vault upwards, aiming for the pinnacle of the tower. However, the stairs stopped short at least one level, forcing them back into twisting corridors. Always one pace behind her, Lucius stopped short when Grayling held up a hand.

"Guard coming," she whispered. "Get him looking at you."

With no other words, she skipped to the left, nestling herself within the shadows of a support buttress that stood proud of the passageway's walls. An instant later, Lucius heard booted feet and the clink of mail from ahead, and realised Grayling's hearing was far more acute than his own. A second later, an armoured guard rounded a corner a few yards down the corridor, coming to a dead halt when he saw Lucius standing in his path.

They stared at one another for a brief instant, the guard surprised at the sight of an intruder, Lucius' mind fumbling for something to say.

He held up both hands. "I surrender."

Frowning now, the guard jogged down the corridor, arm outstretched to seize Lucius, but his motion was arrested by Grayling's foot. Catching the guard off balance, she snaked from the shadows, tripping him with an easy movement, then following his body down with her own. Throwing his helmet aside, one blow to the back of his neck rendered the guard unconscious.

Moving quickly, Grayling tugged at the guard's belt, freeing his weapons. The sword she passed to Lucius, while she grabbed a dagger for herself.

"Sure you don't want the sword?" Lucius asked, surprised she had taken the smaller weapon. She gave him a disparaging look.

"You men are always so worried about size."

Her smile might have been meant purely in jest, but it retained such a look of viciousness that Lucius found himself swallowing involuntarily. Grayling glanced over her shoulder, looking down the corridor.

"Grab that and pull it into the shadows," she said, indicating the motionless guard. "I'll scout ahead."

As quietly as he could, Lucius dragged the guard next to the buttress Grayling had used to ambush him, deeply aware of the grating sound the man's mail made on the stone floor. He tried lifting and shuffling the man as best he could, but it was a dead weight, and he kept flicking glances up and down the passageway, expecting to see half the Vos army bearing down upon him.

By the time he had finished, Grayling had returned, and he noted a triumphant look in her eyes.

"I know how we are getting out of here," she said. "But there is a problem. Come."

Pacing down the corridor behind her, Lucius followed Grayling past two junctions in the maze like arrangement of the tower. They came to a half open door, from which he heard the voices of several men. Following her gesture, he looked inside.

Lucius saw the problem immediately. Four more guards were inside, in various states of unreadiness. Two were reclined on cots, propped up against the far wall as they spoke with their colleagues, while the other pair were seated at a table, evidently finishing off their evening meal. Only one was fully armoured, his helmet lying discarded on the table, while another wore only his mail coat. The two on the cots wore only leather under-tunics, their mail hung from crosspieces on one side of the room. Quickly scanning the room for weapons, Lucius saw a wooden rack against the far wall in which rested a variety of swords, maces and daggers.

Grayling nudged him in the side, and he followed her eyes to a corner of the barracks. A ladder rose from the floor to a large trapdoor in the ceiling.

"To the roof," she mouthed.

Lucius frowned at her and jerked his head to the guards. Despite having the advantage of surprise, he was not sure they could defeat all of the men inside before they could launch a highly effective counterattack. If it were just him, with both armour and magic as his allies, he would be confident. However, he had nothing but the sword Grayling had managed to recover for him, and he did not fancy her chances at all, fighting well-trained soldiers with only a dagger.

She grabbed his arm and pulled him back down the corridor. When they were a safe distance away, she whispered her idea to him.

"I go in first. You move as soon as they spot me, got it?"

He nodded, but she took hold of his arm again, squeezing it to underline her point. "As soon as they see me, understand? If I am caught alone in there, I'm dead. I'm relying on you – can I do that?"

Lucius took a breath, still not liking their odds, but he nodded. "You can count on me."

"Good, "she said, smiling. "I had heard that."

He frowned at that, but Grayling had already left his side, pacing stealthily back towards the door, dagger held low. Watching as she reached the door, Lucius saw her drop into a crouch and then, slowly, silently, she passed the threshold and entered the room.

Using the half open door to shield his presence, Lucius watched in amazement as Grayling padded towards the men in the cots. She moved with exceptional grace, each footstep slow and deliberate. He had heard tales in the common room of some thieves with the ability to blend into their environments to such a degree that they practically became invisible, but he had not really believed it up to now. Keeping her back to the wall, Grayling moved with a slow but irresistible motion. Never completely still, yet never drawing attention to herself. One foot was placed in front of the other in total silence. Lucius marvelled at her ability, but felt her luck could not last.

It didn't. A casual glance from one of the men at the table became a double take as he focussed on the creeping woman who, battered and bruised with a naked dagger, must have looked for all the world like some evil spirit come to exact vengeance.

"Assassin!" the man cried out, stunning his comrades into inaction as he whirled around for the weapons rack.

Lucius was already moving, sprinting for the table. Out of the corner of his eye, he saw Grayling uncoil from her crouch, turning her stealthy pose into a killing strike in an instant. The man in the first cot was dead a second later, blood gushing down his tunic.

The last man at the table reeled back from Lucius' charge, falling from his chair and upending the table as he hit the floor. Kicking the table to one side, Lucius hacked the man down before he could cry out. The blade dug easily into the side of the guard's skull, and blood flowed across the floor as he yanked it free.

A hiss from Grayling caused Lucius to look up, and it was by reflex alone that he managed to raise the blade of his sword in time to catch the downward swing of the other guard's mace. The guard snarled at Lucius – spittle flying from his lips – before he reversed the direction of his weapon, and swung the mace again.

Unable to parry such a close blow, Lucius backed away and nearly tangled himself in the body at his feet. Seeing the guard advance and ready another swing, he reached down and grabbed the fallen chair, raising it just as the mace came towards his head.

The chair shattered into a dozen wooden splinters while the force of the attack caused him to stumble. As he went down on one knee, Lucius swung his sword in a backhanded blow intended to disembowel the guard, but the tip of his weapon just skittered off mail. Pressing home the advantage, the guard raised the mace above his head and brought it rushing down, perhaps hoping to blast Lucius straight through the floor and back into the cells.

Caught off balance, Lucius rolled back toward the door, hoping to gain a little ground. The guard followed immediately, seeing a helpless enemy before him. Kicking out, Lucius stalled the advance with a blow to the guard's shin, but his foot just glanced off the metal greaves. Another swing forced him to dive to his left, and his sword clattered on the floor as it fell from his grasp. On his rump and completely defenceless now, Lucius desperately kicked at the floor, trying to drive himself back, away from the guard, whose face was now triumphant with victory.

He felt the wall at his back, and knew there was nowhere else to run. Raising his arms in a futile effort to ward away the guard's finishing blow, he looked up to see the man staring down at him. The guard's fury had disappeared and his expression was almost serene. Lucius frowned in puzzlement, then opened his mouth in shock as the man sank to his knees and collapsed at his feet. Behind the guard stood Grayling, her dagger dripping with blood.

"Can I help you up?" she said.

Grayling was the first to the ladder and after reaching the top, she heaved with her shoulder to force the trapdoor open. Lucius looked past her slight form to see the blue sphere of Kerberos leering down at him, and he felt a rush of relief as he breathed in fresh air.

Vaulting up the ladder, he found himself at the top of the tower beside Grayling, looking down from the parapets. The roof was dominated by a huge trebuchet – its timbers harvested from Vos forests – the massive stones it threw piled next to it mined from quarries close to the city. A single pole rose higher even than the mighty war machine, but no flag flew from it this evening, that honour having currently been taken by one of the other towers of the Citadel.

The view of Turnitia from this height was spectacular. He could see the entire expanse of the city, from the ocean cliffs guarding it, up the slope to the townhouses on its far side. To the east and north, rows of blank roofed warehouses held the wealth of the city, while the Five Markets lay empty below.

Closer, the construction of the Citadel was equally impressive. The four other towers stood silent and imposing, acting as sentinels for the entire city, while the main keep – invisible to the rest of the world behind vast stone walls – nestled between them. Those walls ringed the entire complex, high above the level of most buildings in Turnitia, and were lined with troops. More soldiers were scattered in the courtyards directly below, and Lucius saw the frantic movements of an ongoing battle. Some of the thieves had escaped from the tower at ground level, only to find themselves cut off and surrounded.

"We cannot help them," Grayling said, perhaps wanting to forestall any foolish heroics Lucius might be tempted to perform.

"Agreed," he said after a moment, nodding. "So, what now?"

"Still thinking," Grayling said as she looked left and right for a solution to present itself.

"I thought you said you had a plan?"

"Got us this far, haven't I?" she retorted, though there was no venom in her voice. Slowly, Lucius began to realise that she was actually enjoying the moment, their brush with danger and the bid for freedom. He could not decide whether that was a good thing.

"We've got this," Grayling said, scooping up a coil of rope that lay next to the Vos banners that were draped down the sheer sides of the towers on special days marked by the empire. "But we can't just drop it down into the courtyard."

Staring out at the city, an idea came to Lucius. "If we could stretch it to the walls, they would be the last obstacle."

She looked at him doubtfully, as if he had suddenly turned simple. "Even if we had a hook to tie to the end, could you throw it that far?"

Walking to the edge of the battlements lining the tower, Lucius stared at the wall, trying to gauge the distance. As a horizontal throw, it would be impossible, but from their vantage point, they had height on their side. If they had just a little help.

"Find something," he said. "Anything that can act as a grappling hook. We need something that can dig into stone."

Grayling disappeared back down the trapdoor while Lucius scouted the roof of the tower. He had hoped to find something useful among the tools and supplies surrounding the war machine, but he was unsuccessful. When Grayling reappeared, he could tell from her expression that she had been no luckier.

She looked up at the trebuchet. "You know, there are stories of thieves making their escape by using catapults."

"Any thief telling that story is either a liar or a good deal shorter than he once was."

Grayling sighed. "We might have to go back down into the tower."

Closing his eyes, Lucius cursed. He knew what he had to do, but it would very likely mean an end to his place among the Hands.

"Grayling," he began. "You counted on me before. I need to count on you now."

"Of course," she said without hesitation.

"I mean it."

Something in his voice checked her, and she frowned at him. "What are you planning to do?"

It was his turn to sigh. "Stand back until I say. And you'll need a strip of cloth or short length of rope."

Still clearly puzzled, Grayling nevertheless followed his instructions, and dug around the trebuchet's supplies until she found something suitable.

Lucius took a deep breath as he began coiling the rope in his hands, staring fixedly at a portion of the opposite wall that seemed to have few guards on its ramparts. He turned his attention inward, seeking the threads of magic that constantly turned and twisted and, like an old friend, they came flooding back under his control.

He began to swing one end of the rope above his head, whipping it around faster and faster as he manipulated the threads to bring those he needed into the real world. An otherworldly strength flooded into his body briefly, hot and fast, and he felt himself shudder as the power whipped about in his chest. Then it was gone, the energy passed to the rope spinning above his head, and suddenly it was moving with its own momentum. Letting go with one hand, he retained a grip on its length with the other. The rope coiled above his head as it span, reaching ever higher speeds.

He heard Grayling gasp in astonishment but his conscious mind was elsewhere, directing the magic that now sung along the entire length of the rope. With a command that was part gesture, part vocal the rope arced high in the sky across the face of Kerberos before plunging down towards the wall. A bright flash of light surged along its length, pulling it taut as the tip rocketed downwards, plunging deep into the battlements of the wall. Feeling the magic spent as the conjuration was completed, Lucius pulled hard on the rope to ensure it had taken hold, then ran to the trebuchet to tie the loose end firmly. He cut a short length from it, and then returned to the battlements.

Throughout this, he avoided eye contact with Grayling, but was aware that she was giving him suspicious sidelong looks.

"Come on," he said. "You first."

With the briefest of pauses, Grayling threw her legs over the side of the tower and wrapped the cloth she had gathered around the rope. He saw her shift her weight in preparation to throw herself into clear air but she stopped, and turned to face him.

"I think I know what you are," she said.

He stopped for a moment, then looked directly into her eyes. "The others cannot know."

She nodded in understanding. "I'll make you a deal. We survive this and escape, it will be our secret. If not... well, it won't matter either way."

Cocking a half smile, Grayling put her dagger in her mouth and pushed off. Grasping the cloth wrapped round the rope in each hand, she quickly gained speed as she flew through the air, down to the wall below.

Lucius sat on the edge of the battlements as he twisted his short cord around the rope then, testing the strain to ensure it could bear him as well as Grayling, he jumped.

He tried to pull the ends of the cord across one another in an attempt to control his speed, but he gathered pace at an alarming rate as he shot down the rope. Feet dangling helplessly in the air, he was aware of shouts rising up from the courtyard, but whether they were directed at him or were the result of the ongoing battle below, he could not tell. Ahead, Grayling had already reached the wall and had dropped from the rope into a graceful roll. Even now, she was throwing her dagger at the chest of a guard but Lucius had greater concerns on his mind.

The wall was approaching at a terrible pace, the thick stone rearing up in front of him, growing ever larger. Belatedly, he tried to find the threads of magic, tried to summon energy that would enable him to avoid the inevitable collision that loomed. With the air whistling past his ears and the feeling of being utterly out of control, he was ashamed to find his concentration completely spent. As the wall approached, he tried to gauge his increasing speed and then let go of the cord.

For a brief second, he seemed to float through the air, and he fancied he might land neatly on his feet, coming to rest lightly on the ramparts of the wall. Instead, he barrelled forward helplessly. Tucking in a shoulder by sheer instinct at the last minute, he smashed into the battlements and the wind was forced from his body.

Lucius was completely dazed, and his head rang as he tried to take in air. He briefly thought he had been run down in the street by a racing wagon, and that well meaning citizens were trying to get him to stand once more. Not caring for their attentions, he tried to tell them that he just needed to sleep, but the words came out wrong. He was not even sure they were audible. Tucking his head under his arms, Lucius was irritated when someone dragged him to sit upright and started shouting in his face.

A sharp sting hit his cheek, and he shook his head. The voices seemed clearer now. He blinked and saw Grayling draw back her hand for another slap. He raised his own palm to show he was back with her, and it was sufficient to forestall the blow.

"Can you walk?" she hissed.

"I think so," he said, feeling the complete opposite. With her help, he stood, and though the world reeled at first, everything quickly settled down as he took a deep breath. The motion was accompanied by a nagging pain in his chest, and he reached down to hold his side.

"A rib, probably," Grayling said. "You were lucky that was the only thing you broke."

"Got to get out of here," he managed to say, and he found no argument from her.

"That's the easy part. Grab that man's sword. I don't know if there are others on this part of the wall, but we can't have gone unnoticed."

"Where are you going?"

Watching Grayling retrieve her dagger from the guard's chest, Lucius leaned heavily against the battlements, aware that the streets of Turnitia — and freedom — were just a few yards below on the other side. No other guards rushed their position and for this, he was grateful, as he did not think he could fight effectively in his current condition. Lucius yearned for a bed and a long rest, but steeled himself for just a little more discomfort before he could claim them.

Grayling had gone back to the rope and, wrapping her legs around it, pulled herself back along its length, hand over hand. After she had gone out a little distance, he saw her look back at the wall, as if sizing its dimensions. Then, taking the dagger from her mouth, she began to saw at the rope. Lucius frowned, as it seemed to him to be a remarkably foolish thing to cut a rope one was using for support. And sure enough, it snapped with an audible twang. Grayling dropped from view.

Stumbling to the edge of the rampart, Lucius looked down to see Grayling grinning up at him as she ascended the rope again. He leaned down to give her a hand as she threw a leg over the stone threshold, and instantly regretted it as pain lanced up his side.

As she stood next to him, Lucius looked at Grayling, the rope she held, and the wall.

"Don't get it," he said.

She rolled her eyes. "That fall robbed you of your senses. Watch."

Holding the rope in front of his face, she then threw it over the other side of the wall. It draped itself over the battlements to dangle gently just a few feet from street level.

"You see?" she said. "Simple."

CHAPTER 14

Hovering on the border of consciousness and deep sleep, Lucius was only barely aware as his imagination and dreams ruled his mind. He only dimly recalled the flight through the streets of the city, supported by Grayling as he stumbled, taking seemingly random turns as they tried to shake any attempt to follow them. There was no memory of arriving at the guildhouse, but images of mighty Shadowmages commanding vast hordes of creatures from the darkest depths of the sea ran riot, the dreaded demons sweeping through Turnitia, claiming it as their own. He thought his wounds were tended to by the smooth and soft hands of a dozen half-naked virgins, but they were soon replaced by the threads of power twisting around one another, before fusing into a terrible energy that burned his eyes and boiled his blood.

Lucius did not know how long he had lain like this, assaulted by confusing scenes and half-remembered dreams, but a cold, wet touch to his forehead made him groan as his mind slowly travelled through the mental fog, back to the real world. A quiet voice forced him to open his eyes, though he quickly half-closed them again as light flooded his vision.

"You're awake. Finally."

Wetting his lips, which suddenly felt deathly dry, Lucius tried to focus on the woman sitting next to his bed.

"Grayling," he managed to say.

"Indeed."

"We made it then."

She gave a short, humourless laugh. "You nearly didn't. You damaged more than a rib in that outrageous stunt. I had to virtually carry you the last quarter mile. We had to give you honeyleaf-dram to get you healthy again."

Lucius sighed. That, at least, explained why he had been barely sentient. The dram was known to induce fever, and in sufficient quantities, coma and death. But the Hands had long used it to aid the healing process. With other concoctions from the guild's laboratory, many serious injuries could be countered in a relatively short space of time, as the body's own mechanisms were accelerated. Widely used among the nobility of Pontaine, the dram was eschewed within the Empire of Vos, but the hands had learnt how to use it with only the merest chance of fatal results.

He coughed and accepted a mug of water from Grayling. Sitting up and taking a sip, he tried opening his eyes fully, and found his senses rapidly coming back to him, though he felt quite nauseous.

"How many got out?" he asked.

"Not enough. We've counted seven in so far, but I

do not expect there to be any more. There has been no word of hangings, so we are assuming the others were killed trying to escape."

"Well," Lucius said, then fell silent for a moment. "It beats a noose."

"Yes, it does. But Luber was one of those who did not come back."

"I'm sorry to hear that." Lucius had not known the man very well, but was surprised to discover that he *was* sorry. Sharing a cell with Luber, however briefly, had forged something of a bond. "We might not have escaped at all if it were not for him."

"Maybe," Grayling said, watching Lucius carefully. "Maybe not."

Lucius returned her gaze, becoming increasingly uncomfortable. This was a moment he had been hoping to avoid for some time yet, but it looked as though there was no way out.

"Listen, you and I have to talk. What you saw at the Citadel –"

"You're a Shadowmage, aren't you?" Grayling asked, her voice low and secretive. He also detected a hint of curiosity, and maybe wonder. "I had heard you had all been wiped out when Vos entered the city."

"I left. But others stayed, hiding."

"There are others?" she asked, a little too eagerly, and Lucius winced. This was not a wise conversation to have when his senses were still addled, he realised.

"I can't discuss this. But, Grayling, I beg of you –"

"It's our secret," she said, guessing his next words. "I know why you kept it hidden. Some of the others here are not ready to accept a wizard in the guild."

He shook his head. "I'm no wizard."

"If the stories are true, you are so much more."

"Well... some of those might have been exaggerated. Like thieves that can pass through solid walls, you know?"

Grayling nodded slowly. "Are there others in the Hands too? No, don't answer that. As I said in the Citadel, you can count on me. Mind you, I think the others might be more ready to accept you than you think. Especially now."

"Why, what's happened?" he asked, noting the change in her voice. He suddenly realised that the dram he had been given might well have knocked him insensible for longer than it had seemed. "How long was I out of it?"

"Three days."

"God." He tried to sit up and was pleased to discover that the pain lancing his side had been replaced by a dull ache. His head still swam though, and he took another sip of water to settle his stomach. It was only marginally successful. "Fill me in then. What's been going on?"

"They're calling it the Thieves War."

He sighed. "It's started."

"In a big way. Killings have spread across the city, and regular operations have all but ceased. Thieves are going round in groups, many with orders to do nothing more than hunt down those in the Guild. They have similar teams, and have been quite successful. We've lost nearly a quarter of our number already, and many are now too afraid to leave the guildhouse. There is a lot of talk about defecting. Of course, all of that just makes this place a bigger target."

He thought briefly of the twins, and the price they had already paid in all of this. "What about the pickpocket teams?"

"Ambrose has completely shut them down. It's just too dangerous. However, some have decided to go freelance, and others have been killed. Magnus sent enforcers to watch over them in the Five Markets, but that turned into a running battle with the Vos guard and more Guild men."

"Is there no good news?"

Her expression was grim. "None to speak of. We've had our victories, but they have been too small and too slow in coming. Caradoc succumbed to his wounds, never responded to the dram. They're talking about poison now. The docks have become a complete no-go area, at least in the dark hours. The thieves we had operating there have just disappeared. Bodies were found the next day, horribly mutilated, but we can only guess as to whether they are ours. The Guild must have hired real savages for that work. I am not sure what manner of man could do something like that."

"I think I know," he said quietly, but ignored her searching look. "What is the Council doing?"

"Panicking, mostly. At least, that is the word among the rest of us. Magnus told me to tell you that he is convening a council of war this afternoon, and your presence is requested if you are fit. I'm not sure though –"

"You can tell him I'll be there."

"I thought you might say that. You do need more rest though."

"I'll rest until the meeting. But this is more important. We're fighting for survival now."

When he walked into the Council Chamber, Lucius' first reaction was one of alarm. The large table that dominated the room seemed empty; only four seats were occupied. Magnus took his usual place, and had been joined by Elaine, Nate and the weather-beaten thief he had come to know as Wendric. Magnus' bodyguards, Taene and Narsell were standing behind the guildmaster, and Lucius had heard they had not left his side since the war began.

With so few member of the Council remaining it would appear that the Guild had been all too successful in its murderous campaign. Lucius found himself desperately hoping that others were engaged in secret missions for Magnus, that some plan was already being enacted that would secure final victory in this dirty war.

Magnus waved him forward, but the motion was slow and weary, and Lucius could see the strain and exhaustion the guildmaster was battling. He guessed Magnus had not seen his bed for the past three days.

"Lucius, good," Magnus said. "I had hoped you would be well enough to join us here. Are you fit enough for action?"

"I'm ready," Lucius said, without hesitation.

"The Hands are in need of every able-bodied thief now. I wanted you to take your place in this council of war, to advise and, if necessary, carry out the plans we make here. While you are not formally part of the Council itself, I believe that may only be a matter of time, to be resolved after this war is done. But that is something we need to set aside for now."

"Of course," Lucius said, surprised at the casual way the promotion had fallen into his lap. He forced himself to focus on the matter at hand.

"We have taken too many losses over the past few days, and it is clear that the Guild of Coin and Enterprise is much stronger than we gave them credit for," Magnus said.

"That may be true," said Wendric. "But it may just be they were better prepared to start a war. While we were concentrating on business, they were planning this from the start, picking targets and building alliances."

If Wendric's remarks were a reproach to Magnus' leadership, no one commented on it.

"We've got to start hitting back in a meaningful way," Nate said. "We've got to pick our own targets. Show the Guild we will not lie down quietly, that we are still to be reckoned with. At worse, we can slow down the assault. At best, we can deliver a killing blow."

"Jewel," Elaine said.

"That's right," Nate said. "They struck at our lieutenant, we must hit at theirs. Tit-for-tat. Loredo clearly prizes her. Removing Jewel will make him less sure, and it must at least damage his own standing within the Guild."

Wendric cleared his throat. "I'm... a little uneasy about that."

"Why?" Magnus asked.

"Well... if we meet Jewel on the street, if she is struck down during a battle, that is one thing. But to plan an assassination on a woman? It seems, distasteful in a way. Beneath us."

"Ha!" Elaine's bark preceded her incredulous gaze. "Best hope she is not assigned to take you down, Wendric. I doubt she will show you the same mercy!"

Lucius discovered that he had been swayed by Wendric's argument. He did not relish the thought of striking a woman down from the shadows. However, he thought of Adrianna and Grayling, women who were clearly at least as skilled as the men around them, and he had seen Jewel was a cold-blooded killer.

"I agree," he said. "Her reputation is well known, Wendric. How many of us is she already responsible for? It might well have been her who attacked Caradoc."

"I concur with Elaine and Lucius," Magnus said softly. "She must be removed. Elaine, with Agar gone, I am making you our Master of Assassins, temporarily at least. See to it."

"With pleasure." Elaine's easy, even grateful, acceptance sent a chill through Lucius, and he was once again reminded of the strength present in some women.

"So, where else is the Guild vulnerable?" Magnus asked.

"What of the Guild's alliance with the Vos guard?" Lucius asked. All eyes turned toward him, and he realised that none of the Council were aware of everything that had taken place during the raids in the merchant quarter.

"What alliance?" Nate asked suspiciously, and Lucius could see a tide of fear and doubt rising in the younger man.

"No one else reported it then?" Lucius asked, though he already knew the answer. He kicked himself, for he should have known that with so many of the raiding parties killed during the escape from the Citadel, the chances of one surviving who had seen the direct co-operation between guard and Guild were greatly diminished. Luber had seen it, but he had already paid the price.

"When the Guild responded to us in the merchant quarter, fights broke out in the streets," he explained. "It did not take the guard long to respond, and the area was soon full of patrols."

"Well, that would be as dangerous to the Guild as to us," Elaine said.

"No," Lucius said firmly, shaking his head. "They had code words. The Guild, I mean. I heard them. When the guard waded in, code words were being used to identify the Guild from us. When I saw what was happening, I told everyone to scatter. But the Guild started tracking us, and leading patrols onto our trail. It was hopeless."

Nate thumped a hand down onto the table in frustration.

"Well, that's it then," he said. "We can't fight the Guild *and* the Vos army!"

"Calm yourself, Nate," Magnus said smoothly, but they could all see he was troubled by this new revelation.

"Magnus, the Guild are already stronger than us," Nate said, suddenly very animated. "Maybe, just maybe, with a careful selection of targets and a great deal of planning, we can pull even with them. Maybe win. But there is no way we can send thieves against the Vos army. They know how to fight. It will just be a slaughter."

"So why not just wander over to Loredo and ask if he needs another thief?" Elaine said, caustically.

Nate looked hurt at that. "I'm just saying."

"One way or another, better or worse, I'll stand with you Magnus," Wendric said. "But Nate is not wholly wrong. The combination of a thieves guild and a city guard – especially one formed from the Vos army – is a dreadful thought. Even in peace time, they could completely shut us down. During a war..."

Lucius considered the sea demons the Guild also evidently had on their side, and he looked up at Magnus to find the guildmaster staring back at him. He thought that Magnus was perhaps thinking the same thing, that the Hands' position in the city was far less tenable than even the surviving Council members believed.

"Then it is obvious," Magnus finally said. They all looked at him with clear relief, clinging to the hope that their guildmaster would still be able to steer them through this difficult time. "If our enemies have built up their strength, then we must do the same. If they increase their reach by building alliances, then we must do the same."

Wendric frowned. "But who can we go to that would be both willing to support us, and provide us with real muscle?"

"We can pull mercenaries in from the Anclas Territories. Battle-hardened soldiers. We'll have to disguise their presence here in the city, but I fancy they will be a match for the Vos guard."

"Expensive though," Nate pointed out. "And we could never afford enough to swing the balance entirely."

"The vault does us no good if the Guild wins this war, no matter how full it remains," Elaine said in reply.

"That is true enough," Magnus said. "We filled the vault before, we can do so again – but only if we survive this war. As for numbers, it will be more important as to how and where we use such men. Our goal is not to launch a coup, remember, just to defeat the Guild or force them to terms. We only need employ mercenaries when we risk running into the Vos guard."

"I'll arrange it," Wendric said. "I have a few contacts I can tap for this."

"It will take time," Lucius said, recalling just how large the Anclas Territories were, and how long the journey to Turnitia could take. That was assuming a company could be persuaded to employment quickly.

"There is something else we can do," Magnus said. "Loredo is acting like a warlord, gathering as much strength in arms to his cause as he can muster.

Somewhere along the line, he has forgotten how to be a thief. That will be to our advantage."

"What do you mean?" Nate asked.

"A thief never confronts an enemy head on," Magnus explained. "Instead, he studies his mark, picks the weak points, bypasses the defences and traps. Only if absolutely necessary does he strike, and then only from the shadows."

"We avoid open battle?" Elaine asked. "Seems obvious."

"It is," Magnus said. "But to do so effectively, we need information. We all know this. Information is what drives a thieves guild, it's what ensures the flow of gold into the vault. We need access to better information – we need to know exactly what the Guild is up to at all times, what their ties to the Vos guard are, and what is happening within the Citadel itself."

"Ah, I see where you are going with this, Magnus," Wendric said. "But you cannot know whether they have not been bought already. They could already be working for the Guild."

Lucius was confused and, from Nate's expression, he was not the only one.

"Who are you talking about?" he asked.

"He wants to bring the Beggars Guild on side with us," Wendric said.

"The beggars?" Nate said derisively.

"Nate, the beggars are eyes of this city," Magnus said. "They are ignored by everyone, and yet they can be found in every corner of Turnitia. From the docks to the Five Markets, you will find them huddled, lost, abandoned and forgotten. But it is exactly those qualities that allow them to get close to others, to see and hear everything that goes on in the city. How many times have you left a house you have just robbed, and ignored the beggar across the street outside, happily thinking you have escaped notice? I promise you, nearly every one of your operations is known to the beggar's guild."

"They actually have a guild?" Lucius asked.

"Oh, there is quite some etiquette involved in begging," Magnus said. "And, like any industry, like us, efforts have to be organised if the maximum profit for all is to be realised. You've worked with our pickpocket teams, Lucius. You know how we strategize their efforts. The beggars are no different, with each assigned a rotating territory that ensures no one area is flooded with them, and no purses are drained too heavily or too quickly. And they can actually be quite vicious towards independents who break the system."

"Do they have a guildhouse?" Elaine asked.

"The streets are their guildhouse. However, I think I know where to find their master."

"You're not thinking of going yourself?" Wendric asked, suddenly alarmed.

"You'd be making yourself too easy a target," Elaine joined in. "The Guild will be waiting for something like this, one mistake that would reveal you and allow them to decapitate us."

Magnus held up his hands. "My friends, I will not be swayed in this. We need the beggars with us, and we need them now. If one of you were to go, the negotiations might take too long. If I can locate their guildmaster, and I have a good idea where to start looking, I might be able to make the right promises and forge an alliance on the spot."

"It is far too dangerous," Wendric said.

"Too many of our members have already paid too high a price," Magnus said in reply. "If I do not share the same risks, I am not fit to be guildmaster in the first place. Anyway, I'll have Taene and Narsell with me, and I doubt there are any assassins capable of making their way past these two. If that should prove insufficient, however, I will also have Lucius at my side."

Lucius looked up in surprise. "Of course," he heard himself say. "I would be honoured."

Wendric had the last words of the meeting.

"Be watchful instead."

CHAPTER 15

Lucius had never felt more alive than he did at this moment. Magnus walked within a pace behind him, while Taene and Narsell brought up the rear, flanking the guildmaster. He felt his heart pounding, heard every sound in the crowded street, smelled every scent. Danger lurked in every passerby, in every alley they passed, within every window that opened as they walked underneath, or so he felt. After the Council had broken up, Elaine had approached him, making him swear to protect Magnus from harm whatever the odds. It was a promise he intended to keep.

Lucius' eyes flicked constantly, sweeping over every member of the crowd that thronged the street. The middle-aged woman manhandling several long Pontaine-style loaves and two children; was she disguised to appear older, her bread concealing a weapon as she moved closer? The kids, were they lookouts, gauging the guildmaster's defences in preparation for an ambush at the next junction? Were those Vos guards intentionally flanking them? Was that a shadow on the roofline, an assassin lining up a shot with a crossbow?

More than once, he had felt Magnus' hand on his shoulder, accompanied with an admonishment to relax or, at least calm down a degree. Magnus had taken precautions, wearing a cloak and wide-brimmed hat to disguise his appearance. To anyone casually walking past the tight, protective group, he might well have been no more than a wealthy trader or official with an exaggerated sense of self-worth. Even so, the mail shirt he wore under his cloak and leather tunic was an added insurance.

They had started their search in the Five Markets which, in Lucius' opinion, was close to madness. The ever-shifting crowds and sheer number of potential threats seemed overwhelming, and he noticed that even Taene and Narsell seemed nervous, their eyes in a permanent suspicious squint, heads turning to face every new sound. Looming over them were the walls of the Citadel, and Lucius could all too easily imagine some guard perched on the ramparts, sighting Magnus and feeling lucky with a crossbow.

Magnus, however, insisted that this is where they start, and he made a rough kind of sense. The Five Markets were among the busiest places in the city, and it was a natural congregation point for beggars. They were, thus, the power centre of the beggars and their presumed guild, though Lucius still had doubts about the homeless being able to organise themselves to any great degree.

Insisting on approaching any beggar directly himself, Magnus was met with suspicion at first, and sometimes a subdued hostility. They all feared the beggars had already been bought by the Guild. However, Magnus was lucky enough to be recognised by one – a foul-smelling woman in the later years of her life – who had a disturbing habit of scratching at her nether regions while holding a hand out for coin. Her directions, which Magnus paid handsomely for, led them to Ring Street and a grain house that lay between the two southern markets.

Crates and empty sacks were piled outside and these had been appropriated by nearly a dozen beggars, all looking dishevelled, miserable, and without purpose. A memory triggered in Lucius' mind, and he recalled seeing beggars gather here before. In the past, he had presumed they were the failures of the city's lowest citizens, those whose begging had been less than successful, and were now just waiting around to die. However, if what the old woman had told Magnus was to be believed, Lucius was in fact looking at the power base of the Beggars Guild.

"They don't look much," he muttered, and felt Magnus' hand on his shoulder again.

"That is their strength," Magnus said. "Now, remember why we are here, and that we need their help. Beggars are outcasts, spurned by everyone, and so they expect no favours. But we must treat them with the utmost respect. Understand?"

Lucius nodded as he followed Magnus and the bodyguards as they approached the beggars. It was hard to identify some of them as men or women, but Lucius had the feeling they were a mix of both, young and old. Some slouched against piles of sacks made into makeshift beds, while others perched on top of crates. All seemed weary, and yet they regarded the entourage of thieves with guarded suspicion.

"Greetings," Magnus began, holding up a hand.

"You've got no business here, sir, best you move along," said one, a girl Lucius thought, though there was nothing feminine about her appearance.

"On the contrary, I believe there is business that would interest everyone here."

"We're not looking for work, so if you have a ship or wagon train that needs unloading, go find your cheap labour elsewhere."

"You misunderstand me –"

"It's okay Grennar," said one of the men sitting cross-legged on the crates. He was wreathed in rags, and Lucius had taken him for a leper, or worse. He drew back his hood to reveal a middle-aged face, dirty, unshaven, but otherwise remarkably healthy. "I think we can dispense with the deceptions this time. Magnus here is finding time rather against him at the moment. Is that not right, Magnus?"

"You know me?"

"We know everyone," the man said with a sly smile. "That is why you are here, is it not?"

Magnus tipped his head in acknowledgement. "You have me at a disadvantage."

"I know you are Magnus Wry, leader of the Night Hands and former lieutenant of the Thieves Guild of Turnitia. You already know my position among the beggars. But you may call me Sebastian."

"I have a proposal for an alliance."

"Of course you have," Sebastian said, his voice warm but his eyes betraying a coldness. "Your little den of thieves stands on the brink of annihilation, and you find many powerful enemies allied against you. You, Magnus, are desperate."

"And you are on the outside, Sebastian," Magnus said. "The lowest of all in the city, ignored by everyone. Only I realise your true value."

"So, we have your respect. Well, that is... nice." The comment drew a small swell of laughter from the beggars, and Lucius saw Magnus turn to him, rolling his eyes at the contrived play between the two guildmasters.

"I can give you a great deal more than respect. Employment. Regular income. Work for all the members of your guild."

"We already have work," said Sebastian. "And many of my beggars are richer than many of your thieves. Show him, Grennar."

The girl smiled up at them, revealing a set of perfect teeth, then reached to her face to pick at a boil. Lucius stomach turned in disgust, then his eyes opened wide as he saw her peel the boil off. She repeated the action several more times, then spat on a cloth and wiped the dirt away, revealing a not unattractive face. Sebastian noted Lucius' look of surprise.

"It is all about deception," he said. "And yes, we know you too Lucius Kane, once exile of this city, returned a gambler, now rising star among the Night Hands – whatever *that* future is worth. We know your secrets too. We have seen how you fight the men you cheat, and the... methods you employ."

Lucius looked up at the beggar master in alarm, but kept his face neutral.

"You see, Lucius, we are not thieves or blackmailers. We have no interest in power, territory, or fame. So long as the city continues to exist, so will we. Our guild offers protection and a livelihood to the lowest, the most humble. That is why we are here, and that is the only thing we work towards."

"We can help you," Magnus said.

"It seems you are the one in need of help, Magnus," said Sebastian. "Alliances, you see, are built on mutual goals. You are currently engaged in a war, one that you are losing. The bodies of your members are found every night in dark alleys, and your numbers shrink daily. And now the Vos army itself has targeted you for destruction. Why would we want any part of that? I have no wish to see my own people decimated in retaliation."

"The risks to you would be minimal. No active operations. Just information, a regular flow. That is all."

"The role of a spy can be the riskiest of all."

"I suspect you already have much of the information we require," Magnus said. "You need do little more than you do now. As you said, your guild comprises the lowest and most humble. You are all but invisible to our enemies – else they would have approached you already."

"What makes you think they haven't?" Sebastian asked.

"I know Loredo. I know how he thinks."

Sebastian shrugged. "Not completely useless then."

"In return, I offer you ten per cent of our guild's takings over the next five years. After that, we review the arrangement, see whether it is still beneficial to the two of us."

Lucius stifled a sharp intake of breath. That ten percent would cut deep into the franchise agreements within the Hands, and he could imagine plenty of thieves loathe to share their ill-gotten gains with beggars.

"Plus, we can train any member of yours that wishes to become a thief," Magnus finished.

Sebastian hooted at that, and that encouraged laughter from the rest of his entourage. "I already told you, Magnus, many of the beggars in this city are wealthier than your thieves. And I won't have you sap my guild's strength to bolster your own."

"Then stop playing, Sebastian," Magnus said, allowing impatience to creep into his voice. "What are you after? You already knew I was coming to see you, and if I did not have something you were interested in, we would not have got this far. So, what is it?"

Pursing his lips, Sebastian looked down at Magnus as if considering his options.

"The ten per cent I'll take," he said. "Though only for one year. You will have trouble enough keeping your thieves in line for that arrangement, and you won't get them to agree to it for long when the danger has passed. Maybe we will continue the alliance thereafter, maybe not. It all depends on which guild earns more during that time."

"Agreed."

"Furthermore, you will give us the Five Markets."

Magnus frowned. "I thought you said you weren't interested in territory."

"Oh, we're not," Sebastian said smoothly. "But visitors to the Five Markets all come with a finite amount of coin in their purses. Most they will spend, but some they give to the poor, starving beggars that walk among them. However, a man who has just been robbed has neither the ability nor the inclination for charity, and your pickpockets have become too good at what they do."

"That is too much to ask."

"It makes perfect sense. It is a small price to pay for our support. And what you are doing in the Five Markets is not good for business. People become tighter with their money, the guard move us on that much quicker. It's bad business, Magnus, you only have the greed of your thieves to blame."

Exhaling noisily, Magnus eventually nodded. "For the duration of one year only, Sebastian. I'll withdraw our teams from the Five Markets tomorrow, but they come up for negotiation again when we discuss the continuance of our alliance."

Sebastian, still crouched on his crate, looked down at Magnus imperiously for a moment, then smiled.

"Then we have an understanding. I'll arrange for one of us to report to your guildhouse daily. We'll update you with anything learned, and you can suggest where we concentrate our efforts."

"Good enough," said Magnus. "I presume you already know where our guildhouse is."

He received a look of scorn for his trouble. "Magnus, we already know the knock code to gain entry through your own front door."

"Of course you do," Magnus muttered, and Lucius guessed that the system would be changed wholesale that very night. "Who will be our liaison?"

"Grennar, I think. She is most suited to the task." Magnus looked doubtfully down at the young girl, who stared back defiantly. "Don't let her tender years mislead you, Magnus. She is probably smarter than both of us."

Magnus shrugged. "Fine. Send her to us tonight."

"She'll be there," Sebastian said. "One other thing, a down payment on our side of the bargain. Have a care as you walk about the city, Magnus. Your enemies know you have left the guildhouse, and that disguise is not going to fool anyone"

Lucius looked up at Sebastian in alarm. "How do they know?"

"The Guild's own spy network is not as extensive as ours, but it's still shrewd enough. Loredo is playing his own game at the moment, pulling on the Vos army for muscle and information, while giving as little in return as possible – Grennar will tell you what we have learned there later. But, for now, be careful. Assassins are on the streets looking for you."

"We should go, quickly," Lucius said, turning to Magnus. He glanced at Taene and Narsell, and saw both had their hands on their weapons and were already scanning the nearby crowds for danger.

Magnus agreed, then faced the beggars. "Sebastian, a pleasure."

The beggar master nodded once. "Just make sure you stay in one piece. I don't want to have this conversation with Loredo down the line."

Taene and Narsell hustled them away from Ring Street, choosing quieter side roads and the wider alleys in an effort to avoid crowds. Now their mission was done, there was no need to take unnecessary risks, and the bodyguards placed themselves ahead and behind Magnus and Lucius.

"That was an expensive agreement," Lucius said cautiously.

"It could have been far more costly," Magnus said. "I was expecting him to demand a portion of the vault from the outset, as it will take time for our operations to reach their full potential again, even if this war is won quickly with the minimum of bloodshed. But I think he had already fixed his sights on the Five Markets."

"Ambrose will not be happy with that, nor will the others involved in the pick-pocketing."

"The Five Markets represent a higher cost than that, Lucius," Magnus said. "They are a magnet for everyone in the city, be they resident or visitor. The pickpocket teams are where we have always trained the youngest among us, bringing fresh blood into the guild on a regular basis. Now, those children will become beggars, while we must look elsewhere for recruits. That is the true value of the territory."

Lucius had not considered that, and it began to dawn on him just how complicated the structure of these negotiations could become. Narsell, leading them down a narrow street lined with tanners, ironmongers and other tradesmen, suddenly hissed, and Lucius looked up to see a patrol of Vos guard rounding the junction ahead. They steered right, heading down a short alley behind a carpenters but, as they emerged into the parallel street, they saw another patrol just a few dozen yards away.

"That's no coincidence," Magnus muttered, and Lucius felt the tension rise in both Narsell and Taene. They headed away from the patrols, directly back to Ring Street, with Lucius reaching beneath his cloak to feel the reassuring presence of his sword. They could see the crowds churning along Ring Street just a little distance ahead, but the Vos patrol had already changed its course to follow them, and they were not being discrete about it.

"Get ready to run," Narsell whispered, and Lucius saw him raise a hand in preparation for the signal to take action. Before he could give it, two groups of men stumbled out of opposite alleyways ahead of them, some singing drunkenly, others stumbling as they clutched bottles.

The timing of their appearance set Lucius on edge, and he felt in his stomach that these were no mere revellers in search of another tavern. Magnus and the bodyguards had stopped, and Taene's blade was half drawn. Lucius looked back at the Vos guards, who had not quickened their pace, but still continued towards them relentlessly. If the drunks proved hostile, they were cut off from any path of escape, but he did not relish trying to smash through the soldiers while fleeing.

"Carry on," Magnus urged. "We'll do better with the drunks than the guard."

They moved to obey, and watched as the two groups of men merged with one another, laughing and slapping one another on the back, seemingly oblivious to the four thieves marching warily toward them. However, Lucius had already noted one or two sidelong gazes directed their way, and knew then they were in for trouble.

A woman strode out from among the press of men and, too late, Lucius recognised her as Jewel. He opened his mouth to cry out, but Narsell and Taene were already reacting, drawing their swords and moving to shield Magnus. She raised a small one-handed crossbow and tightened her grip on the lever. Lucius heard a quiet whistle through the air, then Narsell collapsed to the ground, a short bolt protruding from his throat.

Jewel grinned as she dropped the crossbow and drew a dagger from her belt. The men behind her whooped in excitement, and a range of daggers and short blades appeared in their hands. Led by Jewel, they charged.

Taene showed no fear, and little regard for his own life as he met the attack. Side stepping one man and kicking out at another, his sword claimed two lives within seconds, and the deaths checked the momentum of the charge. He was soon fighting for his life, but he always manoeuvred to keep himself between Magnus and the bulk of the pack.

For his part, Magnus had already drawn his own weapon, a finely balanced short sword, but Lucius grabbed him and propelled the guildmaster forward, hoping to break through the gang and then disappear into the crowds just a couple of hundred yards ahead on Ring Street. He glanced over his shoulder and saw the patrol had stopped, evidently happy to let the thieves kill one another before moving in.

"Go!" Taene shouted as he fell under a swarm of bodies, his sword reappearing momentarily as it continued to hack down at those around him. Blood was already flowing across the cobbles of the street but Lucius knew the bodyguard's skill and luck would not save him in that tight press.

The rest of the Guild men, frustrated at not being able to reach Taene because of the press of bodies surrounding him, broke off from the fight and ran to cut off Magnus and Lucius from escape. Knowing he could not fight them all, Lucius cursed as he shoved the guildmaster behind him. He felt the threads of power respond to his call and he grabbed one whose energy was deeply familiar. This time, however, he allowed the thread to spiral and grow until he could barely contain the form he moulded it to in his mind. With a loud cry, he brought his arm down in a wide sweep, and felt the energy pass through his body to push the air away from him in an explosive burst.

Hit by an unyielding wall of wind, the men were tossed back, sprawling on the ground as they lay stunned and gasping for breath. Breathing heavily from the exertion, Lucius staggered as he grabbed Magnus again to spur him on, trying desperately to ignore the look of suspicious amazement in the man's face.

They started to run, feet pounding the street, each step taking them further from the murderous crowd behind. Magnus cried out, and Lucius felt the man stumble against him, the weight almost pulling him down to the ground. Catching his balance, Lucius turned to get Magnus back on his feet, and saw a slender knife embedded deep in the back of his thigh. Blood oozed slowly from the wound, but Lucius knew that, as deep as the blade had gone, the flow would quickly speed up if the weapon was removed.

"Lucius!" Magnus shouted the warning, even as he scrambled to one side, Lucius sensed motion beside him. Ducking low and rolling backwards, he grabbed for the sword at his back even as another blade sliced through the air between them.

He jumped to his feet, and saw Jewel standing just a few feet from him, her eyes narrowed to slits as she watched them both, judging which to be the greater threat. Her face remained flat and expressionless, betraying no emotion whatsoever. She apparently decided that, with Magnus already wounded and struggling to get to his feet, Lucius was her priority. Covering the distance between them in two easy strides, she swiped through the air with her sword, as if testing his reactions; she then crouched low and whirled round in a circle, the blade building momentum as it spun towards his shins.

Lucius sprang back, then held his sword forward defensively, as if warding the woman back. Rising to her full height again, Jewel drew a dagger from her belt. Lucius stabbed forward, but a casual flick of her dagger turned his blade, holding it to one side as her own sword was held aloft for an instant, then brought down to slash his skull in two.

Off balance from her parry, but seeing the danger, Lucius reached up and grabbed her wrist, surprised at her sinewy strength as he strained to keep her sword clear.

He tried to muster his strength to drive Jewel down, wanting to pin her to the ground where his weight would give him the advantage, but she yielded only an inch at a time. Straining with the effort, he suddenly felt the air driven out of his lungs as her knee drove hard into his groin. A spilt second later, his world exploded into stars of pain as her forehead smashed into the bridge of his nose.

Sightless and writhing in agony, Lucius felt the ground rise up to hit him hard. Expecting to feel Jewel's blade pierce his heart at any moment, he shook his head to clear his vision as he tried to get to his knees.

The world blurred in front of him, then suddenly sharpened into stark reality. Jewel's back was toward him as she strode toward Magnus. The guildmaster was limping badly as he tried to circle her, his own weapon held before him. As she slashed her sword at his chest, he met the attack, and a loud ringing of metal echoed off the buildings along the street as their weapons met. Immediately, Jewel drew her sword back and thrust forward again, only to be turned by a desperate parry from Magnus.

Lucius tried to get to his feet but stumbled and he started crawling toward Magnus and Jewel, desperate to aid his friend before the murderess could finish him. He could see Magnus was in a lot of pain, and Jewel was forcing him to keep moving, every step forcing the dagger in the back of his leg to grind against bone. Their swords met again, and Magnus was forced to give more ground, fighting purely defensively, with Jewel giving him no opportunity to attack.

Drawing a ragged breath, Lucius was finally able to force air into his lungs, and he used his sword as a brace to get him back on his feet. He caught Magnus' eye, and a look flicked between them. Magnus hobbled to the left, bringing Jewel round with him, so her back was kept to Lucius. Lifting his sword, Lucius staggered toward her, fixing his gaze between her shoulder blades, where he intended to plant his weapon and so rid the Hands of this dreadful enemy.

Magnus roared as he thrust his sword forward, as much to distract Jewel as score a hit, and the woman easily side-stepped his attack. Lucius was closing on her now and he began to run, painful though the movement was. He raised his sword, its point aimed squarely at her back, and prepared to thrust down with all his remaining strength.

Jewel turned and flung her left arm out, releasing her dagger. It was a hasty attack, but the spinning blade still thumped home into Lucius' right arm. He cried out in pain as his sword fell from suddenly lifeless fingers, his left hand instinctively grasping the wound.

He bent down to fumble for his sword, but looked up as Jewel whirled back to Magnus, her foot lashing out to strike him on his wounded leg. The shock of the impact was enough to make Magnus cry out in pain and he reeled backwards, tripping on the cobbles.

"No!" Lucius cried out as he saw the inevitability of her next action. Jewel calmly thrust her sword through Magnus' chest. The guildmaster coughed blood as he tried to grasp the blade that had ploughed through his chest bone, then he fell limp.

Anger and deadly fury swept through Lucius now, as he saw Jewel casually withdraw her sword and wipe it on Magnus' cloak. Then, she turned back to him.

"Bitch!"

He was not aware of his cry of vengeance, feeling only the threads of power surging forward, each eager to be clasped by his mind and moulded by his rage. Without thinking, he grabbed the brightest and hurled its force, unchecked and barely formed, at the woman.

A burst of argent fire soared from the fist he punched at her, the ball of white hot energy burning the air itself as it shot forth. He saw Jewel's eyes widen a fraction as the magic surged toward her, and she flinched to one side as the silver flames swept past her face. She shrieked with pain and the smell of burnt flesh rolled over him.

Recoiling backwards and dropping her sword, Jewel clutched at her face, the whole left side having been blackened and scorched by the magical fire. Her hair burned and her ear had been shrivelled by the heat. She took only seconds to recover, and then stared back at Lucius, emotion coming to her ruined face for the first time. He felt her loathing, her fury and terrible desire to inflict pain upon him, and he stood to wait the inevitable, having no energy for anything else.

Just as quickly, the hate fled from her eyes, and they flickered down to the corpse at her feet. Seeing no movement, she nodded to herself once, then turned, and walked away. She called out to the men still standing, and they followed her, leaving only bodies lying in the bloody street.

Lucius was alone. Narsell and Taene lay still ahead of him, the latter barely recognisable after having been all but torn apart by the Guild men. He knelt down beside Magnus, hoping beyond hope that he would still feel a pulse in the guildmaster's veins. Magnus, however, had already left.

CHAPTER 16

Upon his arrival, the guildhouse erupted into turmoil. Lucius had entered the building, his face betraying no emotion other than a hard, frozen shock. Taking a place in the common room, questions and accusations rolled over him like the gigantic waves pounding at the harbour defences but, like the monolithic breakers that stalled the ocean, he remained immovable.

The absence of Magnus, Taene and Narsell spoke volumes, and every thief present knew something had gone tragically wrong. Without explanation from Lucius, rumour and paranoia ran rampant, with scare stories growing ever more fantastic and yet all the more plausible for it. Within a few minutes, there were a good number of thieves who believed the Vos guard had marched onto the streets with lists detailing all their names, and were seeking to murder every one of them.

Calm was not restored until Elaine entered the common room and, upon seeing Lucius, she ordered everyone to leave. Many seemed ready to protest her authority now the guildmaster was dead, but her withering look broke any resistance.

Sitting opposite Lucius, she stared across the table at him, the silence of the empty common room seeming almost deafening to him. She reached out to touch his hand and asked him what had happened. Haltingly, he told her. The finding of Sebastian and the alliance forged between thief and beggar. The presence of the Vos guard on the streets, and the ambush by Guild men.

Jewel. Terrible, deadly Jewel.

He fell silent when his tale was complete, and Elaine had no words. They sat together, in silence as they brooded and mourned, contemplating the loss of their guildmaster and what the Guild would now do to finish them off.

Lucius found his own melancholy a little puzzling. He had liked Magnus, of course – who hadn't? He had been a good leader, quick to spot talent and loyalty, and ready to reward both. What Lucius had not counted on was how much the Night Hands had become his new home and family, how much Magnus had really meant to him.

Part of the hurt, he knew, was his own failure to stop the assassination, and now anger boiled within him too. He clung on to that feeling knowing that in the trials ahead, it would prove useful.

Elaine reached across the table to touch him again, this time shaking him firmly out of his darker thoughts.

"Pull yourself together, Lucius," she said. "Magnus trusted you, and so I must too. We are about to fall apart, and we need all the strength we can muster to stop us breaking."

He looked up at her mutely for a moment, then nodded.

"There will be a meeting," she said. "It will be chaotic, so be prepared."

Elaine had not been wrong. With the Council decimated and Magnus gone, anarchy began to take hold within the Night Hands. The council chamber barely contained the riot as the voices of dozens of thieves, all packed into the inadequate space, competed with one another to be heard.

The remaining Council took seats around the table; Elaine, Wendric, Nate, and now Lucius. Some of the thieves forced to stand raised objections to Lucius' presence at the table, but a sharp word from Elaine silenced their criticisms.

Grennar was also at the table, at Lucius' side, and her transformation was remarkable. No longer a young beggar girl wreathed in rags, she sat straight and appeared utterly confident. Dressed in a tight fitting blue gown, she might have been the daughter of a wealthy city official. Most stunning was her face; sharp, lightly freckled, once clean it revealed a girl of perhaps no more than fourteen. Her young age was a great surprise to the Council, some of whom had wondered out loud whether the beggars were taking them seriously. However, Magnus' posthumous endorsement of the alliance proved sufficient for them to invite her to the table.

Before the table, other members of the Hands jostled for position, seeking to get themselves heard. Each with a different idea of how the guild should continue, or not. Of how they could take instant vengeance, or not. One viciously planted a dagger into the table, promising that if the Council were too weak to take the fight to the enemy, others were not.

The overall mood, however, was one of despondent failure, a feeling that the time of the Night Hands was at an end. Most expected the guild to be disbanded in this meeting.

Clearing his throat, Wendric silenced the bickering thieves and all eyes turned toward him.

"As you will have all heard by now, Magnus has been slain by the Guild. The Council has heard Lucius' explanation of what happened, and we are satisfied that he is in no way at fault." At this, Lucius heard someone mutter at the back of the chamber, but he did not catch what was said, and Wendric ignored the interruption. "It was a calculated ambush aided, in part, by the Vos guard. It would have taken a small army to save Magnus. The guildmaster knew the risks when he left this place to forge a new alliance. It is now our duty to continue in his footsteps, to lead the Night Hands to become the kind of organisation for thieves that he always envisioned."

"Well, what's the point?" cried one thief, an old man whose hands shook as he spoke. "We're beaten. With Magnus and God knows how many others gone, the guild is broken!"

"You thinking we should all just roll over and join Loredo, is that it, Hengit?" called out another.

"We split up!" Hengit said, smacking a fist into his palm. "We all go independent. The Guild will never be able to track all of us!"

"Oh, they will," Elaine said, bringing attention back to those around the table. "You can be sure of that. They will track each one of you down and either force you to join their Guild or kill you. If we divide our strength –"

"What's left of it!"

"Yes, Hengit, what is left of it," Elaine said, her anger directed solely at the old thief for a moment. "If we break up the Hands now, we all die. Or, worse, work for a pittance under Loredo. You think he will just welcome you with open arms? He will mistrust all of you, your careers will be broken, doing the worst jobs and taking part in the riskiest operations. No, Hengit, you are far better off among the Night Hands, however long we last."

"And how long will that be, then?" called a voice from the back of the chamber.

"That is what we are here to decide," said Nate. "Elaine, your hit on Jewel clearly did not work as planned."

Elaine sighed audibly. "No. She was spotted on the streets near the merchant quarter but when our agents moved in... well, she either expected their arrival or is far more dangerous than we credited her with."

"What were our losses?" Wendric asked.

"Total." Elaine's simple answer triggered a collective intake of breath throughout the assembled crowd. The assassins employed by the Hands were experts in their field, trained killers capable of evading guards, traps and other defences in order to strike a target down within seconds. For a single woman to not only escape their attentions but strike back so effectively was a stunning achievement.

"After dispatching our agents, she was then able to gather her forces and take down Magnus. We don't know whether it was a chance encounter, or if they knew where Magnus was –"

"They knew," said Grennar. Her voice cut over Elaine's easily and with a measure of grace. In another time, Lucius might have smiled at the ease with which the girl spoke to the thieves but, at this moment, he simply listened as if she were the equal of any in the chamber. In that, he was not alone.

"The Vos army has its own network of spies in the city," Grennar went on to explain. "When Magnus was spotted on the streets, word was quickly passed to the Guild, and the ambush set. Once the guard was used to funnel your guildmaster into a predetermined area, there was nothing anyone could do."

In saying that, she cast a brief look at Lucius.

"So if the Guild has the Vos guard in their pocket, why have they not just finished us off completely?" Nate asked. "It is what I would do. Why not just launch an assault against this guildhouse and wipe us out in one stroke?"

Nate's question had been on everyone's mind and hearing it voiced caused some to start shuffling their feet and looking over their shoulders, as if expecting to see the entire Vos army crash through the door of the council chamber.

"Because Loredo is no fool," Grennar said, and Lucius saw Nate colour slightly as the girl looked at him. "Because the Vos guard have *no idea* where your guildhouse is."

"Well, that doesn't make sense," Wendric said. "The Vos guard won't see themselves as junior members in that partnership. They will want to run the Guild, not the other way around."

"That is exactly what Loredo fears."

"If the Hands fall and only the Guild remains, Loredo wants to retain his independence," Elaine said. "He does not want his thieves to become stooges for the Empire."

"Exactly," Grennar said. "He is playing a dangerous, but – it has to be said – clever game. He has brought the Vos guard onto his side, and that is a powerful ally for any thieves' guild to have, normally only possible in the most corrupt Pontaine cities. He is playing things down the middle, taking what support he can easily get from the guard, while giving them as little information as possible."

"The guard cannot be happy with that," said Nate.

"The Captain of the Guard, von Minterheim, was seen raging in the Citadel this morning. He has been telling his sergeants to lean on their Guild contacts, to start squeezing them for information. He wants this war over quickly, as it is beginning to make the merchants nervous. If they decide it is safer and more profitable to start trading in another city, Vos' hold on Turnitia is weakened."

Nate gave Grennar a strange look. "And how, exactly, does the Beggars Guild know what is happening within the Citadel?"

She shrugged. "As we told your guildmaster and Lucius here, we have eyes everywhere."

"In the Citadel?"

"Beggars can go where others cannot. No one sees us, and so if a few beggars remain in the courtyard after a hanging or two, well they will be thrown out eventually, but no one is going to hurry to do it."

"Magnus was right about you," Wendric said quietly, and Lucius could see the man had a new appreciation of their ally, despite her young age.

"So where does that leave us?" another voice in the crowd asked.

"Without much time," Elaine answered. "If von Minterheim is pressuring Loredo, he will be forced to move quickly. He doubtless feels we are crippled and defenceless, so his end game will start soon."

"One thing is certain; he will want this guildhouse," Wendric said. "There are too many treasures and secrets within these walls for him to ignore."

"A direct assault, then?" Nate asked.

"That will come sooner or later," Elaine said. "The streets will become no-go areas for all of us first. And if they discover our relationship with the beggars..."

"Don't worry about us," Grennar said. "We would not enter an agreement with you if it meant suicide. Our presence will be kept hidden, one way or another."

"In that case, we go fully defensive," Elaine said. "We lock down the guildhouse, use only the sewers when moving about the city, and stay away from the areas the Guild controls best – the docks and merchant quarter. This place, we fortify. We'll get our trapsmiths to work and plunder the armoury for weapons."

"Just sit and wait?" Wendric asked.

"We cannot fight them directly," Elaine pointed out. "They are too many. However, if we know they have to come here, and our friends among the beggars can tell us when, then we regain an advantage. Superior numbers will mean nothing when the fight is on our territory."

"There is a sense in that," a thief said in support.

"We can ensure that any enemy trying to breach these walls, be they thieves or guard, will be hip deep in their own blood within minutes."

"That is no way to gain victory," Wendric said.

"The first task is to survive. Once we can prove we can defend ourselves, once we show the Guild that they cannot wipe us out without sustaining untenable losses, their attacks will stall."

"I agree," said Nate. "Once we break the back of their main assault, then we can think about hitting back. If we prolong this long enough, their alliance with the Vos guard may break down. Without that support, it is the Guild that becomes vulnerable."

"It would be ironic if the guard then decided all thieves were its enemy," Elaine said, thinking through the course ahead. "Suddenly, it is the Guild that is the most visible, while we are hidden here. When the guard starts hitting back at thieves, they will be targeting the Guild. How long will it be before the Guild is reduced in strength to our level? Suddenly, things become even!"

A ragged cheer went through the crowd, though only a handful of thieves added to it.

"That is pretty fanciful," Wendric said.

"Yes, of course it is," Elaine said. "What is important is that we realise that there are many other options open to us, so long as we can survive the next few days. We can make this guildhouse near impregnable. We can play the waiting game now – the Guild cannot."

Seeing Nate nod in agreement, Wendric looked down the table. "So, we have a consensus?"

"No."

Lucius had been brooding, following only the gist of the debate at times. He leaned on one elbow as he sat in thought. He was only faintly aware that he had uttered his disagreement, and it was the silence that followed that shook his attention back to the chamber, as the assembled thieves waited for his next words.

Looking down the table, he saw Wendric raise his eyebrows in surprise, while Nate frowned in frustration. He tried hard to ignore the dangerous look Elaine flashed him, there only for a second, but no less threatening for all that.

"Make your preparations," he said. "Build the defences you suggest round the guildhouse. Whether necessary or not, they are certainly prudent. And yes, I agree that no one should leave unless on absolutely essential business. You will need the manpower anyway to defend this place. But I do not suggest that we simply sit here, waiting for the hammer to fall. That, it seems to me, would be a very foolish thing to do."

"So, what do you suggest?" Elaine asked, and he could sense the coldness in voice, the faint warning that now was not the time for the Council to be divided, that they could not risk the Hands disbanding.

Laying his hands flat on the table, Lucius sat straight in his seat, staring at the wood between them. He thought of the attack on Magnus, the guildmaster cut down in the street like an animal. He remembered Markel and Treal, two children who had been butchered by the Guild, just to make a point. The disaster at the docks, and the inhuman allies the Guild had apparently gained, still a secret to those in this chamber. Too much blood, too much killing, and for what? So one group of thieves could run the city the way they saw fit?

It ended here.

"I say we attack."

The suggestion was met with silence, and Lucius continued, his voice even, measured, dangerous. "We have little else to lose, and they will be at their most confident. We hit them. We hit all of them. We start with Loredo, Jewel, von Minterheim, and work down from there. We kill their leaders, their senior thieves, the guard sergeants, and anyone else who gets in the way. We pay them back for the blood they have stolen from us, drop for drop. In one evening, we finish this war."

Silence reigned in the room, until Nate coughed, then laughed.

"I see," he said. "We just kill them all. Why didn't we think of that?"

"Lucius, we have already tried to hit Jewel, and it failed. Badly," said Wendric.

"Then we do it properly this time."

"And von Minterheim as well?" Elaine asked. "You suggest we just walk into the Citadel and assassinate the military leader of the city?"

"Yes," he said. "That is exactly what I propose."

Elaine threw up her hands in disbelief. "And how do you propose we accomplish this great night of murder?"

"It's war, Elaine, not murder," Lucius said. "Never forget that. This is how we avenge Magnus, Caradoc and everyone else taken from us."

He stopped for a moment, then cleared his throat. "I'll make an agreement with you, Elaine. You carry on with your preparations here at the guildhouse. If we fail to end this war, your plan will be the only one open to us anyway. I will take care of von Minterheim. This evening."

"By yourself?" Nate asked incredulously.

"I won't require any of you to come with me," Lucius said. He managed not to sound evasive, but he already had an idea of who he could go to for help. "If I succeed, the guard will be thrown into chaos, at least temporarily, and their ties to the Guild will be weakened."

"This sounds like madness," Nate said.

"I would listen to him, if I were you," said Grennar. "If I were all of you. If anyone here can reach the Captain of the Vos guard, I think it is Lucius."

"I agree," said another woman, and Lucius saw Grayling throw a quick wink at him. "Though if he does need any help, I will gladly volunteer for that mission."

He smiled back, but shook his head slowly. *No*, his gesture said, it would be too dangerous for an ordinary thief. Silently, she nodded in understanding.

"If I fail, then you will have lost nothing," Lucius continued, turning his attention back to Elaine. "If I reach him, we go on the attack tomorrow evening. I'll form the team to strike at Loredo and Jewel myself. The other targets we will divide up amongst us. Grennar, the beggars will act as spotters, watching the Guild's movements so we can be ready to strike at Loredo when the guard are at their most distracted."

"They won't be able to sneeze without one of us being nearby to see it," Grennar said. "When the time comes, we'll have your target in our sights."

As arguments between the thieves began to break out, some supporting Lucius' bold plan, others counselling caution, Lucius looked down the table at the other members of the Council.

"Do we have an agreement?"

Wendric looked sideways at Elaine. "We have little to lose. Without being callous about it, we risk only one man."

"I think this is the last time I may see you, Lucius," Elaine said. "But if there is the slightest chance you can succeed... it is an appealing idea. Nate, what say you?"

"I still think it is madness," Nate muttered.

"Then we are agreed," Elaine said, her voice suddenly hard and sure, carrying across the crowded council chamber. "We will start our reprisal this evening."

Lucius stood. "I must prepare."

As he strode out of the council chamber, he ignored the looks the thieves threw him, ranging from outright support to complete mistrust. His mind was fixed firmly on reaching von Minterheim. First, however, he had to enlist the help of someone else. And that would not be easy.

CHAPTER 17

Closing his eyes, Lucius half-smiled to himself as he felt the threads of power buckle and twist slightly, their natural movements disrupted by the approach of another practitioner. He still lacked the finesse to decipher everything they were telling him, but Adrianna's approach was becoming easier to monitor the closer she came. Whether it was the magnitude of her skill in magic that caused the little fluctuations in the threads, or her emotions at having been summoned once more, Lucius could only guess. He found himself thinking of her anger acting as a bow wave ploughing through their energy, as a ship made its presence felt across the vast ocean.

The analogy seemed to hold true as she strode across the empty warehouse, dust curling up behind her footsteps.

"I am not yours to summon and command, Lucius," she said, contempt evident in her voice. He sighed inwardly, knowing his mission here was not going to be easy.

"You turn your back on us, ignore the calls of Master Forbeck, abandon the training generously offered to you, and then expect... what? Why have you called me here?"

"Good evening, Adrianna," he said, forcing a grim smile.

"Just get to the point."

"Your current employers are finished," he said. "Within the next day, their hold on the city will be shattered, their members scattered and bleeding."

Adrianna's pace had slowed as she approached him, and now she stopped altogether, her expression a mixture of puzzlement and exasperation.

"Perhaps you have not been keeping up with recent events," she said carefully, and he realised she was studying him carefully. She had not assumed he was bluffing, instead trying to determine the path he had chosen; she was no longer dismissing him as unimportant. "The Hands are in retreat all over the city, your guildmaster and most of the Council are dead, and you are now just waiting for the end."

"I'm waiting for nothing, Aidy. I told you, this war will be over within the next day."

"This is not your fight, Lucius. Leave them. Leave the Hands. There is no future there, and your allegiance should not be to a den of thieves. You could be so much more than that."

"So you have told me."

"Then why stay with the Hands?"

He smiled wolfishly at her. "I like them."

Snorting at that, Adrianna shook her head. "Are they worth dying for?"

Considering her words, he finally shrugged. "They are certainly worth fighting for, and that is what I intend to do. Without me, they will all die, or otherwise be all but enslaved by the Guild. I can make the difference here, Aidy."

Placing a hand on her hip, she looked at him curiously. "And when did you find something to believe in? Where is the selfish Lucius we have come to know and despise, the one who runs from responsibility? They cannot be paying you that much at the moment, I know. If there is no profit, why are you staying to defend them?"

Lucius opened his mouth to answer, then found precious few words. "That is something of a surprise to me as well," he finally muttered.

"If only you had found a similar loyalty for us."

"I still may." The words amazed him as much as they did Adrianna. Somewhere along the line, he found he had decided to stay in the city, to carve his own niche and no one would be forcing him out. Not the Guild, not Adrianna and definitely not the Shadowmages. Turnitia was after all, his home. He was done with running.

"What are you saying?" she asked, suspiciously, still expecting a trap somewhere down the line. As it happened, she was not so very wrong.

"I'll tell you what I am going to do," he said. "And I'll ask a simple request. What happens then is up to you. You will have the chance, at the very least, to protect your employer's interests, and perhaps deliver victory in this war to them single-handed. That would do much for the reputation of the Shadowmages and herald their return to the city, would it not?"

"Go on."

"Loredo has been clever, building alliances and ensuring he has some of the best thieves in the city on his side. Even his thugs are well-directed and motivated. He has a Shadowmage in his employ, and can call upon the services of demons from the sea. But central to his plans are his ties to the Vos guard."

"And these are the enemies you are determined to make?" Adrianna asked. "You have a chance to escape all of this, and there are those within the Shadowmages who would protect you from further harm if you walked away now. Remember, we always look after our own."

"In a way, I am counting on that," Lucius said, but evaded her questioning look. "However, it is plain that we cannot fight them all, not in open battle."

He ran a hand through his hair as he debated his next words. If he had misread Adrianna, what he was about to say could finish the Hands before a single attack was launched. Still, he forged ahead, determined to test his own instincts.

"We are going to strike them down from the shadows, hit the power base of the Guild." He said. "The enforcers on the streets, the contacts that form their network of spies, the highest earning merchants in their protection rackets, Loredo and Jewel themselves."

"You have already tried to take down Jewel," Adrianna interjected. "That did not go so well."

"We'll be prepared this time, and she won't have so many allies to call upon when we make the move. I'll do it myself, if I have to."

"Have a care. She is as dangerous as her reputation suggests."

"Your concern is touching," Lucius said, but when he saw Adrianna about to react to that, he waved her fury away. "By the time I reach Jewel, she will have a great many things to occupy her thoughts."

"Such as?"

"This all happens tomorrow evening. The Hands will leave their guildhouse and kill everyone connected with Loredo that can be found." He was acutely conscious that if Adrianna did not do as he expected, he had just doomed every member of the Hands.

"How can you be sure you will be able to find all the targets you seek? You know Loredo has moved the location of his guildhouse, specifically to avoid any reprisal like this?"

He did not know that, and Lucius hesitated before offering up the final part of the plan hatched by the Hands. "We have the beggars on side. They are watching the movements of the Guild, tracking down everyone we have deemed important to Loredo's operations. They'll find their new base of power."

"The beggars? Clever." Her compliment was muted, and he could see her mind was ticking away, gauging the threat he and the Hands posed, and how it affected her position with her employer.

"It was Magnus, not me, that brought the beggars into the fold. And he paid for the alliance with his life."

"And what, exactly, is your part in all of this, Lucius?" Adrianna asked.

"I'll be there every step of the way, Aidy. I'll lead the attack."

"You realise, of course, that this will likely bring you into direct conflict with another Shadowmage."

"I have no quarrel with you, Aidy. I am not looking to fight you."

"If you are leading the assault, it becomes damn well near impossible to avoid, doesn't it?" she said, her anger finally boiling over. "Do you understand what you risk, Lucius? Not the dangers in fighting the Guild, but in taking a stand against us?"

"I'm not taking a stand against you or the other Shadowmages, Aidy."

"My contract with the Guild predates your involvement with the Hands, and so takes precedence!"

"I have no contract, Aidy. I am here because I have to be, because these people need me. Because they will die without me, and that is not something I can walk away from. I fight because I have to fight."

"God damn you, Lucius!" Adrianna spat, and went on cursing him, decrying amateur practitioners and their lack of respect for the Shadowmages guild. He let her anger ride out, knowing he risked her striking him down on the spot, but also hoping he had understood how her loyalties ran.

When her fury was spent, she whirled back on him. "You don't leave me any damned choice, do you?"

He waited for her next words, though he found it difficult to hold her stare.

Closing her eyes, Adrianna sighed, and with the release of breath, so the fire of her rage seemed to dissipate. "It seems you have a personal stake in this war, Lucius, and it is clear that I don't. I'll release myself from the contract with the Guild. To continue would risk coming into conflict with another Shadowmage and however agreeable that may be on one level, I will not do it."

"Thank you, Aidy," he said.

"Oh, don't thank me, Lucius," she said. "I am well aware I have been played, and there will be a reckoning after this war is done."

He nodded slowly, then played his next card. "After this, I will take up my training in earnest."

That made her look twice at him, and she frowned.

"It is a promise I make to both you and Master Forbeck," he said. "I will dedicate myself to the Shadowmages, learn all I can, and abide by the rules of the guild."

Clearly sceptical, Adrianna cocked her head. "Why?"

"I am going to stay in this city, Aidy," he said. "It is going to become my home again. I'll always have an allegiance to the Hands, but I will also pledge myself to the Shadowmages. I want to learn about our gift. I want to be more than I have been."

"Your record in this matter is hardly sterling."

"True," he had to concede. "But please allow that a man can change. I don't want to be your enemy, Aidy. We should not be enemies."

Taking a step closer, Adrianna dark eyes bored into his own, as if trying to plumb the depths of his mind for the truth. "If you do as you say, Lucius, you will have my support. But my God, if you should prove false..."

"I know," he said simply.

She took a step back, preparing to leave. "We have an understanding, then. I will not interfere with your plans, and will henceforth break off contact with Loredo and his Guild."

"There was... just one more thing," Lucius said.

"Oh, with you there always is," Adrianna said, but waited patiently to hear him out.

He took a breath, preparing himself to see how far his relationship with Adrianna truly stretched. "The Hands' assault on the Guild begins this evening."

She frowned. "I thought you said..."

"Tomorrow is when the Hands move as a whole. In a few hours, however, I will enter the Citadel and strike at the heart of the Vos guard. Their captain, von Minterheim."

Adrianna just looked at him, mouth open, dumbstruck.

"That is the signal for the Hands to begin. With the guard paralysed and leaderless, they will be of little aid to the Guild, for a time at least."

It took a while for Adrianna to find her voice again. "That... is either incredibly stupid and ill-conceived, or..." she trailed off.

"Whatever it is, it won't be easy. However, my request..." he hesitated for a moment before steeling himself to continue. "I wanted to ask you if you would come with me, to fight by my side and ensure the mission's success."

Trying very hard to ignore Adrianna's dark eyes, Lucius began to explain. "I cannot offer you money or anything that would be the equal of the contract you have lost, but this is important to me Aidy, and –"

"Fine."

"What?"

"Fine," she said with a shrug. "I'll come with you. Then we'll see just how good a practitioner you have become."

Lucius had expected argument, threat and disparagement, but not an easy acquiescence. It caught him off-guard.

"You better tell me what you have planned," Adrianna said. "Then I can tell you where you are going wrong, and how to fix it."

The Citadel lay silhouetted against the giant sphere of Kerberos that hung imposingly across half the evening sky. Bands of clouds racing across its surface like the wake from a ship moving at speed. The Five Markets were quiet, just a few late traders desperately trying to hawk the last of their day's stock.

Lucius' initial plan had been scotched by Adrianna almost immediately in favour for an easier and less complicated approach. He had envisioned an assault upon the walls, a stealthy dash through the courtyard and then a sweep of the keep in order to locate their prey. Instead, the more experienced Shadowmage had suggested they allow von Minterheim to come to them. The changing of the guard was an event undertaken with typical Vos regularity, and it was always overseen by the captain so long as he was present in the city. That meant not a dangerous and probably futile attempt to gain access to the keep, but instead a hard-hitting strike executed in the main courtyard of the Citadel.

Quickly warming to the idea, Lucius had seen its promise. The point of the attack was not simply to avenge himself and the Hands on von Minterheim, but to shatter the guard. To paralyse their ability to retaliate to the Hands' next move against the Guild, however briefly. The Vos army could not be destroyed in Turnitia, but it could be made to stumble. The aim therefore, was to eliminate von Minterheim and cause as much disruption as possible while inside the Citadel. It was a mission that two Shadowmages, working in concert, could excel at.

They shuffled along the short line of people heading toward the southern gate of the Citadel, cloaked and hooded. The others entering the gate were, for the most part, visitors and tourists who often made it a point to witness the precision display the Vos military enacted while changing the guard. In just a few short years since the invasion, it had become as much a part of city life as the Five Markets or the great barriers at the docks. It was a piece of what made Turnitia what it was.

Lucius had left behind his sword and mail under Adrianna's guidance. Reluctant at first, she had pointed out that everyone entering the Citadel legitimately was searched for weapons and contraband, and it would do their mission no good if they were detained at the gate and forced to fight their way through. Besides, Adrianna had said, a real Shadowmage had no need of mundane weapons.

Only partly agreeing, Lucius had refused to relinquish the daggers sheathed inside his boots, and he felt grateful for their hard, metallic presence as they paced, ever so slowly, toward the gate.

The delay was down to the more rigorous than usual searches being performed by the gate guards, halting each person in turn and patting them down before nodding them ahead and turning to the next. The rumour flowing down the line was that the guards had been spooked by a break out the other night, and their lives depended upon no more trouble erupting in the heart of the Vos military presence. Few believed such an escape attempt was likely, but it made Lucius smile.

He strode up to one of the guards as they approached the gate, its arch soaring high above them while the eight inch thick reinforced greywood gates lay invitingly open. Raising his arms, he felt the guard's hands sweep over his chest, back and legs, and was thankful he had not tried to smuggle through his armour or sword, as it would have been found immediately. His hood was jerked back, and the guard, barely more than a lad sporting the first wisps of a beard, stared intently into his face. Lucius smiled back pleasantly, playing the part of a curious visitor, and it seemed to work. The guard jerked a thumb over his shoulder, indicating Lucius should continue, and Adrianna stepped up for inspection. Glancing over his shoulder as he crossed the threshold, Lucius had to suppress a smile as her hood was thrown back and a wilful glare dared the young guardsman to get too familiar during his search. Despite his years, it seemed as though the guard had wisdom enough not to take liberties and Adrianna was, quickly, directed through.

The courtyard swept before them as they entered, side by side. It was dominated by the keep and the five towers, but was still a vast expanse of open space within a city where real estate was usually at a premium. Around the walls that ringed the courtyard and keep were a myriad of smaller buildings; stables, storehouses, guard quarters, and forges. It was said that the Citadel could be closed for over a year and remain self-sufficient. It was only now that Lucius began to appreciate the grandeur of its design.

Guardsmen were already assembled across the courtyard, lined up in their respective units as they prepared to hand over the watch, long shadows cast from their stationary positions from the lanterns that bedecked the entire courtyard at strategic points, driving back the darkness. The visitors were shown by other guards to a waiting area in front of a wagon house, but Lucius and Adrianna had already split up, taking positions at either side of the crowd. It was not their intention to involve innocents in the attack, and by avoiding the centre of the on-lookers, any reprisals from the guard were less likely to inadvertently catch one of them.

Taking a step to one side to put some more distance between himself and a family whose two children had thick Vos accents, obviously from the heartlands, Lucius held his breath as a guardsman approached him, arm held out to one side to guide him back into the crowd. Lucius nodded at the man, who immediately spun on his heels to return to his position a few yards away.

Peering through the crowd, Lucius tried to spy Adrianna, but she had disappeared. She had told him that she would wait for his move, that he would initiate the attack, and he hoped she was merely using subtle magic to conceal her presence, rather than leaving him out to dry. He doubted she lacked sincerity, but he could never quite tell where Adrianna was concerned.

A cheer went up from the crowd, as they all realised the ceremony was about to begin. This drew some frowns from the guard themselves, particularly the older men, but one young guardsman waved until a superior bawled him out, to the amusement of the onlookers.

Movement to his left caught Lucius' eye, and another cheer was raised as the main gates of the keep were opened. From the darkness within strode von Minterheim, flanked by his entourage, six guardsmen in full dress uniform, only slightly less ostentatious than their captain's breastplate, braids, feathered hat and jewel-encrusted sword. At his appearance, Lucius began to tap into the threads, beckoning them to his reach, but he held his mind steady. It would be too easy for the captain to retreat back into the keep if he struck now.

He watched as the captain and his men paced the courtyard with solemn duty, passing each assembled unit while inspecting each man. At times, von Minterheim would mutter a word to one of his entourage, and the man would stop in front of some poor guardsman singled out for discipline for some slight in his uniform, while the captain continued his march down the line.

This continued for some time, as every active member of the guard in the Citadel was reviewed, Lucius felt some sympathy for the guards who had been on duty for the entire day and were forced to endure this charade in the name of tradition and discipline before they could finally be relieved. Von Minterheim finally rounded the last unit, and strode confidently to the centre of the courtyard, where he nodded to a junior officer. The man gave an order to a unit of trumpeters who rang out a fanfare, the sound piercing the stillness of the evening air. The assembled units began to move, one watch being relieved as another came on duty.

It was a good a time as any to act, Lucius thought.

With so much movement going on in the courtyard, no one saw him slip from the crowd as he crept along the wall past the wagon house, and on past a set of stables. The horses whinnied quietly as he stalked past them, and their agitation gave him an idea.

Stepping inside, he cast about for dry hay, finding it baled near the back of the stables. Looking upwards, he saw more stored in the loft above, and smiled wolfishly.

Checking once more that no one was nearby, he outstretched a finger and felt the familiar surge as a small jet of flame short forth, instantly igniting a bale. It was a small fire, but it grew hungrily. Even as the horses began to stir, he conjured a ball of fire to his palm before launching it into the loft. There, it flashed briefly as it consumed more hay.

He smelt smoke rising to his nostrils, and hastened out, not wanting to be anywhere near the conflagration when it was noticed. Continuing his pace along the wall of the Citadel, he closed the distance to the Keep, wanting to cut off von Minterheim's obvious escape route should the man try to run.

An cry from the crowd told Lucius that the mission had begun in earnest. Within seconds, guardsmen were charging across the courtyard to the stables. Sergeants screamed orders as buckets were grabbed from one of the storehouses and a chain formed to a well.

Von Minterheim had remained calm, though the man was scanning the courtyard, obviously searching for the cause of the fire, trying to decide whether it was an accident or something more sinister. As the man's gaze swept over him, Lucius stopped in his tracks and crouched, tugging on threads to bring the shadows cast by the wall and its outbuildings around him like a second cloak.

It was then that Adrianna weighed in with her assault. Something crackled in the air across the courtyard before, from a cloudless sky, a bolt of lightning shot down from the heavens to strike one of the Vos units square in its centre. The luckiest men flew through the air as the ground exploded beneath them, while those closest to the descending bolt were boiled in their armour. A cry went up, and Lucius saw guardsmen point to the sky. Following their gestures, he looked, then gasped as he saw Adrianna, her powers manifesting themselves for all to see.

Her cloak billowing out behind her as tightly circling winds carried her aloft, Adrianna rose into the evening sky. Gesturing at the ground beneath the guardsmen trying to fight the fire in the stables, he saw their feet become mired as the earth turned to liquid beneath them. Adrianna paid them no more attention as she rose upwards to alight on the wall, now commanding the high ground and able to see the entire courtyard below her. Under the directions of an officer determined to take charge, squads of crossbowmen assembled in front of Adrianna, cranking their weapons back and sliding bolts into place before aiming them upwards.

With a series of clicks audible across the excited courtyard, dozens of bolts shot towards Adrianna, but she stayed her ground, merely holding up a hand to ward them off. As if striking an invisible wall, the bolts sheared off course just a few feet away from her, scattering themselves as they ricocheted back into the courtyard.

A few fell close to the crowd. Fearing they would soon be caught in a crossfire between Vos guard and Shadowmage, Lucius tugged a thread, and sent its energy surging into the fires of the stable. With a low boom, the flames suddenly swelled with intensity, sending the guardsmen fighting them reeling back in shock. The sudden flare and noise was enough to galvanise the crowd and, screaming, they fled as one to the gate. The guards stationed there were trying to close the massive portal, but the frightened people just surged past them into the city streets.

Directing more men towards Adrianna, who even now was racing along the wall for the cover of one of the small towers set along its length, von Minterheim made his move. Whether wanting to bring reinforcements into play or through self-preservation, he began to run for the Keep, his entourage close behind. Lucius was ready for him.

Drawing a dagger from his boot, Lucius forced powerful energies down its blade, feeling them pulse in anticipation of release. Stepping out of the shadows, he placed himself in von Minterheim's path before launching the dagger with a straight throw.

Guided unerringly to its targets, the blade arrowed straight for one of the officers flanking von Minterheim, no spin upsetting the delicate balance of its flight. It ploughed into the breastplate of the man, a shower of blood erupting as the weapon tunnelled through his body without losing any of its momentum. As it blasted out between his shoulders, the dagger continued on its trajectory, and smashed into the chest of the officer behind, sending him flying to the ground with terrible force.

Instinctively, von Minterheim and his remaining officers drew their swords as they warily approached the man who had materialised out of the shadows before them. Lucius waited for them to make the first move, a faint smile on his lips as von Minterheim frowned in recognition.

"You," the captain said, his voice low and dangerous, promising a slow death to any who invaded the Citadel.

"You have cost me the lives of many of my friends, you Vos bastard," Lucius said, feeling both hatred and exaltation at confronting this man. "You are going to die slowly."

Von Minterheim sneered, ignoring the explosions and lightning behind him as his guards tried vainly to bring Adrianna to ground. He nodded to his officers.

"Take him."

The four surviving officers of the captain's entourage spread themselves out, anxious to be the one to slay their superior's enemy. Yet, they were wary of what Lucius could do, the corpses of their comrades a stark reminder that this stranger should not be underestimated.

"You are going to burn in hell's own fire, warlock," said one as he paced to one side.

"What do you know of hellfire?" Lucius cried out, releasing his anger as another ball of flame circled his right hand before being launched forward. The officer tried desperately to lunge out of the way, but the fire curved in flight to match his movements, striking him squarely in the chest. His dying shrieks were cut off as the fire eagerly consumed the air in his lungs, now exposed through the shattered remains of his breastplate and chest.

Sensing motion behind him, Lucius whirled round, collecting the air about him into a solid wall, before flinging it at his assailants in a single smooth movement. Hurled off their feet by the blast, he watched the officers collapse to the ground, then summoned the thread once more to gather the air above them. Going down on one knee to emphasise the action, he raised his arm high over his head, then swiftly dropped it, palm downwards. A sickening squelch echoed through the courtyard as the officers were crushed. In his mind's eye, Lucius saw ribs break and organs burst under the weight before he released the conjuration.

Standing straight, he looked down at the dead men, their still faces contorted in terrible pain as blood seeped from their mouths. Grinning, Lucius looked up at von Minterheim.

"Who are you?" the captain asked, and Lucius was mildly surprised to note von Minterheim was more curious than afraid.

"Consider that a mystery to contemplate in the grave," Lucius snarled, reaching out with a hand as a surge of lightning wreathed his arm. Unleashing the energy, he was stunned as von Minterheim raised his sword to block the attack, bolts of white light crackling around the blade as they were dissipated harmlessly into the air around him.

He had taken the weapon to be purely ceremonial, but cursed himself for not guessing that there was little in the Vos military that was not functional in the extreme, and that von Minterheim was likely rich enough to afford the best equipment in the empire.

"Nice sword," he managed to say, but was answered only with a derisive sneer as von Minterheim took two steps forward and swung the blade, the rare stones in its elaborate gold crossguard glinting in the fires spreading through the outbuildings of the courtyard. Lucius noted the markings etched into the blade as he pedalled backwards to avoid the blow, a fine script in some foreign tongue. The lettering glowed briefly with the radiance of the lightning he had thrown at von Minterheim, before they finally faded.

Another swipe forced him back, then another. He crouched down to reach for his remaining dagger, but von Minterheim gave him no room for pause.

Behind the captain, Lucius saw that several squads of guards had noticed the fight, and they rushed to join their superior. They fanned out to either side, weapons drawn, cutting off any chance of escape. Conjuring fire to his hand, Lucius held it low, waiting for his time to strike. He took another step back and felt the wall of the keep at his back. Looking left and right at the guardsmen, he saw grim faced men ready to take their revenge for the attack.

"Make it easy on yourself," von Minterheim said. "Maybe we'll give you a quick death. Once you have answered a few questions, of course. Just a gentle chat, then a quick hanging. Believe me, the noose is better than what my men will be wanting to do to you."

The fire at his fingertips began to burn hot, its energies having been kept in check too long. Lucius took a deep breath as he prepared a last assault on the guardsmen as, pace by pace, they closed in for the kill.

"Adrianna, I could use your help now," he muttered, and he was at least gratified to see a few of the guardsmen check their step, fearing he was vocalising some incantation that would bring death to them all.

He saw her then, standing on the wall across the far side of the courtyard. A guardsman lay dead at her feet, and she seemed to be staring straight at him, heedless of the bolts and spears that flew past her. A rush of air swept over him, a gentle breeze that reminded him of calm summer afternoons in the Anclas territories, and the wind carried Adrianna's voice to him, as clear as if she were standing at his side.

"Unleash the power, Lucius," he heard her say. "Let's find out what you are *really* capable of. Let the magic flow through you. Give yourself up to it."

Von Minterheim had ordered the guardsmen to halt, and they stayed, weapons at the ready, less than a dozen yards away. Their ranks were held tight, at least three men deep, forming a barrier of flesh and iron that trained cavalry would have difficulty breaking. Smiling, von Minterheim took a pace forward and gestured to the ball of flame Lucius still held in his hand.

"Want to try your luck one last time?"

Lucius stared ruefully back at him, before a soothing calm flooded through him. With an instant clarity, he could see the threads spinning and weaving their magic in the hidden part of his mind, begging to be manipulated and used, their only purpose to serve his direction.

Sighing, Lucius held up his hand and let the ball of flame fly high into the sky, where it finally sputtered and flashed out of existence.

"Sensible choice," said von Minterheim, and he lifted a hand to direct his men to take Lucius into custody, but something checked him. His eyes widened as he watched Lucius draw in a deep breath, and a sudden tension filled the air. The shadows around the keep seemed to lengthen and grow, appearing to cluster around Lucius as his eyes shone with a pale, inner light.

"Take him!" von Minterheim shouted at his men, not knowing what his enemy was planning, acting purely on instinct.

Primed and ready to obey, the guardsmen leapt forward, weapons raised, as Lucius closed his eyes and caught the threads. With little conscious thought, he fashioned them crudely, trading finesse for power, raw power. The threads responded, eagerly it seemed, and he opened his mind to their energies, not attempting to hold them in check, acting as a funnel for their escape as if they now controlled him.

His eyes snapped open as the power bubbled violently over the brim and with a wide sweeping motion, he flung fire at the nearest guardsmen. A giant sheet of flame tumbled toward them, its green and purple hues making it look almost tame. As it reached them, it turned white hot and the men were incinerated where they stood, the trailing wake of fire leaving only blackened and shrivelled corpses. Their weapons and armour were melted into slag by the terrible heat.

Only narrowly missed by the fires, von Minterheim leapt forward, the tip of his sword aiming true for Lucius' chest as the surviving guards rallied behind him. Only barely aware of the danger, Lucius continued to let the magic flow unchecked, and he felt himself raise his foot before stamping it down hard. The earth rocked as tremors radiated out from him, throwing captain and guard alike to the ground, their feet kicked from beneath them by the force of magic rippling below.

Scrabbling for weapons, they looked up to see Lucius glaring down upon them, the fury in his eyes replaced by something altogether more primal, smouldering in its release. He sought out von Minterheim from the tangle of weapons and limbs, and his gaze bore into the man's eyes.

"You cannot conceive of the power you have unleashed," he heard himself say, then shuddered as he felt the darkest of threads push itself to the fore, snaking out from his outstretched hands to slither over every man who still drew breath before him.

The strangled shrieks of the guards tortured his ears and drew the attention of everyone left in the courtyard. They grasped their throats as their skin turned deathly pale, the life being sucked out of their bodies. Lucius watched as von Minterheim tried to tear off his breastplate with fingers that rotted as they pulled uselessly at the clasps. Flesh dropped from his hands in blackened chunks, leaving only bone, as the skin drew taut across his face. Hair greyed and fell to the ground, while his eyes lost the sparkle of life, dulled and then hardened. Then the screams fell silent.

Full consciousness returned to Lucius, and he retched as he felt the dark energy pulse through his body. Dropping to his knees, he vomited. He could smell nothing but death, and it seemed like a poison in his veins, charring every part of his being and staining it forever. He spat to remove the foul taste from his mouth, but it felt as though nothing would remove the darkness that gathered in his body and mind.

Standing, he took a shaky step forward, trying hard not to notice the shrivelled corpses that lay all around him. But their sightless eyes seemed to catch his, the dark husks accusing him of a crime humanity had no word for. He felt his stomach heave again, but he continued his march, limping with exhaustion and disgust at himself. Glaring at the remaining guards he passed, Lucius dared them to move against him. After witnessing what he had done to their captain, none did.

The gate was closed as he approached it, and he cast about, looking for a guard to intimidate into opening it, but they had begun to flee back into the keep. He eyed the wooden barrier, knowing he had no strength left to summon the magic, and little desire to give them free reign.

The air became agitated around him, and he felt a gale sweep past his body, the current running just inches from his skin, leaving him unmolested. The wind seemed to be formed from a sweeter form of magic, and he felt physically charged as he bathed in its purity, the sickness of his soul slowly receding. Taking a deep breath to savour the feeling, he watched the wind now whistling with shrieking hurricane force, smash into the gate. The timbers exploded in a shower of splinters, leaving the wrecked gates hanging by ruined hinges.

Beyond, the streets of Turnitia lay as they always had, a scene of complete normality somehow removed from the devastation of the courtyard behind him.

He felt Adrianna's presence before he heard her footsteps.

"I said you had potential," she told him, placing a hand on his shoulder.

"I swear to you," he said when he found his voice, "I am never doing that again. The magic is... evil. Black. We are not supposed to be using it, not like that."

"Don't you dare blame the magic for that! The power you manifest is a reflection of you, and you alone. That darkness is a part of you, and the sooner you realise that, the more powerful you will become."

"I don't want it," he said plaintively.

"Not your choice. Right now, you need it."

Damn her, Lucius thought. He knew she was right.

CHAPTER 18

Murder exploded across the city.

The surviving Hands were astounded at the stories coming from the Citadel: Captain von Minterheim slain in the cruellest fashion, the corpses of guardsmen littering the southern courtyard like so many rag dolls discarded by a precocious rich girl and powerful magic unleashed against their enemies. Many presumed that Lucius had forged an alliance with great wizards, or brought mercenary warlocks into their guild's employ. A few guessed the truth, but their suspicions were over-ridden by a new feeling of optimism among their fellow thieves.

For the first time victory seemed possible. Maybe even likely.

There was little opposition to the next phase of Lucius' plan, and no attempt on his part to curb the enthusiasm of the more bloodthirsty thieves. In the morning after the assault on the Citadel, he unleashed the Hands into the city while the Vos guard were paralysed and the Guild was reeling from the loss of its greatest ally.

Working in concert with the Beggars Guild, shambling mounds of filth-ridden disease providing accurate descriptions of where targets could be found, the thieves hunted down their enemies and showed no mercy. They killed collectors working extortion rackets, their bodyguards and any client known to sympathise with the Guild. They killed enforcers, lookouts, spies, fences, anyone remotely connected with the Guild and who might raise opposition to the new swing in the balance of power. The assault on the Vos guard continued, with a dagger or crossbow bolt launched from a high rooftop or dark alley to strike down sergeants and corporals. The net closed, with the Hands leaving nowhere for Guild men or their supporters to run to. Everyone in the city knew what was happening, and those with no interest in the outcome – the thousands of ordinary traders, craftsmen and their families – kept clear of the streets, not wanting to inadvertently be caught up in the slaughter. The Vos guard, by now, were powerless to protect them.

Throughout the day, a constant stream of beggars reported to Grennar, now permanently stationed at the Hand's guildhouse. They were bringing back vital information of the Guild's response, allowing the Council to pull their own men away from areas of the city where thugs and mercenaries prowled, looking for the chance to repay the Hands for the blood being spilt. All the time, the beggars tracked the movements of Guild men until, finally, they were ready to reveal the expected location of Loredo's new guildhouse.

As evening approached, a final Council meeting was called, attended by every thief not still wetting his blade with the blood of the Guild. The mood was jubilant, for the day had seen the Guild all but cut down. Now, just the final stroke remained, the last attack that would see their enemy smashed forever.

All eyes were on Grennar as she outlined what her beggars had learned of the Guild's last hiding place.

"They've retreated to the docks," she said. "Their operations have always centred in that territory, ever since it became a no-go area for you."

"I heard they had demons on their side," one voice from the crowd said, and was greeted by a few nervous murmurs. "That's what put paid to Lucius' operation."

"You've been drinking too much, or else listening to old wives" tales," Nate said scornfully. "They employed mercenaries who took Lucius and his men by surprise."

Lucius was aware of Ambrose among the thieves, his eyebrows arched questioningly, and he sighed.

"We will be walking into the heart of our enemy's territory this evening," he said slowly. "They will be at their most dangerous, cornered, afraid and desperate. I would not have you walking into their lair without knowing the truth."

The council chamber was suddenly still, and a few of the older thieves leaned forward to catch every word. Lucius ignored the eyes of the other Council members, especially Elaine, who frowned at him dangerously for withholding any information from her.

"Magnus knew what happened, and he swore myself, Ambrose and Sandtrist – the only other thief to survive that evening – to silence. We knew the Guild had brought new allies into their fold, but we knew nothing of where they came from or what they were."

"They are truly demons, then?" asked the same voice.

"I don't know," Lucius confessed. "I know they are not human, that they came from the sea. That they have brutal strength and are utterly savage. How the Guild contacted them and negotiated an alliance, well, I don't know that either."

"So, what do we do if they are waiting for us?" Nate asked.

"Run," Ambrose said.

Lucius nodded. "That is fair advice. From what we saw, the further they are from the sea, the slower and clumsier they become. Even so, you don't want to be anywhere near them when they attack. They slaughtered almost my entire team within a few minutes."

"Then the Guild might still win?"

"Not if I have anything to do with it," Lucius said. "I have some ideas. If they appear, get out of the way and leave them to me."

"And what makes you so special, Lucius?" Elaine asked. "We have heard strange tales from the Citadel. If the Guild has brought these terrible creatures onto their side, who or what have you brought onto ours?"

He hesitated. "That is a topic for another time," he said, finally.

More mutters floated from the crowded thieves, and they were not charitable ones. Elaine leaned forward in her seat to look Lucius straight in the eye.

"If we are trusting you with our lives, Lucius, we all deserve to know who and what we are fighting for."

He returned her gaze for a moment then, deliberately, turned to the thieves in front of them.

"You are fighting for your lives and continued prosperity," he said evenly. "As for myself... I have brought you all this far. I ask you to continue trusting me for one more evening. After that, I'll tell you what I can."

The thieves were far from happy with that. Once, seemingly a lifetime ago, a word from Magnus would have silenced any dissent, and each thief would be content with knowing what he was supposed to know and no more. Now, with every thief able to take part in the Council's meetings, they all wanted to know every secret. Muttering turned into open growls demanding Lucius reveal what he knew, to answer for the rumours of what happened in the Citadel. Of whether he was in league with Loredo.

"He doesn't have to tell us anything," a clear voice said, riding above the noise of the other thieves, and he saw that Grayling had walked out from the crowd to stand between the thieves and the Council's table. "Lucius broke us out of the Citadel and, without him, I can truly say I would not be standing here now. I would be dead, either by the neck or with a Vos sword in my stomach."

"Aye," said Ambrose, standing forward to join her. "I brought Lucius into the Hands, and fought alongside him against these sea demons. I tell you all, if he had meant to betray us, he has had plenty of opportunity before now."

"Before Lucius killed the captain of the guard, we were ready to huddle in this place like trapped rats," Grayling said. "Now look at us! We are on the eve of victory, and still you want to quibble!"

"He has the support of the beggars too," Grennar spoke up.

The testimonies to Lucius' character made him feel a little uncomfortable, but they were sufficient to silence the thieves. To his right, Elaine stood up.

"The Council, at this time agrees," she said, looking pointedly at Wendric and Nate, who both got to their feet to stand alongside her, though Nate hesitated for a second, appearing reluctant to do so.

"We proceed with the plan," Wendric said. "Tonight, we win the Thieves War."

His words gained a few grumbles of grudging assent from the thieves, but if he had been expecting to rouse cheers of support, he was disappointed. Lucius nodded his thanks to Wendric, but his eyes were drawn to Elaine, who had fixed him with a doom-laden stare. He knew that if anything went wrong this evening, he would find one of her daggers planted in his back when he least expected it. Either way, she would be demanding a full explanation from him.

From the guildhouse, small bands of thieves left through the secret entrances to the sewer system and spread out across the city. Vos guard and the few brave Guild men looking to make reprisals were ignored. For once, they were not the target.

These bands divided themselves and regrouped in new locations, expanding across Turnitia like a dark cancer, taking streets least used and alleys least watched. Slowly, they converged upon the docks, a secret army preparing for its last assault.

Finding Lucius on the roof of a warehouse near the cliffs, Ambrose reported that a dozen sentries had been located and eliminated, leaving the path clear for their own thieves to gather and assemble into an attack force. Nodding his thanks, Lucius gave him instructions to report again when each band of thieves was in position. Watching Ambrose withdraw, he returned his attention to the building he had been scanning.

The beggars had found the new guildhouse by the same manner they discovered everything else. Throughout the city, the ostensibly penniless and dispossessed watched known Guild members, tracked their movements, and informed their spymasters. These senior beggars then worked together to piece disparate nuggets of information together into a meaningful whole. There was little happening within the city that escaped their attention.

Perched on the side of the cliff, at the furthest edge of the sprawl that was gathered around the docks, the warehouse was a two storey affair, designed to accommodate a growing business as well as serve as a repository for goods. The Hands were well aware of the layout of such warehouses, built to a specific design as it was, under the direction of the Vos military when they rebuilt the city. Storage area on the ground floor, offices and living quarters above. However, they all expected the Guild to have modified the interior, even in the short time they had been present. No beggar though had managed to approach the building without being turned away.

It was a well positioned site, right at the edge of the city, providing an easy ingress for those wanting to avoid the main entrances. Grennar had told him they suspected that tunnels bored into the cliff led to caves at the base of the cliff face, making it a superb location for anyone wishing to engage in smuggling. A ship need only dock at the harbour and, during the hours of darkness, a small boat could be hauled over the side to deliver high value goods without incurring dock taxes.

Lucius had to admit, it was all very neatly done. Tapping his fingers on the roof of the warehouse on which he had taken position, he mentally urged his thieves to get into place. With the sentries gone they had limited time to launch their attack, as the failure of any sentry to report in would set the Guild on the highest alert. A guildhouse could easily be turned into a fortress, and Lucius had no wish for his thieves to cover dead ground while under fire from secret arrow nests. They had to attack while the Guild was blind to their approach.

There was also the problem of his Shadowmage talents to contend with, and this had occupied his mind greatly since Elaine's silent warning to him. One way or another, he guessed the Hands would know the truth after this evening. Though he knew he had the support of some, there were still too many suspicious of those capable of using magic. Still, he could always look on the bright side – there was a good chance he would be killed tonight, saving him from any explanation.

A low whistle echoed off the walls of the warehouses close by, and Lucius scrambled across the roof to drop a rope off the side of the building. Swinging down, he was greeted by Ambrose and Elaine.

"They're in position," Elaine said quietly. Dressed all in black, she bore two short swords at her hips. She was rumoured to be one of the best blade fighters among the Hands.

"Ambrose, give the nod to the roof-hoppers. Tell everyone else to move on their signal."

Nodding his understanding, Ambrose disappeared into the shadows. Lucius took a place at the corner of another warehouse, allowing him a clear view of the Guild's headquarters. Elaine joined him, drawing a sword and rubbing its blade with a cloth. Gradually, its bright edge lost its lustre, dulled by a lotion concocted to eliminate any chance of light catching the weapon's edge and giving away her position.

"You think this will work?" she whispered.

Lucius considered the question for a moment. "I would give us evens."

"No better?"

He shrugged. "I am pretty sure the Guild has no idea exactly what to expect, but they must know we are coming for them. They will be alert, and traps will be waiting for us."

They were silent for a time, with only the sound of the ocean crashing into the dock's barriers breaking the stillness. Lucius saw thieves move across the skyline, skipping across the roofs of warehouses as they made their way to the guildhouse. When buildings were close together, they would leap across the gap. When the distance was too far to jump, short, stocky crossbows were employed to send a bolt across the chasm, pulling silken rope with it.

"You and I will be having words after this, Lucius," Elaine said.

"I know," he sighed.

"For what it is worth, I have few doubts about your loyalties to the Hands," she said. "You started as an outsider but then, we all did. I know you now have friends among us."

"For what *this* is worth, I count you among them," he said, turning to face her briefly.

"But there are still too many unanswered questions," Elaine said, as though she had not heard him.

He turned away from her, back to face the guildhouse. The thieves on the roofs were about to make their final crossing to the Guild's lair. "You know I wield magic," he said.

"Of course I do. And that is something you are going to have trouble reconciling with some of our members. I am not stupid, Lucius. You left the city soon after the invasion, and now return a spellslinger. I think I know what you are."

"Then you know you have little to fear from what I do."

"I also know that you have obligations to others. But, that aside, we also need to redress the balance of power within the Hands. We are an anarchic mess at the moment."

"We need to rebuild the Council and appoint a new guildmaster," Lucius said, understanding where Elaine was going.

"If we are successful tonight, there will be many who want you as guildmaster, magic or no," she said.

He gave a low laugh. "I don't want it. Truly, I don't. Up until a few days ago, I was not even sure I would be staying here after this."

"You now think you will?"

"These thieves are growing on me," he said. "Look, I'll make a deal with you, here and now. You support me against those who may have trouble accepting what I am. In return, I will do everything to convince the others you should be guildmaster."

She was quiet for a moment. "You really don't want it, do you?"

"That is not where my ambitions lie. You have the experience and knowledge. You also have the assassins in your hand, which should ease the conscience of any doubters to your claim. For my part, I would like a place on the Council – I feel I owe Magnus that much, and some of his more controversial decisions will need a champion. His deal with the beggars, say. That's too important to let slide in any reorganisation."

"I agree. Both to the beggars, and your terms."

"Wendric should be your lieutenant."

"I was thinking you might be more suitable, especially after tonight."

"I told you, I really don't want any of it. Besides, you don't want to split the guild between myself and Wendric, and then let Nate through."

"Then I think we have an understanding," she said.

"We do. We also have the signal."

Gathered on the roof of the guildhouse, a dull glow flashed twice as a thief caught the low radiance of Kerberos on a hand mirror. From warehouses and alleyways, more thieves detached themselves from the shadows and began the rush to the guildhouse, keeping low. Lucius and Elaine watched them for a moment, then darted forward to follow.

A flash erupted from the windows of the first floor of the guildhouse, quickly followed by a muffled blast. The rooftop thieves had pried open a skylight and thrown bundles of flash powder down into the offices. Cries and screams from inside split the evening air as the thieves followed their flashpowder, blades drawn. The killing had begun.

The nimblest thieves had reached a side door and one of them jammed a crowbar into the frame, wrenching it hard. As the door flew open, Lucius saw something dark and heavy inside move with speed, and the thief had no time to scream as a large stone block swung down on chains to catch him square in the chest. The impact sent him sprawling several yards and he landed heavily on the street, completely motionless. More shouts came from the main entrance, where the heavy double doors had been forced open, the thieves there greeted by a hail of arrows and bolts, cutting down any not quick enough to dive out of sight. The assault was stalling before it really began and Lucius knew that if they did not gain entry quickly, those who had entered by the roof would be quickly killed.

"Come on," he shouted to Elaine. "We've got to get inside."

She ran for the side door with the sprung stone block trap, seeing fighting had erupted at its threshold. The Hands could only enter one at a time, and he imagined several Guild members inside, easily overpowering anyone who made it through. Whenever the Hands backed off, they were chased by thrown blades. Already, four bodies lay in front of the door.

Lucius threw himself against the wall of the warehouse next to the door, and looked about for support as Elaine joined him. Another thief was on the opposite side of the door.

"There's a dozen of the bastards inside," the thief shouted across to him. "Bloody death-trap in there."

Risking his neck, Lucius quickly poked his head round the corner, then hastily drew it back as an arrow thudded into the door frame, its metal head jutting through the wood just inches from his face. He shook his head in despair, having seen the defences inside; three armed men just inside to ward off any attacker, and an overturned table behind them, lined with archers and blade throwers.

"We can rush 'em, but the first of us inside will die," the thief said, clearly not volunteering for the duty.

Lucius cast a quick look back at Elaine, who raised her eyebrows expectantly. He sighed.

"The hell with it," he muttered, then shouted for the other thief's attention. "You, get your men ready. You'll follow me."

Incredulous, the thief grinned, happy not to be the first in.

"Whatever happens, you follow me in, right?" Lucius reiterated.

"We'll be right behind you," Elaine said, and Lucius felt he could trust her at least to threaten and cajole the others into obeying.

"Right," he said to himself, and half-closed his eyes to seek the threads amidst the chaos of the battle. They came to him, ready, almost desperate to be used. "Shut the door!" he said to the thief across from him, and the man swung the heavy wooden door shut.

Stepping out in front of the closed door, Lucius took in a deep breath, and summoned the air around him to his control. A breeze whipped around the clothes of the amazed thieves close by as he raised his fist, the air rolling into a tight twisting wind that followed his movements. Punching forward, he released the magic he had infused into the air, and it blasted forward to crash against the door. The structure had no chance.

The door, smashed by the force of a typhoon, burst from its hinges and was hurled inside, crashing into the table and those taking cover behind it.

Not hesitating, not waiting to see whether Elaine would succeed in forcing the thieves to follow, Lucius dove inside. The upturned table was before him, pinning several Guild thieves to the floor, while others lay on the floor, groaning as they nursed vicious looking wounds caused by the splintering door. He kicked at one who reached for a sword, then rushed forward.

Lucius was in the main storage area of the warehouse, littered with wooden crates, furniture and equipment, all recently transported from the original guildhouse. Much of it had been reformed into defensive posts, and he saw movement everywhere. To his left, stairs hugged the wall, leading up to the floor above, and they were lined with thieves armed with bows and crossbows. Almost immediately, a hail of fire was directed toward him and he rolled for the cover of a crate, missiles impacting on the floor around him.

Behind him, Lucius saw Elaine leading the other thieves in, and they quickly set about ending the lives of any who had survived Lucius' entry until the arrow fire was redirected towards them. Two fell immediately, long shafts jutting from their bodies as they collapsed to the ground, and he heard Elaine order the others to take cover and prepare to charge their attackers on the stairs. Above the din of the battle, he heard cries and thuds from above, and knew the thieves who had entered by the roof were fighting for their lives.

On the other side of the warehouse, he saw more makeshift barricades in front of the main entrance, the doors now wide open to the evening air. Lanterns and torches had been positioned strategically throughout the building, casting their light around any entry, yet keeping the defenders shrouded in darkness. Every so often, a Hand would dare to peer round a corner to let loose a bolt or arrow, only to be driven back by a hail of return fire.

Seeing a chance to tilt the battle in their favour, Lucius pushed away from the crate and started to creep toward the barricades. He felt a thread come to the fore and eagerly seized it, beginning to mould its energy to his wishes as a familiar ball of fire leapt to his fingertips before his quickly extinguished it. It would be very foolish to set light to the warehouse while they were still in it.

Instead, he pulled upon another thread, and the lanterns near the main entrance seemed to pale and shimmer, as if losing their radiance. Concentrating, he mentally tugged at the shadows cloaking those behind the barricades, lengthening and stretching them towards the open entrance.

Confused for a moment, the defenders ceased their volley of fire, no longer able to see their targets through the unnatural darkness that swept between them and the enemy. The Hands did not question their good fortune, and they swept inside en masse. A few thieves fell to quicker-witted Guild men, the rest leaping over the barricades to engage the defenders with blade and club. The warehouse quickly filled with dozens of individual melees as thief battled thief, swordplay interrupted by an arrow or dagger in the back from a concealed enemy, men howling as poisons burned through their bodies from minor scratches. It was a dirty way to fight, and both sides were very good at it.

Missiles were still coming from the direction of the stairs, picking off anyone too slow to dive for cover once they had dispatched the man or woman they were fighting, and Lucius kept low as he sought to make his way back to Elaine and the men she led. A loud cry made Lucius turn to see a thief running toward him, sword outstretched and eyes wild as bloodlust overcame him.

Suddenly realising he had yet to draw his own weapon, Lucius stumbled backwards as the sword sliced through the air in front of his eyes, and he sprawled over a motionless body. The thief, now screaming incoherently, held his sword in both hands and raised it above his head, ready to cleave Lucius in two. The weapon descended, and Lucius, panicking, held his arms before him, desperately seizing the first thread that spun across his mind's eye. With a loud metallic ringing, the sword stopped suddenly in its downward motion, as if it had struck a thick, invisible shield.

The thief, looked puzzled, jolted out of his bloodletting by what must have appeared as Lucius halting the blow with his own arm. With a grim smile, Lucius rolled out of the way and stood, drawing his own sword. He stabbed forward, and the thief parried wildly, pushing Lucius' blade to one side. Closing the distance between them, Lucius grabbed at the man's throat and felt a warm pulse of energy rocket down his arm. Twisting savagely with his magically enhanced strength, he felt the bones in the neck of the thief grind together, then snap. Releasing his opponent, Lucius discarded the body as it collapsed to the floor.

He found Elaine crouched behind a jumble of hastily piled furniture, surrounded by the bodies of the men she had led into the warehouse. Only a handful now remained alive, the rest having been picked off by increasingly accurate fire.

"We're winning," he said breathlessly.

"We'll win nothing if we don't take those stairs," she said, her frustration evident. "Can you clear the way?"

"Easy."

He closed his eyes, visualising the thieves on the stairs, counting their number and summoning the energy for what he planned to do next.

"Get ready," he whispered, and he was dimly aware of Elaine rallying her remaining men, forcing them to prepare for a charge. They appeared doubtful, then stared, wide-eyed, as the furniture they were hiding behind began to tremble and shift, as if caught in an earthquake.

With a loud shout, Lucius hurled the energy he had been building forward, and the furniture responded to his direction. Heavy chairs, desks and wardrobes flew through the air with deadly speed, crashing into the stairs and the thieves upon them. Most were crushed instantly by the force of the flying furniture, but a few were fortunate enough to merely have limbs smashed into bloody pulp. Their moans and screams were ignored by the cheering thieves below.

"Up there!" hissed Elaine, and Lucius followed her gaze to the ruined stairs, to see Loredo surveying the carnage in the warehouse, his pointed beard quivering in either rage or excitement.

"He's mine!" Elaine said as she leapt forward and began leaping up the tangle of bodies and smashed furniture balanced precariously on what was left of the stairs.

"I want Jewel!" Lucius shouted as he followed her.

Elaine was a few yards in front of him, but where she leapt lithely up the obstacles to Loredo, Lucius found his greater weight was causing the ruined stairs to shift disturbingly, and he was forced to regain his balance time and again. He looked up to see Elaine draw her second sword, intent on duelling with Loredo, but the man smiled down at her as he produced a small hand crossbow.

Screaming a warning, Lucius fumbled with a thread to block the bolt, blast Loredo apart or otherwise alter the course of events, but he saw he was too slow, as the crossbow was aimed at Elaine's chest and fired.

Flattening herself against the wall, Elaine's twisting motion was almost a blur to Lucius, and he was forced to duck as the tiny bolt went skittering through the air past her and shot over his head. Giving no time for Elaine to recover, Loredo dropped his crossbow and drew a sword, a long, thin blade weighted for speed. Leaping down the stairs, he picked his way over the obstacles and broken bodies of his own thieves to confront Elaine. Balanced precariously, they traded blows in a fast display of swordsmanship, he with the advantage of height, she able to bring a second weapon into play to defeat his lightning fast thrusts without losing the momentum of her own attacks.

Within the warehouse, the battle was turning in favour of the Hands, scattering the defenders and overwhelming them through teamwork and foul play. Someone had started a fire near the entrance, whether intentionally or not, and the warehouse was beginning to fill with smoke. Lucius could see there was little danger of the fire spreading out of control before it could be tended to.

Looking back up the stairs, he willed Elaine to make the killing blow, ending Loredo's life and allowing him to vault up the stairs to find Jewel. He was tempted to join Elaine and fight at her side, but he also knew his life would not be worth living if he robbed her of the kill.

A terrible crash reverberated through the warehouse, causing the many fights to cease for a few seconds. Over the far side, a tall stack of crates had been toppled, and thieves on both sides lay under the debris, calling out piteously for help from their comrades. Leaping across to the remains of a wardrobe for a better look, Lucius saw what had caused the crates to topple.

Within the smoky shadows behind the scattered crates, he saw movement as a heavy trapdoor was swung open in the floor, and he recalled Grennar telling them of smuggler tunnels leading to the foot of the cliff. When he saw the scarred face of Jewel vault from the blackness within the trap door, he knew what was going to follow her.

"Hands, to me!" he shouted as he leapt from the wardrobe. "Get behind me!"

A few were quick enough to heed his instruction, while others were either cut off from reaching him, or too shocked by what they saw emerge.

Moving with a terrible grace, Jewel drew her blade and began moving through the thieves, slashing out at anyone she did not recognise from the Guild, leaving a trail of broken and dying men behind her. Clawing their way from the lip of the trap door, Lucius saw scaled, black-eyed creatures, their talons black as the deepest night. One look at their fanged maws was enough to send thieves scrambling away, but the creatures moved with inhuman speed, claws snaking out to gouge bloodied chunks from any victim who strayed too close.

The creatures began pouring out of the trap door, and Lucius rushed ahead, seeking to gain a vantage point. A score of the monsters had leapt into the warehouse before he clambered onto a table propped up against a pile of sacks, and more were slithering out of the open trap door. Bellowing a challenge, Lucius raised his arms to the ceiling and focussed on the energies he felt bubbling above. Some of the creatures looked up at him, their dark alien eyes puzzled as electric tension filled the air, its crackling just barely audible over the screams of the dying and terrified.

The power he sought mastery over erupted, only just within the edge of his control, and the ceiling above burst apart in a shower of splinters and rafters as a bolt of lightning snaked down to explode within the darkness of the trap door. The shrieks of the creatures caught in the blast pierced the ears of everyone in the warehouse, galvanising those who kept their wits to flight. A few made it outside, but most were cut down by the creatures moving among them, or by Jewel whose expressionless face seemed all the more terrible in the half light spilt by the remaining lanterns and growing fire near the main entrance.

Exalted by the energy he commanded, Lucius shouted in a joyous rage as he saw the creatures move away from him, and he sent another bolt of lightning down into their ranks, then another, leaving charred and boiled corpses scattered across the warehouse, strewn throughout the human dead. More holes were punched through the ceiling as he brought lightning down from the sky and he directed the blasts back to the trap door as he saw more movement within, the creatures rallying for another attack.

With a loud crack, another bolt descended, and he smiled as he anticipated the terror and pain of the creatures below, only to see the bolt shatter into a thousand shards of light a few feet above the opening. Bolstered by this failure, creatures started flooding from the trap door again, and he summoned the threads to his aid, intent on halting them in their tracks.

A sharp pain blasted inside his head, and he reeled, feeling as though his mind was being squeezed by a giant hand. Staggering, he fell to the floor, trying to take in air, but discovering his lungs no longer worked as they should. Suddenly, the gripping agony was gone, and he sucked in precious breath, leaning against the table on which he had been standing for support as he tried to gather his mental energies to launch another attack.

He raised a shaky hand, and fire rolled down his arm. With a flick, he sent the ball of flame flying across the warehouse towards the creatures now scampering toward him but, as he watched, it simply snuffed out of existence before it reached them. Frowning in confusion, he took a step back, raising his sword defensively, and he felt the threads of power twist out of his reach, seeming to fly away from his grasp at speed.

The creatures started to circle round him and, as they parted, he saw one different from the rest. With greying scales, it walked with a stooped gait, and held a coral-encrusted staff upon which it leaned for support. Its eyes were milky and without any life, and yet Lucius knew the creature was watching him.

Raising the staff, the creature pointed its end at him. The pain came once again, forcing him to the ground as he clutched at his head, trying to pull his own skull apart to relieve the pressure. He grabbed, helplessly at an elusive thread, even as his sword slipped from his twitching fingers, but the magic would not come to him. Lucius raised his head to stare up at the grey creature as it approached, shuffling its clawed feet across the stone floor. He raised a hand, hoping — praying — that so much as a tiny ball of fire would come to fingers. But just as the thread started to jerk towards his will, the creature waved its staff in a tight, circular motion. The magic just fled, disappearing into the darkest recesses of his mind. It was quickly replaced by the agony, and he screamed in pain and terror as he grovelled on the floor.

Opening his eyes, Lucius saw a claw just inches from his face, and he looked up to see the grey creature staring soullessly down upon him. Its coral staff pointed down at his forehead. He was paralysed, utterly unable to order any of his limbs to move, and he began to gasp for air as his lungs and heart began, slowly to shut down. Tears came to his eyes as the pain intensified and he tried to mouth a curse at the creature, but no words came.

His world exploded then, and Lucius thought the end had finally come for him, that the light and sound was part of the journey to Kerberos where he would meet his family and roam among the clouds forever more as a free spirit. It was not until the greying creature collapsed next to him, its milky eyes ruptured and oozing a dark black liquid, that he realised he was still alive.

The pain and agony were gone, and with his heart pumping to restore the flow of blood to his body, Lucius managed to claw his way to his knees as he looked about him. It was a scene of complete chaos and carnage.

Panicked, the creatures were moaning in a strange alien tongue as they ran, seeking shelter from something near the main entrance. He struggled to his feet to get a better look, but was forced back down as the warehouse wall behind the trap door exploded inwards, nails and shards of wood whipping through the air to shred the fleeing creatures. As debris rained down, Lucius saw four figures standing outside the warehouse, each gesturing at the creatures and each gesture was followed by a wave of magical energy. Fire and lightning, stone and ice lashed out at the creatures as they were consumed by the onslaught.

The figures walked steadily into the warehouse, annihilating any creature they saw and any human foolish enough to attack them. Lucius stared, open-mouthed as he recognised Master Forbeck at their head, his genial face now a mask of hatred and vengeance as he wreathed himself in fire, sending out bolts of multihued flame to engulf every creature that dared to make its way past him.

Near the main entrance, some of the creatures were trying to follow thieves out into the streets, but a solitary figure stood at the threshold, hurling ice and blasts of solid air at any that made the attempt, while planting a sword into any who survived the maelstrom, and Lucius cried out loud in relief when he recognised Adrianna. Stumbling across the warehouse, he ran to greet her.

The battle was over within seconds, and an eerie silence fell across the shattered remains of the warehouse punctuated only by the moans of injured thieves. A few remaining creatures croaked as life fled from their dull eyes, and able-bodied thieves were only too happy to hurry them to their deaths.

Breathing heavily, Lucius stopped as he reached Adrianna, who stared down at him imperiously, and he thought he might be in for another of her jibes or criticisms. Then she smiled, warmly.

"One day, Lucius, you may curb your ability to get yourself into trouble."

"But not today," a voice said behind him, and he turned to face Forbeck. The master was flanked by three young men and even if he had not seen their display just a few minutes earlier, Lucius would have known they were Shadowmages from the magic he sensed emanating from them. He realised he was standing before practitioners of great power.

"What..." Lucius started. "Not that I am ungrateful, but what you are doing here?"

Forbeck nodded to the corpse of one of the creatures, it's back arched as though still in agony. "We heard a Shadowmage was in trouble, had brought more down upon his head than he could handle."

"You knew about these things?"

"We suspected," Forbeck shrugged. "And we had you as a witness to their activities previously. It bore further investigation. When Adrianna released herself from the Guild's contract, it allowed us to take a legitimate interest in what was going on. Though we are still unclear on exactly what that is."

"This may help," Adrianna said. As she stepped to one side, Lucius' gaze was caught by a motionless form on the floor behind her. Jewel.

"She's still alive though, I suspect, she may regret that when you take her back to your guildhouse."

"You are handing her to us?" Lucius asked, visions of vengeance suddenly flashing through his mind.

"We are neither thieves nor inquisitors," Forbeck said. "You'll get more out of her than we will. I trust that, as one of us, you will keep us informed of anything we need to know."

Lucius turned back to Adrianna. "Thank you. I mean it. For everything."

She sniffed, avoiding his eyes for a moment. "Just remember your promise to me."

EPILOGUE

The shadows cast by the single lantern hanging in the centre of the low ceiling did nothing to hide the baleful malice of Jewel's glare, the hatred she bore for all of them was plainly visible. The greater part of her enmity she held for Lucius, the wreck of the left side of her face a twisted mass of burned and ravaged flesh. Her left eye seemed slow to react, but its twin was as fast as ever, seeming to almost glow with smouldering fury whenever Lucius walked in front of her.

He was impressed. With the concoctions she had been plied with, recipes brewed by the expert interrogators of the Night Hands, the woman should have been barely conscious, mumbling truthful replies to every question set before her. Instead, she still spat curses, promising slow death to them all. Elaine was getting impatient.

"Has she been trained to resist?" she demanded as she limped to Lucius' side to stare Jewel full in the face.

Her stomach was wreathed in bandages, the legacy of a single thrust from Loredo's sword that had skittered across her lower ribs, smashing one. The guildmaster had fared far less well in their duel, falling to the ground with both of Elaine's swords jutting from his chest. "Has she taken something that nullifies our potions?"

Wendric shrugged. "Either is possible. Or both. For the latter, we may need to just wait for the effects of the counteragent to subside."

"We should increase the dosage," Elaine said flatly.

"No," said Lucius. "She has already taken more than you or I could bear. And I want to know what she knows."

Folding her arms, Elaine regarded the other woman. "She's playing us. We should move to more direct means."

Lucius guessed that Elaine had been itching to say that since they had brought Jewel into the bowels of the guildhouse two days ago. A few yards above them, in the common room and throughout the permitted areas of the guildhouse, thieves still celebrated, getting drunk and retelling stories of their rise to victory. The tales grew with each telling, but no one objected. From daring hits on the Guild's enforcers to the final assault on the guildhouse, every thief had the opportunity to become a hero.

Elaine had granted the Hands a week of celebration, but had made it painfully clear that open Council sessions were a thing of the past and that anyone defying her law as guildmaster would answer for it. She had been accepted smoothly enough, and even Lucius had avoided too many awkward questions, such was the elation throughout the guild. That, he knew, would likely not last.

Picking a knife off the single table in the small, dank room, Elaine crossed back over to Jewel and held the blade in front of the woman's face.

"It will do no good to work on her face," Elaine said, trying to goad her. "You already worked her over well, Lucius. She might have been pretty once, but now she looks like a freak. Like one of those creatures we slaughtered. Remember those? The ones we threw back into the sea."

Silently, Lucius shook his head. He had a fair idea that Jewel had never concerned herself with looking good and that, if anything, those scars aided her line of work. For her part, Jewel just held Elaine's gaze, her face completely neutral and without emotion, except her eyes, which spoke of nothing but promised agony.

"No, we must do something more... permanent, I think," Elaine declared. "Perhaps a few tendons cut, or the loss of a few fingers. That would bother you, wouldn't it, bitch? Not being able to kill any more. Life wouldn't be worth living."

Jewel muttered something then, but it was lost by Wendric's caustic comment. "I think she could learn to kill if you removed all her limbs. And maybe her head too."

Lucius held up a hand to silence him, and leaned over Jewel. Though she was tightly bound to the chair they had placed her in, he still did not get too close. He did not expect her to spit acid or poison into his face, but it would not surprise him if she did.

"What was that? What did you say, Jewel?"

With utter contempt, she stared back up at him and, for a moment, he thought she was going to fall silent again.

"I said, you are all dead and you don't even know it."

"We were the ones that won the war, Jewel," said Elaine. "You might have trouble recognising defeat, I realise, but what you are feeling right now, that is it. Wendric, give her another dose."

"I told you, she is already dangerously high."

"Apparently not," said Lucius. "Go on. Risk it. She's no good to us silent."

Grabbing a small opaque vial from the table, Wendric stood over Jewel, and regarded her as he held the vial aloft.

"We've done this before. You can have it easy, or have it hard." As he reached down, she twisted as far as her straps would allow.

"Hard then," Wendric said, grabbing Jewel's nose and wrenching her head back. For a minute he held her like that, waiting for her to draw breath through her mouth, but she remained resolutely still. Losing his patience, Wendric punched her hard in the stomach and, when this elicited the required response, drove the vial between her teeth, emptying its contents before slamming her mouth shut.

Still Jewel held out, twisting to break his grasp as a trickle of the potion ran from the corner of her mouth. She was finally defeated by the basic need for air, and Wendric finally released her when they heard her swallow.

For a moment, she gasped for breath, then spat at their feet. For a few seconds, her eyes lost focus and her head began to sway.

"It's beginning to work," Lucius said, taking a step forward. Then, as if a torch had been snuffed out, the dullness disappeared from her eyes and she snapped back in her restraints, staring past them as if watching something a great distance away. Both Lucius and Elaine looked at Wendric, but he just shrugged.

Lucius crouched until he was at her eye level, but she just seemed to stare right through him.

"Jewel, how did you contact those creatures?"

"They contacted us."

"What did you offer to get them working for the Guild?"

"Idiot."

Behind Lucius, Wendric smirked. "If the truth drugs are working, I would say that gives you little credit."

Ignoring him, Lucius pressed on. "Jewel, what are they."

"The power of the ancients, the rulers of the past," she said, then added an afterthought. "And the future."

"I don't understand."

Jewel sighed then, long and exaggerated, as if failing to get through to an ignorant child. He decided to try a different tact.

"What do they want?"

"Everything."

"What do you mean, everything? All the gold in the city? The city itself? The Empire?"

"Everything."

"That doesn't make sense, Jewel," he said, wishing the others would join in. "Why would they fight alongside you? What could you offer?"

"Revenge. A tip in the balance."

He stopped, thinking that one through. Turning, he faced Wendric. "Does she have to be this literal?"

"It works differently for everyone," Wendric shrugged. "Some appear drunk, others desperate to please. I always thought it was a reflection of the personality, though I am not sure what that says about her."

Scratching his head, Lucius confronted Jewel again. "You said they wanted to tip the balance. You weren't paying them in gold or goods, were you?"

"Of course not." Again, that exasperated tone.

A thought struck him as he saw her head begin to sag. "Jewel, listen to me. They weren't working for you, right? You were doing their bidding."

"We served them."

"But why?"

"Idiot."

"She presumes the answer is obvious," said Wendric.

"Yes, thank you Wendric, I am beginning to get that," Lucius replied testily. "They served something more powerful than them because they would be rewarded. I withdraw the question – happy?"

In response Wendric shrugged as Elaine pushed past him. As Jewel's eyes began to close, she slapped the woman hard across the face. The sharp sting of pain seemed to revive Jewel and, for a moment, she seemed lucid.

"What are they, Jewel?" Elaine asked. "What do we have to fear from them?"

"They have been here forever," Jewel said slowly. "They commanded us and we obeyed, for that is the only way to survive the war."

"The war is over Jewel," Lucius said. "You lost."

"No, the war has gone on for centuries, and will continue until every man and woman is dead or lies enslaved at their feet."

Wendric cleared his throat. "I recall hearing stories of the Older Races, those that came before man, and the great empires they built. Is that what you mean?"

"Idiot," Jewel spat. "They were ancient when elf and dwarf walked this world. They fought them too, and won. Now it is our turn."

"But why?" Elaine asked.

"Because they understand hatred. Because they know it is not enough to simply exist."

"What do you mean?" Elaine pressed, but Jewel's head was beginning to hang to one side, as if it were too heavy for her neck. When Elaine shook her, they all saw a slither of froth between her lips.

"She's going," Wendric said. "I warned you."

"Stay with us, Jewel!" Elaine demanded, shaking her harder. "What do you mean by that, why is it not enough for them to just exist?"

Jewel coughed, flecks of bloodied spittle flying across Elaine's face. Her words were barely more than a whisper, forced from her throat by the power of the drugs alone.

"Our presence is an affront to them. War has come, but now they can join the old power with the new. Now, they are unstoppable."

"I don't understand," Elaine said. "What do they want? What *are* they, Jewel?"

She slapped the woman again to bring her back to consciousness, then shook her when she failed to respond, until Lucius laid a hand on her arm. Jewel had stopped breathing.

"It's too late, Elaine."

"Damn her!" Elaine spat, as she pushed away from Jewel's body and stalked across the room in frustration. "She told us nothing!"

"She told us little," Lucius corrected her, but Elaine was in no mood to be placated.

"Riddles and fairy tales! And you Wendric," she said, turning on her new lieutenant. "You should know better than to spout myths about goblins and elves!"

He seemed ready to respond, but wisely kept silent. Lucius was lost in his own thoughts as he tried to piece together what Jewel had told them. Could her words be trusted? If she had the power to resist the truth drugs, did she also have the power to defy them outright? Still, he had witnessed the power the creatures from the sea wielded and that scared him more than he cared to admit to either of his fellow thieves.

Either way, he had just got this guild back onto its feet, and he was not about to let anything tear it back down. Even if the threat lay at the bottom of the ocean.

THE END

MATTHEW SPRANGE

With a solid history in roleplaying and miniatures game design, Matthew Sprange has written over three dozen gaming books, including the *Babylon 5* and *Judge Dredd* roleplaying games, and has won two Origins Awards for his miniatures games. *Shadowmage* is his third novel.

Abaddon Books

COMING AUGUST 2008...

Now read a chapter from the second book in the
Twilight of Kerberos series...

TWILIGHT of KERBEROS

THE CLOCKWORK KING of ORL

MIKE WILD

A KALI HOOPER ADVENTURE

COMING AUGUST 2008

ISBN: 978-1-905437-75-7

CHAPTER 8

Kali looked down and couldn't believe it. *This* was Slowhand's alternative escape route? Bloody great steaming pits of Kerberos, there were *birds* below!

Their flight from Makennon's guards had taken them up, up and up, and finally, inevitably, to the highest accessible point of the cathedral, a rope and plank walkway that at some point had been strung around the outside of its main steeple and hung there now as loosely as a whore's belt. Some fifty feet below where the steeple's tapering spire took over, the narrow, drunkenly undulating and half-rotten platform had perhaps once been used for repairs because as far as any other purpose went it was good for nothing, led nowhere.

Damn Slowhand! She should have known better than to trust him. What the hell did the idiot expect them to do now – run round and round the thing until the guards following fell off, either through dizziness or exhaustion?

She stared at Killiam as he slammed the hatch behind them. Barred it. No more than a second passed before there was an insistent hammering on its other side. If the hatch were as neglected as the walkway they balanced upon it would not be long before they had company.

"So... " Killiam shouted casually above the winds that roared and buffeted here, taking a moment to sweep back his hair, "... you're a tomb raider these days?"

Kali steadied herself on the swaying wood, positioning her feet with great care. Through a triangular gap between two planks she could see the toy-like rooftop of a Scholten factory belching a tiny plume of white fog in her direction. It was indeed a long way down. "A-ha."

"Like, erm – ?"

"No! Not like 'erm'."

Killiam nodded vigorously, swallowed. "Fine. Fine."

Kali jammed her hands on her hips, regretting even that tiniest of movements when the walkway shifted beneath her and slapped against the side of the steeple, creaking loudly. "Look. Do you have a clue what you're doing up here, or not?"

Killiam took a moment to reply. He was inching away from her along the precarious platform, his palms pressed against the side of the steeple, presumably for stability against the worst gusts of wind. "Hooper," he shouted back, "have I ever let you down?"

"Yes."

"I mean *apart* from the Sarcre Islands..."

"Slowhand, those things almost had me *stuffed*. And yes, *apart* from the Sarcre Islands."

"Okay. Right. But let's get this straight. You have never, have you, actually come to any... *permanent* harm."

Rain suddenly began to hammer the walkway, soaking the two of them instantly. From beneath dripping, slicked-down hair Kali stared hard and ground her teeth.

"*Nooooo...*"

"And that's because," Killiam shouted slowly, "*you... always... plan... ahead.*"

He plucked a cloth-wrapped bundle seemingly by magic from the steeple's side, and Kali realised he hadn't been pressing his palms there for stability but searching for a hidey-hole. From the shape of the bundle, it contained one of the weapons that had once been Killiam's tools of the trade.

"You hid a longbow up here? Why on Twilight would you do that?"

Killiam stripped away the cloth, hefted the impressively-sized crescent, and pursed his lips. "The amount of anti-Makennon rhetoric I've been spouting of late, I knew it wasn't going to be long before she sent her goons to have a word. I just thought of every eventuality... "

"Actually, I meant *what use* is a bow *up here*? What are you planning to do – spear a cloud for us to ride away on?"

"*Oh, funny,*" Killiam said. Acting quickly, he pulled a coil of thin rope from the same hidey-hole and attached one end to an arrow, the other to one of the more secure parts of the walkway. The coil certainly looked long enough to be able to reach a cloud.

Killiam squinted down at distant buildings, eyeing a trajectory, then aimed the bow high into the air.

"What the hell are you doing?"

Killiam ignored a louder banging on the hatch. It sounded as if Makennon's people were almost through. "Little idea I came up with. I call it a death slide."

"Nice," Kali said, and then put two and two together. "Hold on... you're going to fire that rope at a building down there and expect us to slide down it?"

"Nope. Building's no good – from this height you'd

slam right through the wall. Need to hit somewhere open, target it through a ring."

"A *ring*?"

"Okay, a big, iron ring," Killiam said. "One I tied between the Red Rum Tavern and Ma Polly's, actually." He pulled back on the bow and winked. "Cocky little bugger, eh?"

Kali said nothing. She couldn't even make out the places he talked about. She knew Killiam was good – very good – but to make the shot he planned over such a distance, at such a target, and in *this* weather? Impossible.

Then Killiam reminded her why he had gained the sobriquet Slowhand.

In the space of a second her ex-lover seemed to shut the world away. The wind and the rain and the hammering and the shouts seemed no longer to matter to the man at all, and an aura of great calm enveloped him, as if he lived now in a universe entirely his own. Gone was the happy-go-lucky troubadour he had styled himself as of late, and back was the famed archer who, for what had seemed like an eternity, had tested the hearts of the men he had fought beside at the battle of Andon eight years before. Kali had heard the story told in a hundred of that city's taverns... how their forces were in danger of being overwhelmed – were *being* overwhelmed – and Killiam had stayed his hand as his comrades had clamoured at him to loose his arrow and take one more of the invading bastards down. But Killiam had waited – even as enemy swords and axes had cut and sliced about him, he had waited – because he had chosen his target and would not fire until he knew his aim was true. Finally his arrow flew. Just one arrow across the length of a battlefield that was sheer chaos – through the flailing, bloodied forms of a thousand battling warriors and their dense sprays of blood – unerringly on until it found its home in the forehead of John Garrison, the commanding enemy general. One arrow into one man, but a man on whose survival the morale of the enemy depended. And with his death the tide of that battle had been turned.

Killiam let fly. His arrow sang into the sky then arched downward. He must have calculated its flight perfectly because seconds later the rope it had carried with it ran taut.

"After you," Kali said.

Killiam stared at her, hesitated. "There's just one thing. I'm not going."

"*What?*"

"There isn't time for two runs," he said, looking towards the hatch. "And in this weather it's too dangerous to risk the rope to two."

"I see. But you expect me – "

"Listen to me. I saw how you handled yourself during our escape, your reflexes, your speed – what you could *do*. There's something different about you, something changing... something *better*." He tested the tension in the rope that stretched out into the night sky, wiping the moisture from it on his tunic. "I knew it when I came up here. To be honest, in these conditions I don't know if I *can* make this slide, Hooper. But I know you can."

"I'm not just going to abandon you here."

"Call it payback for the Sarcre Islands."

Kali faltered. Was this Killiam Slowhand being *serious*?

"Use the bow," he said, quickly stripping it of its string then handing it to her, nodding in reassurance. "It'll hold. Go, Kali. Find your friend. Now."

Kali knew there was no other choice, not if she was going to save Merrit Moon. Even if that meant not only abandoning Killiam, but abandoning him defenceless. She slung the stringless bow over the wire and pulled down until it became a horseshoe, gripping either end as tightly as she could. Then she felt Killiam's hand in the small of her back, for a second almost tenderly.

"Enjoy the ride," he said. And as he spoke, Kali heard the door to the walkway crash open.

Kali looked down and let her body go loose. "Slowhand, I'll be seeing you again. I'll be – "

Killiam slapped her off the walkway.

"Bye, bye."